CW01665729

Not Everyone Lives

By Ben Dunn

For My Sisters, Nik, Kel and Rae

Copyright © 2023 Ben Dunn.

All rights reserved. No part of this publication may be reproduced, distributed, or transmitted in any form or by any means, including photocopying, recording, or other electronic or mechanical methods, without the prior written permission of the publisher, except in the case of brief quotations embodied in critical reviews and certain other noncommercial uses permitted by copyright law.

Any references to historical events, real people, or real places are used fictitiously. Names, characters, and places are products of the author's imagination.

ISBN: **978-1-7394208-1-9**

Second printing edition 2023.
Book Burn Publishing

Prologue

He was running as a child, and they were chasing as men.

They were faster, he knew that.

He didn't look back, only ahead, watching images bounce and shake as he forced his body forward, trying to hear anything above the noise of his panting breath and the slap of his feet on tarmac. He glimpsed his brown leather School shoes he'd bought himself. They were all about fashion and not about speed. His black trousers, red and grey striped tie, and his blue shirt and blazer with school badge were all new and clean and slowing him down. The chasing group were shouting and people were watching, stepping out into the autumn drizzle from shops that lined the local high street. He was looking for help, looking to be filmed, looking to buy enough time for someone to call the police. But most were scared, no one ever spoke, and why would you risk your future to call in a crime between teenage kids who only ever destroyed the place they live?

This part of London was no longer a community, it was fear.

He knew they were closing, he saw the faces of shopkeepers and customers and pedestrians moving for shelter, back inside, into doorways, and behind parked cars. It was like seeing little children playing hide-and-seek for the very first time. He heard the screams and shouts of the chasing pack, a wild bunch of dogs in their tracksuits. He thought about the stupidity of arrogance he had felt being the man with money and friends with strength.

They weren't here now and he should have known, should have seen this coming.

He had walked out the gate, the end of the school day in which he had done nothing and teachers had left him be. A year eleven with no hope of qualification.

School buses were parked outside, teachers big enough not to be heckled, standing guard to make sure the commotion was never enough to cause criminal damage. He had strolled, smiling at Lucy, and she smiled back and he knew she was his, or could be and would be. She moved in her skirt, black tights and white socks and he recognised the sway as he had watched before. But then he had heard, and looked to his left, his flirtatious smile dropping into a word. He swore, dumped his bag, hoping they would be thrown, and ran, sprinted, wanting to make the distance too much for them to believe they should give chase.

He could run forever but never fast.

This wasn't a shake or a warning, they were not thinking of leaving a mark and a message. This was the end. He saw the machete, the knives, and the wood. He saw them all recognise him, all rise in volume and point and shake weapons. He knew they were there for him and he knew why. He didn't have time to count the number but there were more than ten, and more than enough to have speed and violence in numbers. Them in trainers designed to look cool but shaped for a comfort in stride, and him in a child's business clothes.

He ran, top speed, lungs burning instantly, legs pumping, mind racing, looking for a way out, wishing he could lose them in the streets. But they knew them all as well as he. He had to be smart and take turns he shouldn't choose, streets they wouldn't guess and create confusion so they stopped.

He was running away, he knew that, but not to a place, he had no destination in mind. He was running to break their spirit and make them quit.

His place of sanctuary was closed.

He saw the corner shop, run by a dodgy old man of mottled skin and bone who was happy to serve cigarettes under the counter. The boy slid, grabbing at the brown brick corner, pulling himself to his left, turning into the next street. He looked back to where the chasing pack were making noise. One of them, a face covered in a scarf, his hood up, black gloves, black top, black tracksuit, and black trainers was two metres distant. Someone who was in shape with natural speed and desire to show his loyalty.

The boy span into the street, stopped, turned, and braced. The kid in black came round the corner, ready to push forward again, and the boy drove his forehead into the chaser's face. There was no blood to see, it was all encased in expensive sports fashion, but the guy dropped, and the boy's own head spun. He was dizzy but not out, his legs worked, his mind less so.

He wanted to be sick.

He looked at the weapon on the floor. It had been the kid with the machete. He picked it up, stood his ground, saw the group metres away, they had slowed, not knowing what to do, not knowing why he would stop and take up arms.

He couldn't see any of their faces, but there was white skin, dark skin on show. Blue eyes, brown eyes, and not a wrinkle to be had. They had slowed and stopped, watching him as he watched them. If they came as a wave he would be dead, but none of them wanted to die on the journey. When you can fight as he could, people give pause to attack. Here and now, any skills he had learned were nothing but no one was sure of that. When a group wants to stomp you, there is nothing to do but run or die.

He needed to breathe, think but not fight, take oxygen in and this was the break he wanted. He stepped toward them and they didn't move, he nodded and they nodded back. They figured him to be making the dumbest decision of his life, but that one had already been and gone and had led to this. The boy stepped forward, the shop door to his right, open, the owner at the front window looking out not knowing what to do.

The boy leaned forward, looking like he was about to laugh, hands dropping down so they touched his knees, the machete still in his hand.

He knew they would all be smiling behind their masks, smiling at the futility, the kid who thought he had an escape. Maybe they were waiting for him to beg.

The boy stood up slowly staring at his blade, moving the machete back and forth as if he had discovered something new. They looked at its shiny surface, all of them transfixed by the glint and the danger. He was misdirecting like a poor magician pulling tricks in pubs for drinks. The boy straightened nice and slow, ticking off all the moves for a man about to stand his ground and invite conflict. They tensed in reaction, ready to swarm. The boy twisted his body, pushed power through his feet and sprinted into the shop. He moved fast to the counter, went through the gap, flipping down the wooden extension to block anyone following. The shop keeper shouted, more interested in keeping stock safe than a kid alive. The boy darted into the back room, one he had never seen before, boxes of sweets, cleaning products, a table and chair, kettle and mug, and a back door with a push bar. He sprinted to it, pushed with his shoulder, the door flying open into a back alley, he turned left, back to the school from where he came, sprinted past bins and overgrown grass and rubbish and fallen brick. He pulled bins over as he ran, sprinting, hurting, not wanting to give up. He reached the end, ran out into the road, turned right, knowing his only escape was to head for hiding. He couldn't go home, couldn't call police, couldn't do anything here anymore beyond vanish and wait for the Farm to open.

He looked down the alley, his chasers too far back, the obstacles too many, the distance too long. He smiled, the luck, the thoughts, the decisions. He was a chosen one, too smart to fail, to cool to be caught. But he knew he was done. This told him he had to go.

The chasers had given up. They stood, at a distance, jammed up in back alley, pointing and shouting but not moving.

The boy smiled. Another time.

The noise stopped his thoughts. He turned to look, the end of the road, a red car, Japanese, standard and stolen. It swerved in too fast, shook and straightened and accelerated forward. It revved and he ran. The road was narrow, yellow lines on both sides, no parked cars, the alleyway full of boys with weapons, the next escape ten metres ahead, across the road. He ran, sprinting, the machete in hand, his face grimacing, the rain on his face, in his hair, in his clothes. The noise was coming, the car in the wrong gear and screeching as it burned forward. He darted left, making for the alley, running, breathing, screaming, fighting, the hope and belief never going and driving him forward.

He could see it, feel it and he smiled at the hours in a gym that gave him the endurance to survive.

Three more steps and he would be free to run through a narrow gap between terraced houses. He slowed, ready to swerve left, smiling, hoping, thinking but not knowing he couldn't be caught.

The contact was heavy into his back. But he didn't flip, he flew. His forward momentum pushed with horsepower through a plastic grill, his feet lifted from the floor, his body flipping, the pain in his legs making him scream as he sped into the wall to his left. Eight feet tall, topped with wire. He didn't get high enough to be slashed, but his left shoulder hit brick, his legs, loose and hanging, flipped around so they led the way, he span more and gravity started to win and pull him down. His speed not decreasing, only his height. He hit the floor on his chest, his legs buckled up, over his head, and he rolled, slid and bounced to a stop after ten metres in a second of ripped skin and smashed bone, to a heap of flesh beyond the alley he had seen as his escape.

He knew he needed to rise, needed to run, needed to think. But nothing worked, only his eyes. He lay there staring up at clouds that drifted in white, grey and black. He saw no blue, no sun and no way out. The pain ran through him and the ability to communicate with his body was all gone. His muscles worked but they pulled on broken bones and only his head could roll.

He heard the screech of brakes hit hard, the thump of a door opening and slammed shut. He saw them, two figures above him, looking down, their eyes on show but scarves and hoodies covering every other feature.

"He isn't dead," the one on the right said.

The one on the left reached down, his hand clasping a six-inch hunting knife, a shiny sharp edge and one serrated. He drove it into the boy's chest and the boy screamed, short and loud. They watched the blood bubble out and the man leaned back in and dipped the blade through the boy's throat. The boy in school uniform could feel the warm blood cover his skin, his lung stopped bringing in air through his mouth, releasing only blood through the slash in his chest. He stared at the two men because he couldn't move and they watched him back, waiting for the dead.

"He is now," the man said, wiping his blade on the boy's blazer.

But he wasn't, not quite. A second too soon.

The boy watched the two men, two men he had hoped to be, he watched them as they waited for him to go. And he did, in his school clothes, on a street, with no one around to care and for no other reason than being the one they chose.

1

They walked in and no one stopped.

They were not here fishing for facts, they were here for their own amusement.

Raucous knew this because their excitement in the set up was spoken in actions and moves. Four uniformed police and two plain-clothes up front. They were strolling and smiling and dragging out their moment, wanting and needing everyone to watch.

The Fight Farm was his. A gym to compete with no one. It was not new, not clean, not heated, and because it sat in prime estate in London, not cheap. The pristine gyms where plastic people in perfect clothes worked machines and took classes were not stealing his clientele. Here there were free-weights, mats, bags to hit, mats to wrestle, and in the corner of the large, white painted brick room above several shops, stood an octagon for the fighting to take pace.

It was evening, dark outside, cold wherever you went, and boys, men and women were here in his gym to train, be taught to fight, and feel safe. There were many who came that could beat Raucous in a fair fight with rules, and referees, and tap-outs and counts. But none of them would try outside the confines of organised conflict. Without rules, Raucous was left alone. He felt good at that, because at forty-one, he was in shape, six-feet and strong, but he knew the shaven head and scowl was becoming an act, and his rage was pointed not at the world but only those that caused harm.

This had been his retirement, a non-profit project to keep him busy with the air of legitimacy. He had money from illegality, and no more ties to crime because everyone he knew was dead. But here the police were, and he wondered as he smiled about what mistake he had made.

No matter how perfect the outcome, somewhere, at some point, an error occurs, a small piece of evidence, a witness that should never have been, a camera or a passer-by remembering, identifying. An alibi broken, a small piece of DNA, a confession or just bad luck can do for the most well-executed plan.

Raucous wondered where he had made his error.

They wouldn't be here if he had done it all perfect. He must have made a mistake. Raucous thought about that night, about how he had taken every effort to cover his tracks, not just for the police but for him. The kick back was always going to be revenge, but if they didn't know, they couldn't attack, and he'd left it late. Revenge served cold. He hadn't wanted people to know, didn't need the notoriety, the reverence from people saying Raucous got his justice. He just needed them dead, and now they were. Another should have gone but now that would have to wait. Maybe wait for another man to do the job.

He had hidden the weapon after cleaning it down. The blade dipped in bleach, left to rest for an hour and then thrown into trash in a bag in a park. His clothes and shoes burned to ashes in an oil drum at the allotments. The bodies left to be found where he laid them down in pools of blood fifty miles from here in a cottage in the country. The fight had been nothing because it had never started. He entered, he slashed, the second attacked and Raucous snapped his arm and put a knife through his chest and then his throat. That had been what he wanted and what he did. The car he used ran false plates, and was burned out within the hour.

A simple plan from a simple man putting right a simple wrong.

It was easily executed but clearly with a flaw. One these men of law had discovered and were now here to tell all, and walk Raucous away.

He knew one of the suits, the woman was tall, straight brown hair, a trouser suit in dark blue. She smiled and her face was not yet ravaged by stress and the horrific sights of her job. She was yet to hit thirty-five. She was called Kathy Simpson. She had been the one to tell him of Mack, she had been the one to tell him one of his lads had been hunted down, hit with a car and put down in a street.

She had told him well. He had thanked her.

She wasn't here now for a death notice.

The noise of bags being hit by hyperactive youths and the sound of iron weights being dropped and then picked up had faded. They had their audience and Raucous stepped toward the police, smiling, wanting to know how they knew.

"Inspector Simpson," Raucous said, and she nodded her response.

Raucous looked at the others and didn't know names. He'd seen them before, the uniforms, they were local, as much as that can be. Probably Simpson's favoured men. But the suited man was new.

"Who's your friend?" Raucous asked.

He answered himself, knowing enough not to offer his hand.

"Inspector Locke," he told him, an accent from the south, Brighton way.

Raucous looked him up and down, smiling, trying to grate. He saw what he always saw, a man in a suit thinking his smarts were more and the thinning hair, and the mid-thirties face of a runner thin with stress, would hang around long enough for his wedding photos. He wore no ring. The same height but half the mass.

Raucous nodded again and waited, he was not going to ask why they were there, he was not in the mood for inviting conversation.

"You must be wondering why we are here," Locke said.

"Nope," Raucous replied, looking at Simpson.

"We brought news, not out in the press yet, or in circulation. But we thought you'd like to hear. Seemed only fair after Mack," Simpson said.

Raucous tried to keep his smile, and he figured he had, but Simpson saw enough of something to squint herself.

"MarQuick is dead," she said.

Raucous wasn't sure of the reasons, he'd figure them soon enough, or have a short list of possibilities and try and narrow them down to the most logical option. He looked at the floor, thinking, recalculating, angry at the news. He shook his head as plans he had made evaporated into nothing beyond fantasy.

He looked up.

"Disappointing," he said.

"And how is that?" Locke asked.

Raucous still wouldn't turn to look at him. He stared at Simpson, and spoke his answers to her.

"Because it wasn't me that killed him."

"Know who did?" Locke asked.

"Are you being forced to have this guy around?" Raucous asked.

He saw Simpson smile, and knew she was laughing at him, not his words.

"Know anything?" Simpson asked.

"Whoever got him was either good, lucky, or on the inside. Probably all three. How did he go?"

"Can't tell you that," Simpson told him. "But hopefully it will comfort you that it was not easy, nor pleasant."

Raucous nodded.

"There is some comfort in that."

Raucous looked at the room, and the faces staring, the people trying to figure out the whys and the words. Raucous thought about how he would not have his moment, how Marquick would not end at his hands. How someone else had taken his hate and killed the man who had caused Mack's death.

Raucous took a deep breath, and told himself to move on, to think of this, to place it all in order when alone at home, when he could speak to Charlotte, when he could hear her words.

"Why the guard of honour?" Raucous asked.

"No reason," Locke said.

Raucous turned his head slowly, taking a deep breath like the irritated man he was.

"There is always a reason," Raucous told him.

2

Charlotte had a key. Raucous had thought it the right thing, a move to something he couldn't define, but something he wanted all the same. She had taken it with a smile he thought had been knowing. She had offered one for him but he turned it down. He would never be able to walk into someone else's place unannounced. Welcoming people into his world was a strange sensation, giving Charlotte a key meant something to him and he didn't know how much it meant to her.

Raucous had wrapped up at his gym, cleaned, put equipment away and locked up. He had received the looks he expected from the people that came in and sought advice and practice and fame from building techniques. Back when he had been a kid, boxing was the skill, the sport that singled you out as a man of violence. Old school gangsters in unlicensed fights where referees could rarely control and heads and teeth were fair game and laces across eyes was a skill they taught. There was little refinement, only tough men hitting hard and taking shots because to avoid was soft. But now he saw young men and women able to wrestle their way free of confrontation and take people to the ground tie up or leave them open to cheap-shot blows. That is what they came for, a combination of styles, the melding of the catch wrestlers of a bye-gone fairground trade, who hooked and shot their way to pain filled domination. Brazilian Ju-Jitsu designed to control one-to-one fights and take a puncher to the ground where size and strength could be countered with skill.

Charlotte had shown him moves, holds and submissions. She had made him quit, tap out and writhe in pain. She knew how to use her skills to defend and hurt. But there needed to be a gap of knowledge, a gap of skills. Straight up, she would lose to most who knew the game.

Raucous hoped she wasn't there, a rarity now as he wanted to see her more. He had made his promises and he hadn't lied, not outright because he couldn't break his word, not to her. But this had been a stretch of credibility, a word game to hide his involvement in a play he should never have joined again.

He popped the door next to the café and walked the stairs to his flat, the only one he had known. First with the kindness of his grandmother, and then on her death, after his time inside as his alone. Nothing had changed much since it was decorated by a woman old before her time and looking to see how dark wood furniture could fill all corners.

He knew she was there when he turned the key, the smell was different, it always was when she came round. But he knew she had heard. She probably knew before the police had come.

Raucous closed the door behind him, took his shoes off and paused at the door which opened into the front room. He was in that small area that held coats and shoes, that docking space between the outside and the inside. A small cubicle of a room where feet were wiped and the cold from outside held up from breezing through a property that was in need of modern insulation. He took a deep breath and fixed a smile looking at the red sports shoes she had taken off and left where she always did. He pushed the door and walked through to the small front room.

Charlotte was stood in the kitchen, the door open and the hatch in the wall that was never used to serve food was open too. The smell of coffee filled the room. Charlotte was bringing it to the boil on an old and stained shiny metal contraption his grandmother had heated every morning for fifty years. She gripped the Bakelite handle. Charlotte smiled, and Raucous smiled back.

"What did they want?" she asked.

Raucous knew from experience that playing dumb was not an option as she would rile at his attempts to use intelligence to sway conversation from what she had decided would be the topic of the day.

"Wanted to pass on information. They seemed to think I'd like to hear."

"Did you already know?"

Raucous knew what she meant, knew what the answer would mean if it were wrong.

"I don't have your contacts," he told her.

She stared at him, looking for his face to fail, he knew this much. He let her look and held his smile without thought although uncomfortable.

"Did you kill him?" she asked, and he could hear she wasn't mad or angry, she just needed to know.

"I wish I had, I can't lie about that. Feels strange that I don't have that option anymore."

Raucous moved into the kitchen as Charlotte opened cupboards and took two small coffee cups. Like binge drinkers moving to shots, the big mugs of filtered caffeine had been replaced by small cups of high strength ground beans. She didn't look at him as he moved and came to stand beside her. He smiled inside as he often did about how small she seemed next to him. She was not more than five feet four, but muscled and her blonde hair short. He understood why some thought she wouldn't be into men, but he knew she was.

Raucous leaned in to kiss her and she returned nothing but a shake of the head.

"Too much of a coincidence, Raucous," she said. "Mack's death and then MarQuick goes."

Raucous stood up straight and took a small step back.

"I'm out," he told her. "I promised you that. I'm not seeking out trouble. I had nothing to do with it."

She looked up again, searching for the signs, as if he had a poker tell and she knew every time he played it.

"I would have, and I thought of it, and with the opportunity I would have taken that. But I would never have got close, never been able to take him out without a lot of people knowing. Without plenty seeing. And I'm here now."

"So why the group of police and not just a quiet word?"

Raucous had thought, tried to figure why, and the possibilities were too many and he had too little information to make a good call on the reasons.

"I don't know," he said. "Maybe they figured it had been me, maybe they thought I'd run on seeing them? I don't know. Maybe they are trying to shake something up."

He smiled as she looked at him, looking for forgiveness for something she had no idea he had done. He looked at her and thought of the men she had killed, the times she had saved him from being a victim, how someone so small could be a person who he owed his life.

"They burned him," Charlotte said. "Smashed face, beaten real bad."

"I don't care how he went," Raucous said.

Charlotte nodded and poured coffee from a hissing pot. She filled the cups, which didn't take much at all. She dropped milk into hers and left the other black.

Raucous waited as he had learned to do, waiting for the final words.

She sipped, clicked her tongue, and stared into the coffee as if she could see where the imperfection lay.

"He died from stab wounds," she said. "One to his chest and the second through his throat."

3

Mack had come into the gym like others. Some knew him, the lads that had stayed. It was a pattern. A group arrived, all eager and nervous and crackling energy, some thought themselves already mean, already skilled because they had faced only peers, peers who were scared. The best students were those who had never risen to the top, who learned and listened and had no false persona to protect from the embarrassments of defeat in front of friends.

Mack was one of them. He spoke and people listened. He was not ruling through fear but charisma. Raucous could never figure why these people achieved their presence. There was nothing about him, nothing that he could see. He looked like the others, smiled, and said similar things, only when he spoke they all nodded. Raucous knew he could say the same words, in the same order, with the same voice but with little effect. The kid had a politician's presence. The confidence of what he said could be heard in his every sound.

But he didn't mind being beat, didn't mind the bullying from instructors who simply didn't like the kid's popularity. Mack took more than most, held down in submission for longer than others. He knew what was happening, knew it wouldn't go away. He smiled, never broke, thanked people who hated him for teaching it the hard way.

Raucous watched, waiting, yet he never quit.

But he made a mistake, made it obvious, made it so people knew and gave him respect gained from the men above him. The easy way to money was through drugs, moving, selling and protecting. That was how it was, had been since Raucous was young. But where Raucous had fought and earned his time through violence, these kids earned their money through small slices off the top of deals and deliveries. They spoke with words Raucous did not know, although he gained a working knowledge. He heard of the houses they set up, the owner inside, involved or hostage, it didn't matter, and turned into a dirty hub of activity. They had their special names, their code words that had moved from secrecy to the common tongue. The kids in posh school, in posh streets and with all the prospects you could need, used the words too. Roadmen was a term, an endearment, a way of being one with something bigger than the average life.

Raucous could see in most who came to his gym what their life was worth, how that changed, and the reasons for money.

Raucous bought into Mack's charisma more than most. He saw the kid with the clothes he couldn't afford, walking round, being quiet but seen. No words, no brags and no need to shout look-at-me because everyone already did.

Raucous knew he had killed for Mack and not because of a sense of pride in protecting the boys that came from the life Raucous had led. He realised as he burnt the car that what he had done was no social act of kindness but a means to protect Mack. He had thought about it since, thought about it more than he'd like to admit, and Charlotte had seen him drift away into questions he was asking himself, questions he could answer but not with conviction. Raucous knew he had caused Mack's death. Had caused the way it happened.

There was nothing he could do. He could go deeper, continue on the path for what he would have once called justice but what he now knew was only ever pathetic revenge.

It had to end, it already should, and that was the decision, the way to live.

His punishment was knowing, and living.

He hadn't intended to kill, had not seen it as the only solution. There were ways he had seen to bring it to an end. They chose the end through their own stupidity. He had warned and they had ignored. Their deaths were nothing at all, a social cleansing to be replaced within hours with another, similar strain of nasty. He had killed them and the knock-on was someone killed Mack. Raucous saw and repeated the cause and effect, couldn't help but play out the blame game, and while he knew time would reduce the looped thought of self-disgust and regret, he also knew he didn't have the time to hide it all from those who mattered.

4

"Where were you?" Charlotte asked as soon as Raucous sat down.

They were meeting in the Coffee shop below his flat. The owner knew Raucous now, and knew Charlotte was someone to respect. Every time he said they didn't need to pay, but each time they did.

A bohemian café that sat out of place, as if the street had already been gentrified, when it had yet to truly start the process. There were incursions of cool, the alternative scene that would be pride of place in a city like Brighton, but here faced opposition from the old-timers and the middle-aged who loved their heritage. They didn't need university educated people coming in and transforming it all from what they knew to what the hipsters wanted.

But they served good coffee and sandwiches that they had learned not to call Paninis. A ham and cheese toastie had no need to be called a brie and prosciutto Pita bread.

The chairs didn't match but were all taken from the 1950s comprehensive science labs as were the tables, and the rest was decorated with salvage from old churches and buildings. There were places on the backrests to hold bibles.

Raucous was sat with his coffee, that even he would call a cappuccino. Charlotte sat opposite a small wooden table, cupping the flat white she had ordered.

Raucous smiled and didn't answer.

"I covered for you. Lied."

Raucous had known some was coming, knew the outline of what would happen. He had thought things through.

"You didn't lie," Raucous said. "You were where you said you were, doing what you said you were doing. You told the truth."

"But you didn't."

She hadn't paused, her words followed his.

"I didn't say anything that didn't happen. We went to bed, we woke up in bed."

"No, I woke up and you weren't there."

"I was in the kitchen."

"But you hadn't been in bed. I had to lie."

"Neither of us lied."

"That is just a technicality. We bent the truth."

Raucous sipped on his drink, the frothy milk covered in chocolate powder the barista knew not to make into some stupid shape like a coffee bean. Maybe this is how they do it, Raucous thought, that small step, that ever forward march through incremental advances until he was ordering spiced pumpkin lattes and talking politics without realising he had become one of them.

"I am out. No more. I promised," he said.

"What happened?"

Raucous looked down at the table, looking at marks scratched into wood from years gone by. Schoolboys, it was never the girls, carving names or symbols, and burning rings of black in science lessons and now they are left to be chic cool in what currently passes as the modern version of a red and white plastic table cloth.

"I got Mack killed," he said. "I thought I was doing the right thing."

Raucous looked up as Charlotte moved her hand across and grabbed his clenched fist. She wasn't looking for a loving gesture, she grabbed and squeezed. Raucous looked up, saw her eyes, knew he had to listen.

"We are done, Raucous. No more. We are lucky to be alive, lucky to be able to still walk without fear. You understand that? Mack was gone, dead already. You know that. Whatever you did, it is over."

Raucous nodded, he knew her words had meaning and truth. He knew that she was warning him as well as caring.

"I'm out," he said."I'm too old and too slow and too soft to be chasing down revenge. There is no revenge to have. Just a shot at people who don't care and retaliation from the same."

He knew they would come if he caused trouble. He couldn't keep his involvement quiet. He had been lucky. The police, he knew had him as someone of interest, someone they believed could be the one. But they had nothing beyond logical thought and a hunch that felt right. They could squeeze, push for a crack but he was too smart and too experienced to fall for anything as simple as the word games they used.

The police would have him as a man operating under the instruction of whoever came next, whoever killed Mack. With his history they would be stupid to eliminate him from their thoughts. But they had already seen Raucous standing alone and their theories would fade and adapt and change. They had nothing for if they had he would now be dead.

"I don't want to be back in," Charlotte said. "I'm done."

She squeezed his hand so the blood ran away leaving white skin.

"Promise me you are out," she said."No word games, no one-off going back. A promise. One that if you break, I am gone."

"I already gave you my word."

"Our future is something else."

5

The discomfort he felt came from what he saw. They were being subtle but not enough to be hidden. Anyone watching would see nothing, but Raucous had been in the game so long that he saw it all in real time.

There was no danger, it was early but people were around, the dawn was in the past and shops were doing business. His gym was not for the early birds, the old ladies who had been awake for hours wanting to walk in water and chat to friends, nor the business men who needed the rush of an early morning sprint to get them through the day. His business thrived from late afternoon to the night, manual workers and students and school kids turning up to learn defence, or learn to attack, and be held accountable to the men inside.

Raucous walked slowly and he knew that he had spotted them. Two kids in grey hoodies, black tracksuit bottoms and whatever trainers cost the most in the current fashion.

The gym was a first floor barn, a warehouse from when the shops below had been one large store, the name of which no longer exists. A huge area that many would want for flats, or student accommodation but which was bought and paid for, and rarely heated. White walls covered in posters of fighters and fights, beams from which heavy bags hung, and an office in back where nothing happened and a book was kept of names,

names of the people who came in. You showed ID and they knew who you were. No alias, no pretence, no hiding, you came here and Raucous knew who you were.

The door was solid wood with aluminium panels, the type used on industrial stairs, all rough to stop sliding and here to stop holes being kicked and urine soaking into wood. It was an alcove and people would use it for all manner of things. Raucous opened the door and took the steep, narrow staircase. He had left the front door unlocked. He reached the top and unlocked the large, thick blue door, opening it into the gym. The air seemed colder inside than out. There were ten large windows, all single glazed and most always open. The circulation of air could never wipe away the smell of sweat and damp and age, but it took enough of an edge for the air to be palatable.

Raucous waited, listening but couldn't yet hear what he expected. He waited a little more, heard nothing and walked across the large open floor, between the metal pillars holding the ceiling, over the hard, worn linoleum floor that was covered in mats strategically placed to hide the holes made by the workers of years gone by.

He entered the office, with its desk and chair they had inherited when they moved in, ones that they could sell as props to a movie set in the nineteen twenties. The top covered in worn green felt, and the chair a design classic in wood and beaten red leather.

He sat down and waited, watching the door that rose up alone, through the floor, like someone had placed a cupboard in the middle of the room.

6

He didn't wait long, the steps were bare of carpet, the white paint chipped away and wood visible and the dips caused by the friction of feet clear to anyone who stood and looked. He could hear feet going slow, taking their time as they walked one step at a time.

Raucous wondered who it would be, and what they would say, and whether what he was going to tell them would make any difference at all.

The head came into view and Raucous wanted to smile at a man he knew and respected. But he couldn't bring himself to do that. The meaning he thought he would understand upon seeing was now gone. It shouldn't be him.

Big George ambled to the top and took a large breath, not through nerves but exhaustion. Thirty years ago he would have been past his prime but still very much a danger, now he was a man whose respect came from his presence rather than fear.

He was still large, but deflated somewhat, loose skin hung on his face where once a muscled jaw tensed at all times, and skin hung down joining his throat. He wore his three-piece suit, the one he had taken as his upon his official retirement from violence.

A large bald man, elegantly dressed. He had been around so long he seemed to be a hundred, but he was just short of seventy and didn't have many years left.

"Come on in, George," Raucous said, waving George forward.

George nodded, accepted the invite he had been waiting for and walked toward the office.

Raucous knew this was an old-school move, probably an intelligent one. There was no direct intimidation, no warning, and George was not one to be forced into delivering idiotic messages. Raucous thought of scenarios and reasons as George ambled forward. He should use a cane, Raucous thought.

Raucous waited for George to sit opposite him. Raucous hadn't risen, offered a hand, or started small talk. This wasn't a business meeting, and any such move was weak.

"I didn't think it would be you George," Raucous said. "Someone younger. Someone still involved."

George nodded, smiled, and accepted his place.

"It wasn't my choice either."

"The last of the old guard. If you were a politician you'd be the father of the house."

"I don't know what that means, but I'll take it as a compliment."

"I thought you were retired, had no affiliations."

"I sell cars."

"So why are you here?"

"To talk to you."

"On whose orders."

The old George came though. As a young man, Raucous knew, George would be looking to fight. He tensed, wanted the power to surge in his muscles the way it did when he was considered the man such a long time ago. The straighteners, the unlicensed fights between men who represented factions and gangs. Educated cock fights for the black tie crowd who struck deals between rounds.

He'd lost a couple along the way, run doors to nightclubs, but had made his change, realised that life was worth living, and become a grandee and grown into the role.

"Who do you think would have won?" George asked.

Raucous looked, knowing where he was going but wanting no part.

George smiled.

"You know what I mean. Me and you, prime of our life. Who would have won?"

Raucous leaned back but kept his hands on the table palms down, a sign he was trying nothing. George was doing the same.

Raucous had heard the stories, seen grown men, hard men, show their respect in words and actions. But myths built up wherever mystery lay and people told stories that should be the same but are added to over time, embellished, numbers increased and the shock and awe blowing up exponentially over time. George was an old man, already in his suit by the time Raucous was young and lively enough to be someone the locals knew. There was no way of ever telling. George would fight, showed outrageous aggression, always coming forward and the skills he had were those from street conflict and trying to keep what he owned. He was a large powerful man with speed and anger and that was the combination to keep everyone wary. There were no challengers to him, none that ever came to much. He had retired, chosen his own time to walk away, and left his place for others to scramble over. He had earned his later life peace.

But Raucous didn't know, didn't care, talking about heavyweight greats and who would beat who was a chat that went on forever, and listing names of local psychopaths was much the same.

"I don't care, George. That is for others to talk about and make their own judgements. Different times."

Raucous thought more than he wanted, briefly saw himself young and wanting to show the world he was the top dog. He would have come for George way too soon and been sent on his way with ease. His youth was one of arrogant disregard.

"That it was. But at a certain point, with our difference in age, there was a time along the line where you could beat me. Right now, a stand up row, me and you, on the street or in a ring, there is only one winner. And that is you."

"You are an old man, George. That wouldn't be a fair fight."

"There are no fair fights. But that balance, that tip away from at the very least a difficult-to-call conflict to a one-sided humiliation, that happens, somewhere along the line. You don't know where, it is only long after that the dominance shows."

Raucous could see George look at his arms and his gut and sneer with disgust. This was a man who worked, was strong like a farmer is strong, and now here he was as weak as he would ever be.

"You walked away," Raucous told him.

George smiled and looked up again.

"Not unbeaten, certainly not untouchable. But still feared. And that little bit of notoriety, that is what made me get to an old age, and I am old now Raucous, I can barely make the stairs. Isn't that something? I could run five miles in army boots, spar all day and workout all evening, and here I am now, as an old man, sat talking to you knowing I couldn't hold my own against a housewife."

"Does it mean that much to you?"

Raucous knew the answer, it was all that mattered but George would never say as much because none of it was left.

"What means a lot to me is that I made it this far. That I am this old. That I got out, carrying respect, people knowing me, and giving me enough to live on. You understand what I'm saying?"

Raucous leaned forward again, he understood but he didn't understand why he needed the message.

"I'm out George. I have nothing to seek out, no one to kill, nothing to balance. It is all gone. All over."

George smiled and Raucous knew that he didn't believe what he had heard.

George wasn't the only one who had reached old age, there were others, but they all drank their lives away, or found weaklings to bully so their aggressive self-esteem could be boosted despite the obvious failings of their aging bodies.

"Whoever it is that sent you, you can assure them I am out."

"And the boy?"

"Mack?"

"That boy."

"He is dead. There is nothing I can do about that."

George took the words, tried to remember them as best he could. Raucous knew he would be repeating them soon.

"It has changed Raucous, from my time unbelievably so. I don't know what you see or what you feel. You spent a long time inside. I only had short spells. I never killed anyone."

"You just never got caught," Raucous told him.

George smiled.

"It never happened if you don't get caught."

They sat a while staring at each other like an old people's home weigh-in stare-down taken in comfortable chairs. Time dragged and Raucous was sure George was lost in thoughts of his youth and how he would have walked through Raucous. But Raucous wanted his time.

"Who are you reporting to?" he asked.

George came back into the present taking a deep breath to force memories away.

"Not one person, a lot of people. Boys come here and respect you. I don't know what your angle is, don't care. I boxed in a club all those years ago. But that boy wasn't the first to die, and there will be more. There are always more and for the same reasons. There always needs to be someone in charge, and when they aren't, there is chaos. MarQuick is gone and everyone is scrambling round looking to take control, but it is all kids. Not men."

"It is always kids, George. How many grown-ups did you know?"

"That is it though, isn't it Raucous? It is the kids, and we old folk need to stay out."

And there it was, the reason Big George walked the stairs and sat down and talked. Raucous tapped the table top and removed his hands from its surface.

"You came here to tell me that? Stay out and watch?"

George looked at his body and arms again.

"I'm too old to threaten anyone. Look at me, I get taken out by a slippery floor or a tumble from a step-ladder. Leave them to it, Raucous."

"So why send you?"

"Old ties, old beliefs. I don't know. But leave them to it. We can't change anything."

"Leave who to what?"

"None of that matters. There is nothing you can do."

7

They have done this before, spoken about their plan, each told their role and where and when to come in. Like a violent troupe on a primetime dance-show they start from a point of practised choreography.

Raucous smiled at the quote running through his mind, Machiavelli or Tsu he didn't know, maybe some civil war bearded general, but it mattered little who said them first, No plan survives first contact with the enemy. Charlotte had told him that, corrected his idea that the bastardised version in boxing was the origin. He preferred the pugilist description.

Raucous had locked up and walked away. An evening of watching classes, taking part, being the victim or perpetrator in self-defence lessons. Women and men and kids defending themselves against his faked attacks. Techniques beyond clenching keys in balled up fists, techniques he had learned, he had developed and he had practised in the real world. Breaking grips, creating space, making sure you got out unharmed.

Throat punches, wrist-locks, weak spots, wrestling techniques from American high-schools and Judo holds, and above all knowing that running away is the best form of self-preservation.

Not a single person in the gym subscribed to the notion, but it was truth. But Raucous never could.

Raucous felt it before he saw. There shouldn't have been that much movement. A hushed breeze or sound that was just not right. He saw two, realised there were four and simply stopped and turned. The two who were coming from behind were carrying blades, long and only useful for chopping. The two coming cross the street were carrying bars, possibly cut down scaffold poles. A beat down, a scar or two but not a death. Their plan, what was left of it, was based on surprise. They had blown it before it began.

Raucous lifted his small kit bag from his shoulder, the strap coming over his head, he twisted it so it acted like a wrap around his left fist. He had no plan on punching, but he had no desire to be sliced by a long blade across the face or head.

The four were young, how much Raucous couldn't tell. He had long reached a stage in life where anyone under twenty three could be fifteen or thirty in his eyes. They all looked young, and they all looked small and they all looked weak. But if they were old enough to come at him in a group, carrying weapons, and ready to harm, they were old enough to be beaten.

"Can I help you?" Raucous asked the four boys, in their black wear with white trainers, and covered faces, and hoodies up.

Raucous glanced at them all and saw little muscle, no thickness to them, all scrawny. Maybe with their shirts off you could see six packs and muscle definition, but that was not through strength and size, that was through nutrition, or the lack of it. Just because you can see the sinew doesn't mean you can demonstrate strength.

He checked their hands and saw the knives and bars. It would be a straight up fight, no bottles or sprays of acid, no cheap evil to pretend they were the devil. One with a knife looked to the other three and decided he was the voice.

"You talked to the police. That isn't cool. We are here to remind you that isn't allowed."

"I consider myself reminded," Raucous said. "Very kind of you all to help me of the fact."

The voice nodded.

"You see, the message we need to pass on isn't supposed to be words. We need to make sure you truly understand."

Raucous breathed in, nice and deep, as much oxygen as he could take in one inhale. He thought, composed, fought the shakes of adrenaline, but encouraged the rise in anger. But he knew it had to be controlled, knew he needed a sequence. Four of them, two with blades he wanted to avoid, two with bars they almost certainly couldn't use well. They would need big swings, and Raucous wouldn't give them that.

He couldn't wait, although they seemed to think he would. They could be thinking he'd run and they would chase him down. Maybe in their time people took the harm they gave out.

Running away was always best, Raucous had said this not an hour before to a group of people who paid money to hear his expertise.

They were out of reach, each of them more than a step away so he had to choose who was first, which wasn't difficult. The voice had volunteered by taking the lead. The boy was watching Raucous, never taking eyes away and that was a requisite for not getting hurt easily. It was always best to start rather than wait and retaliate. But these boys weren't taking their shirts off and using insults to rile an opponent or show a crowd who was the alpha male through baring a torso. They were waiting, for what Raucous couldn't tell, but he was sure they thought the fear they imagined they carried would result in a chase.

He was the centre of a four point compass with each boy standing at North, South, East and West. In front, behind, and side to side. Each of them the same distance from him, knives front and back, bars to the left and right. A fight illuminated by street light and a moon reflecting enough of the sun to give shape to anything within touching distance.

Raucous saw the first twitch from the boy who spoke and he grasped the handle on his bag. It contained a sweaty tracksuit and damp towel, with the canvas material he figured it would hold up to slashes.

They all moved at once, which made defence difficult, Raucous encased as if four walls were closing in.

Raucous reached out to his left as he stepped that way, the boy was swinging the foot-long bar, and Raucous grabbed it in his right hand, the slap of metal numbing his palm. He didn't catch it right and his thumb bent and a fire of pain shot up his arm. But he grasped as he stepped toward him and felt a glance at his right shoulder as the other boy took a swipe. Raucous pulled on the bar, hoping the boy wouldn't let go, and would pull himself forward as Raucous drove his head into his nose. But the lad released his grip. Raucous ducked, stepped to the side of the boy moving forward, and pushed the end of the hollow pole into the kid's right knee. No ligaments broke, but the knee-cap snapped with a crack. The kid hopped and fell as Raucous straightened and stepped out of the group. He turned and stabbed the bar into the other boy with a bar, he hit just below the chest, in and up through the solar plexus, hoping to bruise his heart. The kid's eyes bulged, his tongue shot out and Raucous stepped into him and dropped his forehead onto the bridge of the kid's nose and the kid lost all contact with his body, unconscious before he started on his way down. Eyes rolled up, he fell sideways, hitting his head hard on the concrete slab pavement.

Raucous heard the swish, something he knew would leave a scar running through his scalp, possibly remove the top of his ear. He held up his sports bag, and the long blade sliced into its side, straight through the large white branding. Raucous had a moment where he couldn't tell where the second blade was coming so he pushed against his bag, pushing against the boy, pushing his way distant from the only boy left to hurt. He released his grip on the bag strap, loosening, letting its length fall, he pushed against the boy, who offered no resistance as his mass just wasn't enough to stop momentum. He tied the boy's wrist in two loops of canvas, and pulled down. The boy held the knife, but Raucous controlled his arm. Raucous pushed him against a shop wall of rough red brick, pulled the strap so the boys hand flew out and to the side, still holding the knife. Raucous drove the scaffold pole into the boy's clenched fist, hitting knuckles, slicing through skin, exposing the white of bone. The boy screamed, and Raucous dropped the pole as the knife fell from the boy's broken hand.

Raucous felt the hit on his back, up by his right shoulder and he winced, not from instant pain but from the thought of the pain to come if the contact was the blade. He reached forward and down and grabbed the handle of the knife the boy had dropped. He leapt sideways, to his left away from the blow, no screaming pain, only a dull thud. He stumbled further away and turned. He saw the boy with the blade coming for him. The kid whose knee was shot was rolling behind, holding his weapon. Raucous knew he'd been slashed, hoped the jacket and shirt he was wearing blunted enough of the impact to not have exposed muscle. The kid with the knife stepped and slashed down as if were about to partake in a test of strength at the fairground with a hammer. He slashed down and Raucous pushed up, the blade he now held parallel to the ground and moving up toward the boy in a straight line, not an arc.

The boy slashed the blade down with speed, and Raucous closed his eyes through instinct. Raucous felt his wrist bend back with the impact, he opened his eyes as the boy screamed, he saw the blade fall to the ground, he saw it bounce off the tarmac at the same time as two half-fingers. The boy held his own wrist, staring and screaming at his open hand, his index- and middle-finger just stumps pumping blood.

Raucous stood. The kid had tried to put a blade though his skull. Raucous kicked out at the kid's knee, snapping it back and the kid fell.

"Who sent you?" Raucous asked.

None of them answered, none of them could concentrate on anything but their own pain. Raucous held up the blade above the kid whose knee was gone.

"Who sent you?"

"The Darts," the boy said, holding up his hand. "The Darts."

Raucous heard the sirens and saw the blue lights at the end of the street. He could run but there seemed no point. He dropped the blade and waited, leaning against the wall, trying to block out the cries of the four boys, knowing he would be brought in, knowing self-defence was going to be what he claimed, knowing these kids would already be known to authority. But most of all he thought about The Darts, and who or what the hell they were.

8

Raucous rode an ambulance. They patched him up at the scene, the back of his hoodie and shirt sliced open and his flesh cut through. The impact and depth not the incapacitating kind, but requiring medical attention not available in the street. He rode to the hospital not the station.

The nurse asked Raucous if he wanted anaesthetic, and his mind went back to his teenage years where through stupidity, arrogance and violence a grown man not as drunk as he seemed had thrown Raucous into an old red weighing machine with large glass dial. You never see them anymore, Raucous thought. The young small Raucous had smashed forehead first into the large circular face and the glass had shattered, a large sliver embedding in his forehead. The nurse then had asked the same question, and despite there being no friends or females around to impress, Raucous had declined. The pain had made him scream, as if a jagged knife was being twisted and scratched on his nerves.

"I'll take the painkiller," Raucous said.

He was leaning over a bed, sat on a chair, his shirt off and his back exposed. The nurse had injected and like a dental appointment, the immediate effects of numbness kicked in. These would be his last moments of peace, he thought. There were police to see, and conversations to be had and Simpson and Locke were already in the room, watching.

"I didn't think you'd accept the injection," Locke said.

Raucous grunted, as he felt the needle push through his skin. He felt the pressure, felt movement but no recognition of being pierced. He waited, as the nurse took his time, and finished by adding a large white pad that stuck to his skin and covered the wound.

"Pretty lucky," Simpson said. "That could have been a lot worse. Maybe you still have some of your old skills."

"Any of them dead?" Raucous asked.

"Nope, all alive, none talking, but all in pain."

"Then I've lost my edge," Raucous told him.

The nurse told everyone he was done and left the room. Admitting you are a killer always had that effect.

Raucous stood slowly and felt the adhesive pull on his skin. He picked up his shirt and slowly placed it over his head as the two detectives watched in some sort of reverse burlesque routine for the aged and infirm. There was a large rip down its back where the paramedics had tried to better see the cut. He placed his hoodie on, still being watched and still going slow. He wanted to think, as he had been, about what to say. The no comment would only work in his favour if he needed nothing from them. But he knew he needed information and figured they were willing to offer drips in return for his own participation. They looked eager and had no need to sit through and observe his back being joined together.

Raucous had the choice of sitting on the chair, the bed, or standing, which was no choice at all, and despite his desire to rest, he stayed on his feet, showing his size and taking the small advantages he could.

"So what happened?" Simpson asked.

"The boys not tell you that?"

Simpson and Locke smiled and stared at him, not speaking just eliciting further words. Raucous didn't like the game, even if he knew all the rules and had played so many times that answers and responses were only simple repetitions of previous conversations and moves.

Raucous thought maybe he had got this wrong, that maybe they weren't here to exchange. He knew he was being used, knew they thought they could push him in one direction with or without his consent and he was tired. These two, younger than him, less experience, less knowledge, and most of what they think they know learned in classrooms and lessons and not reality.

"I think they must have thought me smaller than I am, picked the wrong person. Probably having a slow night and needed to extend their range of victims. Can't see that they will be pursuing these types of robberies again."

Simpson smiled, she was gaining experience, had heard a lot and seen enough men of the world to acknowledge when they were playing.

"You think they wanted what was in your kit bag?" she asked. "Come on, Raucous, everyone knows you, you weren't five minutes from your gym, and four teens try and take you out."

"It was a nice bag. Nice enough to save my life."

Raucous knew he would have come up with another option, but it would have resulted in more blood.

"Did you know them?" Simpson asked.

Raucous had already thought and tried to identify anything they had given him. He hadn't checked their faces in detail, the police and medics had removed face coverings and he didn't recognise one.

"Faces covered, voices already broken. I didn't recognise one of them. But I'm guessing you already know who they are so if you want to give me their names I'll check them off in my head."

Locke smiled and looked down at the floor. Simpson smiled too but kept her eyes on Raucous.

"We could charge you," Simpson said.

"Come on, I'm old, tried and tested. Is there some type of obligation to say that? I know there is no truth in it, just like you do. Bring me in for questioning, sure, but to what end? A silent interrogation?"

"Weapons were involved," Locke says.

"Their weapons, against me. Self-defence. I put them down and used reasonable means. I didn't then beat the hell out of their prone bodies."

"One of them is missing fingers."

"Then he shouldn't play with blades."

Raucous looked at them, one then the other.

"There is something you want, either from me, or to tell me. You set me up when you came to the gym. A cheap trick that only the stupid fall for, or those looking for any old excuse will accept. You set this up, or at least put it in motion. If you want to tell me why, go ahead. If you want to play some weird game in which you think you are in some way intellectually superior because you read a book about it once and passed a multiple-choice exam, then keep your voices down while I wait to be discharged."

"You talk a lot for someone who prefers silence," Locke said.

"You don't speak enough for someone who thinks they are smart at drawing out information."

Raucous turned to Simpson.

"I am out. Have been for a year. I keep an eye on things and all I see is a power struggle to see who is going to have control of the movement of drugs. It has been this way for decades. That is where the money is, that is where kids see their fame and fortune."

"And you keep an eye on the kids," Locke said.

Raucous stepped forward and Simpson made a move, putting her arm across Locke's chest.

"Holding him back?" Raucous asked. "Are you kidding me?"

He looked at them, almost huddled, almost cuddling. He knew they were looking for this reaction. He had to think, be smarter than he was, smarter than them.

"I run a gym, the kids that come in, they show ID and I know who they are. I hear of anything they do that doesn't fit with the rules, and crime and drugs and violence are among them-"

"What about Mack?" Locke asked.

Raucous drew breath, a long deep pull on the disinfectant thick air.

"You want to tell me what he was involved in? Because I heard nothing," Raucous said.

"Come on, Mack had money but no job, bought things he shouldn't be able to afford, and he got killed because of it. You know what he was involved in, and yet he was welcome in your place. Protected in you place."

Raucous heard what he was saying, thought about whether Locke believed this to be true.

"I'm out," Raucous said. "The kids aren't mine, I'm not their handler, or whatever word is given to those people now. It is not what it's about."

"You are never out," Simpson told him. "You are what you are, and that is a life-long crook. You can dress it up any way you want with talks of codes and morals and all that old-time gangster stuff that was never true even when thought up. How many of the boys who come to your gym are clean, Raucous? Genuinely clean?"

"I'm not involved."

Simpson shook her head but kept her gaze on Raucous.

"Look at it through our eyes. Almost all the kids that come to your place to learn how to fight are known to us, or have connections to people known to us. And not the low-level vandalism stuff, but the big stuff. And how many deaths have we had in the last ten months? I'll tell you, twenty-four. Tit-for-tat killings, and it is getting worse. Your main guy, Mack, taken out in the street, and you are telling me you are just walking away? I know you Raucous, that is not going to be a thing."

Raucous knew this was the opinion of everyone, and it would have been the way to go. But he had given his word, promised Charlotte. There was nothing he could do about that.

"I'm done. I have given my word. I am out. It is nothing to do with me."

Locke stepped away from Simpson.

"Just like those two boys out in the countryside were nothing to do with you? Stabbed in the chest and throat just like Mack," Locke said.

Raucous had left nothing, it was all hearsay and they knew it. It had been a mistake, one he was paying for, one he shouldn't have made. But there was nothing there to throw guilt on him, nothing that would hold up beyond we think you did it.

"You know as well as I that once someone takes over the deaths stop," Raucous told them. "And then your attention will be on bringing them down so the next gang war can break out and away we go."

"They are not deaths they are murders," Simpson said and her pious tone hurt Raucous hard.

"And what do you care? You don't care about the dead, you care about the numbers, you care about how bad that looks for you, for your area of influence. You can't stand being an officer in a place where gangs are taking each other out. You'd destroy their lives too, just in your way."

"And you are staying out of it?" Simpson asked.

"That is exactly what I am doing. I'll look after my little part of the world, and it is little, and you guys can look after the bigger picture. That is your job."

"You are fooling yourself, Raucous," Simpson said. "You are part of it and your history says you can't walk away."

"The word I gave tells me I have to."

"You keep fooling yourself," Locke said.

They stared at Raucous, not waiting, only showing their contempt. They looked at each other and shrugged.

"You got any more questions for us before we go?" Simpson asked.

Raucous did and there was no reason to wrap it up in something palatable.

"Who are the Darts?"

They smiled, exchanged a look and did not answer.

9

Charlotte was waiting where she said she would be, in the street, engine running. She was the richest person he knew and she was never going to pay ten pounds to leave her car in the Hospital for five minutes. Maybe this was why she was rich, or maybe showed she would not accept a return to being poor.

The car was expensive but discreet, powerful but not loud. A dark grey with a badge that told people of the cost, and one not all would recognise.

"Don't get blood on anything," Charlotte told him.

Raucous slid in, the leather seats soft and high quality. They produced very few per year and so the price remained high enough for them to be exclusive. Everything was smooth, that one step ahead of the conventional, and quiet.

Charlotte indicated and pulled out.

She was checking the mirrors in a constant relay from left to right to behind. She was looking for anything, but saw nothing.

"There is no need to follow," Raucous told her. "They know where we will go, they know what we will do."

"What's going on?" she asked, looking ahead, concentrating on the road.

The question was loose and ill-defined, and not asked with a specific answer in mind. An opening to small-talk, an open chat about whatever theories they could piece together.

"I am being played. Nothing smart. Obvious stuff, but enough for excuses to be made for actions. Both sides are at it but I only know one of them."

"How bad is the cut?"

"I got lucky. Not too deep. It'll leave a mark, but I have a few. You got the names of the kids who did it?"

Charlotte indicated the glove compartment. Raucous leaned forward, opened and saw the paper. He read the names scrawled in Charlotte's hand. He recognised none of them.

"Local?"

Charlotte shook her head.

"Not exactly. All post-sixteen, none of them in education or work. All with records for drugs and violence. All from the Mountford estate."

Raucous knew the place but had never visited, there had never been the need. It was another vast shrine to incompetence, built to house but not look after, as many flats as possible crammed into the smallest space so people could be shovelled under and buried in concrete.

"They were a long way from home. That is an hour on the train. Who runs that?"

"They came by car. Stolen. Found parked, their prints all over. No actual affiliation beyond Mountford. Local thugs, worked for a few people, always the ones on top."

Raucous thought, he couldn't piece it together. Mountford could be a whole continent away, there were no connections, no competition, and boundaries didn't even meet.

"Why come here, and why for me?"

Charlotte looked at him, and he knew she was trying to understand his stupidity, the way he would refuse to accept the most obvious connections. There was nothing in fact, not yet, nothing they held that could explain events. A theory describes what can be observed and measured, an explanation of the real, and what you can see. What they had now, was just hypothesis or supposition, guesses at what truth could be revealed.

"Coincidence exists," Charlotte said, "but not like this. The two guys in the countryside, Mack, and now people who shouldn't be here come after you."

Raucous nodded. As much as he wanted three separate, standalone events, he knew there was a theme and a reason. They just didn't have enough information to give them a working theory.

"Big George came to visit, before the kids," Raucous said.

Charlotte turned to him and he saw her confusion, heard her swear.

"Visit for what?"

"To tell me to stay out. That it is another man's world now."

"And what did you tell him?"

"That I am out. That I gave my word I was not taking part anymore. That I'm done."

Charlotte went back to watching the road, she indicated and turned into the street where Raucous lived. She drove slow, third gear, not topping thirty. She slowed until the car sat idling.

"Doesn't seem anyone is inclined to believe you," she told him.

10

The gym became busy at seven P.M. Kids had eaten, or at least had tried. They came in small groups, and some alone, a few had kit bags but most turned up in the clothes they wore to train. Raucous took the first hour, an intense set of circuits based on old-school boxing. There was a buzzer on the wall that when set would beep, wait three minutes, a full round, beep again, and give a minute's rest. A warm up, a stretch and then ten rounds of movement. Raucous walked and demonstrated but couldn't go the full session. But some of the kids here were in fighting shape, even if not of the fighting mind.

There were stragglers, and those new to the routine, who went at their own speed. Raucous walked and encouraged but didn't shout, didn't bully. That was reserved for the actual fighters, for later when controlled aggression was taught and learned, when the groups were smaller and the real fighters took to mats to practise and submit. This hour was for everyone, the intensity as high as you wanted to take it.

The buzzer sounded and people started jumping, burpees, skips, knees to chest, all the moves he'd seen good looking men, and no body fat women perform on internet videos, dressed in clothes from their high-paying sponsor, and teaching a class full of the aesthetically pleasing nobodies whose life highlight was to be featured on a youtube tutorial for bored people at home.

This was the hour Raucous enjoyed; a mix of people, all ages, and all persuasions, going at different speeds on the same exercises. Some dropped out along the way and were given bag-mits to smash a heavy bag with varying levels of acceptable technique. It was tough to make it to the end.

In the minute break Raucous would move through the lines of people, telling them to keep moving, not to slump, not to stand still, picking out those who were too proud to quit but would never say no to a request from Raucous to go and hit the bag.

The numbers were dropping, the high-tempo music dragging along those near the end like an aural amphetamine, musical doping of the drum and bass kind.

Raucous smiled and performed his fake cornerman routine of encouragement and talking about the championship rounds, coming to an end, almost there, one little push. He was surprised at how many listened and forced that extra effort out, how his words could provide motivation for these people to go a little bit more, simply because he had asked them.

The final buzzer sounded and people slumped, sweating, breathing hard, laying on their backs, some kept standing with their hands on their heads taking in huge gasps of air.

Raucous smiled, looked at them all, their different states of well-being, their pain and the ease with those who had not pushed to the limit. But his smile fell as his eye was caught by the man in the doorway.

Jim was an ex-pro fighter, nothing special, as many wins as losses, usually by submissions. His ground work wasn't good enough, just like most converted boxers he was a danger when on his feet and weak when on the floor. He came in and trained, and helped others with technique in exchange for paying no fees and having access to whatever he needed, whenever he wanted. He was retired a couple of years but he just couldn't stop combat.

Jim was nodding, pointing down and he held up two fingers, and moved an imaginary steering wheel. Raucous nodded.

He had kept someone outside to look as a precaution, the next shift had been his own. Five days on a rolling look-out. He couldn't be here twenty-four hours and had expected at best vandalism and at worst destruction. It was old-school threats, pressure applied, an uncomfortable atmosphere to put everyone on edge.

"Two guys. Sat in a car, watching the front door," Jim said. "Been there thirty minutes. No movement."

Raucous nodded.

"Thanks Jim."

"You want help?"

Raucous placed his right hand on Jim's shoulder.

"If you could keep things under control here, that would be appreciated."

Raucous walked to his office, opened a drawer, pulled out a black safe box, put in the combination, opened it and placed the gun he had stored into the pocket on his hoodie.

11

Raucous left the gym through the rear fire exit. He went slow, knowing anyone who had spent time studying would have the back way covered. He held the gun, concealed in his hoodie, looked slowly left and right along the narrow, single lane tarmac road with its double yellow lines along both sides. He walked right, towards the first narrow alley that led into the main road. Sometime in the past this would have been a loading bay of constant activity providing goods for businesses that could no longer survive. Whole shop floors dedicated to material that would be sized and cut in front of you so clothes, curtains or whatever skill those old ladies had could be put to use and objects fashioned for homes and sales. He had memories, vague and maybe not as accurate as he thought, of times gone by when he was a child, small and in the care of adults.

There was no one waiting, no one watching, an alleyway all would avoid because no CCTV would capture anything here. Jim had told him the car was out front, opposite side of the road, which posed a problem. It was always better to arrive unseen, to surprise and work from the advantage of knowing. Raucous chose to move on to the next alley, one after the series of stores that out front were a terrace of late night stops for drunks and students. Fast food, late night supermarkets, and a taxi rank. Out back they were a long single white wall with bricked up windows at ground level and blacked out glass on the first floor. Three rear doors, each steel, each old and each with the marks of attempted forced entry.

He walked the alley and stopped short of the road. He didn't look or seek out conformation of position, there was nothing to be gained. If he made a movement they picked up he would have lost all advantage.

The street was illuminated, but not well. The lamps were for cars not pedestrians and the patches between them were dark enough to blur images from a distance. Cars were parked, probably for commuters who would need to walk for minutes to get home as the streets they lived in were hives of vehicles parked nose to tail and with the permission of the council on the back of expensive permits. Here the cars were old, broken and worth nothing. To find them gone, scratched, or in disrepair meant little to the owners. They were all but a few worth more in insurance than actual cash.

Raucous pulled up his hood and stooped low, hiding his head and looking to seem smaller and insignificant. On the other side of the road a large van, twenty five years past the date of sale, with patches of rust, and a shape that looked like it came from the mind of a designer long since retired. He walked across the road, head down and covered, aiming for the back of the van. He stopped and leaned against the back doors. There was a makeshift lock bolted into the bodywork and not looking like it would hold up to much pressure. A sticker stated there were no tools stored inside and Raucous imagined that if there were they would be worth little beyond scrap. Raucous gripped the gun tight, his right hand warm inside the thick material. He stepped onto the pavement, turned right and started to walk, trying for a relaxed stride but knowing his thoughts made all the smooth evaporate and he was left with awkward, jerky steps.

Raucous could see nothing other than the pavement and his feet in turn. He wasn't looking, didn't want to be seen scanning the cars. He held his gun and would have preferred to be left handed with it pointing to his right and into the road. He walked, moving his eyes right as he came alongside each new vehicle. Most were white and red and he remembered the game played in the back of a car when he was a child. He always chose yellow. Another ten metres and he would be opposite the gym entrance. He glanced right and saw them, two figures, hoods up, in the front of a dark grey German saloon car. He pulled the gun free of the hoodie, reached across with his left hand, grabbed the rear passenger door, opened and slid in.

"Don't move," he said as he pushed the gun between the seats, against the side of the passenger's head.

They had reacted, the passenger reaching for the glove compartment and the driver under his chair.

"Leave whatever you were reaching for where it is," Raucous told them.

"No," the driver said.

He leaned forward, and Raucous turned the gun, the end of the grip protruding from the side of his fist and he smashed it right into the driver's temple. The driver kept reaching under his seat. Raucous smashed the guy's head again and a deep cut opened up and split longer through the thin skin on the side of his skull. The passenger laughed and reached for the glove compartment, opening it up and Raucous saw a knife, serrated edge like the weapon of a possessed killer in a slasher film.

The passenger grabbed the knife, the driver, seemingly invigorated with the attempt at fracturing his eye socket, turned around with a knife in his hand. Raucous made the decision as they both turned, looking like a pair of demonic Italians with olive skin and wet, tight curled hair, their faces covered in thick stubble. But they weren't the gigolos of beach romances, they were the young faces of boys who would want to be made men in New Jersey. Raucous jumped out of the car, spun to face the two men and watched them step out, smiling at him. Raucous raised the gun.

"If you were going to shoot us, you already would," the driver said.

"I didn't come to kill you, I came to speak."

"That's just a dumb thing to say when you get in my car carrying a gun."

The two of them stared at him, the driver slightly taller than the passenger, but not making it past five feet ten, each was wearing a jacket middle-aged men would buy to go on long treks in torrential weather out in the wolds. Each wearing tracksuit bottoms of the shiny and smooth variety. They had the build of lithe long-distance runners.

"I take it you guys are from the Mountford estate. I'm just guessing here."

They showed no sign of understanding, just staring with limited curiosity.

"And you are Raucous," the passenger said. "Which means you are dead."

They stepped forward and Raucous stepped back.

"I just want to talk," Raucous said.

The driver walked around the car and stepped onto the pavement. Two young men, two knives and the desire to attack in unison. The passenger waited until the driver was at his shoulder, he looked briefly at the wound and blood, smiling all the time.

They returned their gaze to Raucous, stepped forward, knives out.

Raucous didn't want the bloodshed, didn't need the violence. But he knew he had to shoot. Pulling a gun and being called by a pair of lunatics was not his plan. He had lost it, the edge, the fear, the face people knew would kill. They looked and laughed, Raucous had taken a step back. They didn't believe, thought nothing of him, chose to ridicule him through disregard. Raucous didn't want to kill, couldn't, the gun was illegal, no licence, no reason to own it. A relic left over from the life he chose to leave. He saw the two in slow-motion, their smiles, the enjoyment they showed, the rush of what they thought was to come. The pain, the violence, the satisfaction in superiority.

Raucous lowered his gun, away from the head shot he threatened and their smiles widened. They thought they knew.

Raucous fired. The noise exploded, a car alarm set in motion of repeated shrieks. The passenger spun, but not fully, a ninety-degree move to the left so he faced the driver. The pain came on delayed, he looked down, his smile remaining, the blood running through his fingers as he clutched the left side of his abdomen. The knife he held fell to the floor. The driver looked down, his own face breaking into anger, a snarl, but it was a mistake. Raucous took the chance and walked forward, as the driver turned to the movement, Raucous drove his forehead hard and down onto the bridge of the driver's nose. He reached out with his left hand, grabbing the driver's left wrist, twisting and smashing it back against the edge of the open car door. The driver released his grip and the knife fell. Raucous swept his right leg and hip into the driver's thigh, bending and pulling on the driver's arm. The driver flipped up and over, his legs hitting the passenger and his body then hitting tarmac. Raucous stomped down on the drivers head, crushing it against the floor. He wasn't unconscious, but he had no ability to get up as his eyes lolled in their sockets.

The passenger was looking for the knife he dropped, bending at the waist. Raucous grabbed the collar of his jacket and threw him against the car. He pushed the gun barrel into his face. Raucous could feel it now, the anger, the hate, the absolute stupidity of him. A grown man playing kid's games, hurting these small people who did not know the rules, who did not know him. How many times did he have to be this person?

"I am out," Raucous said. "Do you get that? Tell whoever it is that sent you, I am out. I didn't kill anyone, I will not kill anyone. I'm not competition and I am not a grass. The police came to me for all this to be set in motion. I could kill the pair of you now, but for what? I'd just be dragged back in. So get your man here, get in the car and get to a hospital. But tell whichever handler you have that I am done."

Raucous picked up the driver from the floor, the strength in adrenaline still surging, and pushed him into the back of the car. He looked at the steering wheel and saw the key dangling.

"You're driving," Raucous told the passenger.

He marched him around to the driver's side, opened the door and pushed him in. The passenger sat there, staring ahead.

"Start it up," Raucous told him. "And get out."

The passenger breathed heavy through his nose, his jaw clenched. He didn't move nor make an attempt to fight. Raucous watched, knew he needed a push. Raucous pushed his left forearm against the passenger's face, forcing his head into the seat. Raucous pushed his gun into the passenger's gut, and the passenger inhaled but didn't scream.

"Move the car," Raucous said.

He released his grip and stepped away.

The passenger reached forward and turned the key. The engine popped into life. He struggled putting the car into gear, the rip through the left side of his body causing pain. He turned the wheel, pushed the accelerator and Raucous moved to give the car space.

12

"I thought you'd get here sooner," George said.

He was stood out front of his office Portakabin, three-piece suit, at the top of three steps, a scaffold pole handrail to his left. Out back was a vast field, a property developer's dream of an area, filled with second hand cars of any type he thought he could turn a profit. The garage was there too where his men would fix up for the resale. Two of the mechanics were hanging close, and had appeared as Raucous came into view.

Raucous nodded his recognition and walked slowly forward. He stopped at the bottom of the first step.

"I'm here to talk not fight," Raucous said.

George smiled down, appreciating the fact Raucous had given up advantage, had shown respect.

"That has been the opening to many conflicts," George told him.

Raucous nodded at the mechanics who stood close holding tools that were too big to fix anything.

"There are things these guys don't need to hear," Raucous told him.

"That is true," George said.

George looked at his men, nodded. It made little difference if they walked away or not, they would be close enough to catch and fight if Raucous stepped out of line. George was showing his own compliance and respect. The silly games grown men play.

Inside was clean and blue, the light kind that elicited peace. The walls had framed posters of classic advertising, spark plugs, oils and the classic cars of years gone by. British made was a theme, although there were few of them to sell anymore. The desk was neat, wood and dark, the chairs new, black, comfortable and leather.

Raucous sat one side and George the other like they were in negotiation over the price of a sleek European saloon. George leaned across, fingers entwined and elbows resting.

"They know you are here," George told him.

As an opening line it was not what Raucous wanted.

"Who?"

"Everyone. Police or otherwise. You are a man of interest to many people, but most importantly both sides."

This was life, Raucous thought. It has always been so, and now the only difference was he didn't know the why of it all.

"Who keeps sending the kids, and who do I need an audience with to end it all?"

George leaned back, palms down on the table.

"You put yourself in, Raucous. The two they found in the Country. They know that is you."

"They don't know anything. Certainly nothing concrete. I've been accused of many things-"

"Guilty of a fair few more," George told him.

"I've been accused of things I never did."

George smiled and tapped the table as if sending a telegram.

"But found culpable of everything."

Raucous stared, wondering why he had come, wondered why George was involved. The right move would be to attack, to put out feelers. But that would have been right if he were affiliated to something of meaning, something that carried muscle and weight. He had none of that now, he was a single man in a world where gangs ruled.

"Why did you come to speak to me? You haven't been in since I was a boy. Sure, you float around on the periphery, but you are no one's messenger, and you owe me nothing."

George tried for a smile but gave up a third of the way in and pursed his lips.

"I owe very few people anything at all. I'm not dumb enough to realise I didn't have support and help to build whatever this all is here," he said, indicating his porta cabin as if it were a kingdom, and maybe, deep down, that is what he believed it to be. "But enough of it I built alone for me to be comfortable calling it all mine. But I got out, stayed out, and each and every man who came next left me be."

"For a price?"

"Nobody buys me," George said, each word loud and slow.

"Then who sent you?"

"Nobody sent me. I don't work for anyone but myself. But I owe a man a lot of things. And what I thought I was doing was attempting peace. I got it wrong. I got you wrong."

Raucous stared at George, and while he would never say he could read people to perfection, he saw no fake in the face opposite, and George had never needed to pretend, to fake words. He told you, he didn't play or hide.

"I was expecting something else," Raucous said.

"You were expecting threats, a strong arm from somewhere or someone. And you were right, that would have been the way to go for anyone with sense. But I got there first."

"Who asked?"

George smiled again.

"Sometimes you don't need to be asked, you just know it is your turn. You are in trouble Raucous and you have made it all worse, and whatever I said to you, whatever you took from that, just isn't applicable any longer. The problems that come are yours, but not alone."

Raucous couldn't piece it all together, George had been old school all his life, there were few people left from that time, and none of them with influence.

"Who are the Darts?" Raucous asked.

"You are so far behind what is happening. You think you see the whole world you live in, but you have no idea what is coming up behind you."

"Do you know who they are?"

George laughed.

"Are you kidding me? You know the Darts. You shot one of them, and stomped the head of the other."

"The two kids?"

"They are kids, but they are also bone fide psychopaths. And all the other kids are scared of them. Fear gets people to do many things. We know that, it is a tool we use. They will be back for you. And you know as well as I that neither of them make old age happily. Either they soon become a prison problem, or they are found dead. Most likely dead. But they will smash and destroy all the way there. I'm not saying you can't handle them, but you can't handle what they belong to."

"Which is what?"

"Organisation. None of our small time stuff. None of our little territories. Something bigger."

"No one works together, too many places and too many gangs. They don't cooperate."

George smiled and moved his head in a slow shake.

"There is money everywhere. Everyone wants it, more than they need and more than they are worth. The police today can't handle the scale. We are not Mexico or Colombia, we don't have gangs with that much wealth and that much power, but we have enough to outnumber and outthink and out manoeuvre. The ones that get caught, the ones they put up on TV to show the country the good deeds and the clean streets, they are there because they have been given up."

"Where do the Darts fit into this?"

"They are you and me. Modern version. A weapon. They are not known, don't have enough about them to be anything to follow. They are street bullies made big. But they are useful for violence. They have backing that reaches all the way to when I was you."

The meaning was there, the idea of a something bigger, a takeover that didn't eliminate but just made everyone rich.

"And if I kill them?" Raucous asked.

"No one will cry and each side, to some extent will be happy. They are dangerous. They understand only violence. Their go-to method and their whole point of being. It isn't necessary, they enjoy it. They have connections and uses. I couldn't claim to know them all. But there will be kick-back from their death, and I don't know if you could ride that out."

Raucous heard the words but there was nothing there he could use, it was listening to a criminal philosopher musing on the bastardisation of his once great theory.

"Who do they work for?" Raucous asked.

George leaned back further understanding what he was saying made no difference to the large man opposite.

"They are from the Mountford estate. But their family isn't."

"I know this."

George paused and thought, the principles of old school men with a promise given holding strong.

"Do you remember Saint?" he asked.

Raucous had never met the man, but he knew who he had been.

"Used to be the man you protected," Raucous told him.

"Yes, he was. Got killed inside. A simple hit."

"And you stepped away."

"A calculated risk. I would never have been trusted with the new crowd, and I owed loyalty to him. I could have sought revenge and died after I had killed some men. I couldn't see the reason in that. But I gave my word I would help his family. And I have. In coming to you I was trying to avert what I should have known was inevitable. But I did what I promised. All that comes now is beyond my influence. You are who you are, but you are alone now. There is no group to help you stay safe or ward off enemies. You are a capable man, but now you are just you."

"No names?"

"You need to stay away. Make it just you and the Darts. That is something you can win. Beyond that you are out of your depth."

"You don't know me," Raucous told him.

"But I do know them."

"And that is the information I came here to find."

George smiled, coming to the end of his patience, he stared, but Raucous couldn't understand what was meant.

George stood, and walked around the edge of the table, and headed to the door. He wrapped his swollen old fingers around the handle.

"It is all there," George said. "You just don't have the means to see it. It is a different world because there is a different level of money and a poor level of policing. There are kids, and I mean kids, nine, ten, moving drugs and money. Those South American mules, only British and in such numbers you can't stop them all. Some get caught, and they have so little to be meaningless. Thousands of them, Raucous. All day, every day. Money and drugs, and more recently weapons. You see those articles of billionaires buying out the competition, merging all that stuff together. That is what we have, and it hasn't yet settled. Some want in, some want out, some want to stay independent. Only that isn't happening. There is a war, and you blundered in. I wouldn't bet on you getting out. The papers say twenty four dead so far, but it is more, closer to a hundred and it is going to get worse. Nobody wants to save people other than you. Everyone else just wants the money and fame."

Raucous stood, not knowing if he had enough to move forward. The Darts would come again, that much was obvious, but he had seen them off once and they offered nothing but the maniacal belief they could not be killed.

13

They were waiting, all sat or standing in his office when he walked the stairs to the gym. The place only had a sprinkling of people because it was the early afternoon and most were at work or at school. An ex-boxer was jumping rope, slowing down the decline of his body by offsetting the calories of alcohol his evening brought. Two women were stretching, ready to hit weights and Raucous still couldn't believe how many females now wanted muscles.

He saw them as he walked through the door on the first floor. An office with Charlotte standing, arms folded across her, wearing sports clothes more baggy than the norm, and Simpson and Locke sat waiting. Locke swivelling side to side like an agitated child.

Raucous looked to Charlotte, and she gave a little nod. Be careful, all was good. That is what she had meant of that he was sure. A shake would have seen his heart rise.

She had messaged so the surprise Raucous forced onto his face was as fake as the apologies he used to give at school.

"Almost as if you knew we would be here," Simpson said as Raucous walked through the open door.

"With people as predictable as you there is very little thought needed," Raucous replied. He turned to Charlotte. "You Okay?"

Charlotte nodded and smiled, knowing the question was a joke. She looked after herself and Raucous smiled along.

"Nice little bit of love right there. Heartening to see," Locke told Simpson as he stood. "Do you want to hold hands, a little peck on the cheek?"

Charlotte rolled her eyes and the fun that brought blew away the anger he would have once felt.

"Charlotte has been entertaining us while we have waited," Simpson said. "And as lovely a host as she is, we are here for you."

Raucous stood and smiled and waited and they knew he was not about to speak or be kind or offer a hand. The seconds went by and everyone smiled, not through embarrassment but that they were all in on the secret.

Locke broke the silence.

"It has come to our attention there was a small altercation in the street two nights ago. The word is you were involved."

Raucous waited, answering quickly was a mistake in any situation. But he got there with a drawl. He preferred things slow.

"Long time ago, nothing springs to mind."

Simpson stepped in and Raucous wanted to shrug at the alternating routine. They were trying to put him on a verbal merry-go-round and shake up his mind.

"Talk of a gunshot. A person shot. Another hurt," she said.

Raucous turned to her slowly, scratching his cheek, smiling all the way.

"Check the hospitals, maybe you'll find something."

Locke wanted speed and cut in fast.

"We already have, doesn't seem to be any people fitting the description."

Raucous inhaled deeply and slow, turning his head when he could inhale no more. He was having fun, wondering why the up-and-comers always thought the verbal wave of back-and-forth voices was a weapon that always worked.

"Then I'd say your attention has been wasted."

Locke started to walk around the office, touching things as if he had a gift and could read the history of the room through making a physical connection with inanimate objects. Raucous hated the act, didn't need the story, and wanted the reveal. He looked at Charlotte and she was smiling, watching Locke, knowing the game having seen the same story before.

Simpson was watching him too, and Raucous thought he could see a little embarrassment, a small level of uncomfortable in the way she tried to hold her face neutral.

"You hear a lot of things," Locke said. "And you try to piece them together, fill in the parts that aren't there, bridge those gaps in the story, make logical guesses at what hasn't been said."

Raucous hated the way they all spoke as if he hadn't read a book, and had learned nothing at all beyond the simplicity of violence. Anger was there and he knew he should share it.

"And you do that with your intellectual brilliance?" Charlotte asked, her voice she used when mocking Raucous for saying something lacking any credibility. "Or with some creativity you picked up on a course financed by the taxpayer?"

Locke stopped his walking and touching and held his hands behind his back. A military past, Raucous thought.

"You think you have brains because you deal with stupid people," Charlotte said."You think you have insight because you crack the mistakes of the criminally incompetent. You are here now because you want your Agatha Christie moment, you should maybe have grown a waxed moustache and forced a French accent. But if you can hurry up to the great, unforeseen reveal, we would be most happy so we can then show you out and go grab a coffee."

Locke smiled, uncoupling his hands from behind him. Simpson smiled because Locke couldn't see.

"We would like to have a little search of the premises," Simpson said.

Raucous replied without thought. A stock answer to the same type of enquiry.

"I'm assuming you have the legal authority to do so."

Simpson nodded and pointed at a paper on the desk. Raucous couldn't read the words, the print was small and far away. He turned to Charlotte, and she smiled and nodded.

"All official," she said.

Raucous smiled again and spoke.

"I appreciate the request. Always best to be polite. Anywhere in particular?"

Locke made a childish attempt at looking around the room, touching walls and the glass. He came back around to the desk and sat down as if it were his. He opened the top drawer of three, looked inside and closed it. He opened the second, repeating the trick and Raucous wanted to yawn but one wouldn't come. Locke opened the third drawer and made a noise of surprise. He pulled out the black metal box with a numerical combination. He held it up to the light, turning it to look. He shook it and heard the rattle inside. Metal on metal.

"Heavy," Locke sad. "Want to give me the combination?"

"No," Raucous replied.

Locke looked up to Simpson, his eyes sparkling more than hers. She had picked up on the vibe although it didn't seem she could understand what it meant.

"I don't trust you to open it on your own," Locke said. "So if you want to come over here, put the combination in – I promise I won't peek – and step away. I can open it."

Raucous looked to Charlotte again, his heart faster than he hoped. Charlotte nodded in return. The trust you have to have. No one else could make him do this, no one for whom he would ever give away this much.

He walked to the box that Locke still held but was placed on the table top. Raucous entered the combination, his hands not shaking. Raucous stepped away.

Locke opened the box, he looked in, smiled but he looked again. He reached in and pulled out a large metal gun. But he saw it was all wrong. It was heavy with a long barrel, but it was a gun for the Wild West, a gun designed for kids. A silver colour with intricate designs of lassoes and horses. The handle wood, but old and worn.

"I don't have any caps for it," Raucous said. "They don't sell them much anymore, and I'm not too sure it works."

Simpson was smiling behind Locke, who himself was nodding with pursed lips. He was still holding the gun.

"I keep it in a box because it was my first ever toy I got for Christmas," Raucous told him. "Has a special place in my heart. So if you can be careful with it, that would be much appreciated."

"Anywhere else you want to look?" Charlotte asked. "The warrant there gives you access to everywhere."

"Is there anything we need to see?" Locke asked.

He stood, smiling and nodding down. The information he had been given was false. He knew the joke and knew he was the punchline.

"That is for you to decide," Raucous said.

Simpson and Locke looked at each other, accepted their loss. They smiled.

"We're good," Simpson said.

14

He noticed them as soon as he turned into the street. They always chose the same place as it was best for the job they were there to do. A car parked on the far side of the road, in front of a large industrial red brick wall with concrete and glass bottle top. The view was down the street, looking across at the activity, where most shops were and where most people walked. The left side, through a quirk of history, held houses that were now flats, and ground floors that were mostly barred.

The two people in front were watching the street with a clear view, despite busy traffic, of the front door to where Raucous lived.

Raucous saw them and knew them. Charlotte, walking at his side, away from the road, saw them too.

"What is the point in that?" she asked.

It was early afternoon and light. It was not time for surveillance. Locke and Simpson knew where they would be but had chosen to sit on the street and apply pressure through their presence.

Raucous started to change course for their car, Charlotte held his arm.

"They are kids. Whatever they think they are doing, let them do it. They are looking for a reaction."

"It's cool," Raucous said. "I just want to say hello."

Charlotte smiled and shook her head.

"Two minutes," Raucous told her.

They had arranged to meet, sit down and have a coffee. Charlotte had asked and that gut punch moment of convincing yourself of bad news occurred. Raucous rode it, convinced himself it couldn't be, and waited it out till she came by.

She had smiled, held his hand, kissed his cheek, but in a way that told him it was nowhere near final. They knew the heat would never leave and that police were looking and hoping to see them fall. Whoever was moving in to take over the running of drugs was coming too. It had been less than three days since he had met the Darts but all the feelers he had put out for information had stayed unanswered.

Locke and Simpson were silent, looking ahead as if at an American drive-in movie and they had reached the point where one of them needed to make a move.

Raucous tapped the window, and these two trained, expert police officers jumped as if Raucous was walking in on them making out.

Simpson stared, understood and recognised and pressed a button to wind down the window. Her face and body clawing back at the calm she had lost.

"Makes sense you are here," she said.

"It's the street I live on," Raucous told her.

Locke was listening but staring forward, his eyes moving. Watching Charlotte, Raucous assumed.

"You'll get a better view down there," Raucous said, pointing toward the coffee shop. "A simple coffee and chat."

"That's good to know," Simpson told him.

They stared at each other for a few seconds, Locke looking forward, eyes moving left and right. He tensed and reached for the door, pushing it open and stepping out. Simpson didn't look at the noise but her face dropped and she pushed open her car door, smashing the panel into Raucous.

Neither of them, as was the norm, were carrying guns.

Raucous dipped at the impact as the swinging door caught his knee. He watched Simpson step past him, her face angry, her hands coming up. He looked to Locke and saw.

Raucous dipped, going as low as he could without losing his feet. A crouch like young kids do when playing in sand. A deep squat for the gym goers on leg day. He felt the material scratch against his head as he dropped, tugging on the top of his long forehead but sliding off. He placed his palm to the floor and pushed up.

He saw Simpson lash out, scratching, but she had stayed upright and the three kids, faces covered, all in black and all branded were swarming. The lead had slipped a black hood, or string-tie bag over her head and pulled on the cord. She grabbed but snatched the wrong place and was left the impossible feat of trying to break the rope being pulled from behind by a skinny kid in casual sports wear. One of the others kicked at her knees from behind and she fell forward, the other pulling at her arms, forcing them back and using a plastic tie to bind her left wrist to her leg.

Raucous stood and turned and the three kids there for him were coming as a wave, all three, fast and low like an under-fifteen front row of skin and bones trying to take out their large adult coach. They hit low, the impact on his groin, and Raucous leaned down, forcing the point of his elbow repeatedly into whichever back he could see. One boy dropped away and Raucous, moving back, wrapped his right arm around a boy's neck and he squeezed and lifted, his teeth crushed together and eyes wide. He lifted up and the boy lost his grip on the floor. Raucous reached forward with his left arm, forcing his body weight down on the one boy still pushing. Raucous jumped, his feet leaving the floor and his weight, with that of the boy he was carrying, pulled down, and the boy still pushing did not have the strength to hold them up. They crashed in a heap, the boy at the bottom crushed, his chest smashed and his diaphragm a rage of spasms, his breathing fast gasps. Raucous stood, bringing the boy in headlock with him, he leaned back, pulling up and if the boy didn't pass out, his neck would break. The body went limp, Raucous dropped him and he lay motionless on the tarmac. The boy with no breath was on all fours and Raucous punted him in the head and he dropped too, not moving, and struggling for air.

Locke was down, a hood on his head, his left wrist attached to his left ankle. The three boys running away, leaving him blind on the street. Simpson too, but in the road. The one boy who was still mobile and had come for Raucous sprinted away.

Raucous turned, looked down the street and saw. He swore, shouted and started to run.

Charlotte was struggling, a hood over her head but not tied closed. Three boys were swarming her, trying to grab her hands, one swung and connected with her covered head and she staggered away but was stopped by another. She pulled the hood from her head, took in the scene, swung a kick at one of the boy's knees and connected. The snap of a ligament ricocheted through the street. The boy dropped and Charlotte turned. Two boys jumped on her, grabbing for her arms, and she rolled back, onto the ground, bringing one with her, flipping him up and over, until he was thrown, and twisted and landed face up. She stood and stomped down, aiming for his collar bone and breaking it with a snap. The third boy leaped onto her back, wrapping arms around her throat.

Raucous was running but he had never been fast, he saw the car screech to a halt, he saw the door open and Dart step out. Charlotte saw too, and she leaped up and back, landing on the boy who was clambering on her like he wanted to be her shell. They hit the ground and his grip loosened, she flipped and stood. She heard the noise behind her. She turned, tried to parry with her arm, got contact but not enough to deflect the knife that Dart plunged into her back, into her kidney. She screamed as he pulled it out, she twisted to face him. He stabbed again, and she deflected with her right arm, the blade slashing the flesh below her elbow.

Raucous screamed, Dart smiled, and he stabbed again as Charlotte tried to move away but too slow. The blade pushing through her abdomen on the right side. She staggered back, Raucous shouted. He was close. Dart raised his knife, pointed it at Raucous, smiled a big toothy grin. Dart stepped back to the car, got in and the car accelerated forward.

Raucous watched Charlotte sit down, she was holding her side, not her back. Raucous watched the car as it came toward him. He sprinted harder, along the street a game of chicken where he was the designated loser. The car swerved toward him, a tonne of mechanics and metal against his ignorance and flesh. He dived onto the bonnet of a parked car, the car the Darts drove scratched across the side, slowing but not stopping. Raucous watched them and they watched him, the pair of them smiling and nodding as they drove.

Raucous stood and ran the final metres to Charlotte. She was sat up, blood pouring from her. Raucous took off his top, balled it and placed it on the wound to her stomach. He looked up, the café owner was there.

"Ambulance," Raucous said.

"Already coming."

The café owner gave Raucous clean tea-towels. Raucous pressed them against the wound in Charlotte's back. He saw her, she smiled. Her face white but still conscious, still alive. They waited.

15

Raucous hated hospitals. He had been in as a kid, young and in that phase when memories are blurred and are a combination of momentary grabs of information. He couldn't remember it all, only glimpses and segments. He remembered the injection, being asked to count back from ten to one, and reaching nine before vanishing away. He remembered the fish cakes he was forced to eat on tiny chairs at a tiny table. He remembered getting out of bed, needing the toilet and walking slowly, in pain, not asking for help and struggling back. No one came to assist, but they knew he had gone. He remembered waking up, in a bed and no one there, not even a nurse. Alone on a ward with other kids who had family to visit and presents to bring.

He had been back, but always kept it short.

He sat in a waiting room with other silent people, some there knowing their friend, partner or parent was dying and the wait was just a single drawn out step, a long silence for the inevitable end.

The room had four other people, two groups of two, who like him sat with heads down, a plastic cup of coffee or tea or hot chocolate, staring at a blue, marble-effect linoleum floor, hoping that whoever came in would bring them news good enough for them to go, or to visit or to see or to hold.

Raucous had made his own way. The ambulance came, stabilised Charlotte and left. The police swarmed, asking questions, looking for witnesses and massaging the ego of Simpson and Locke. Two lads were in custody, but they wouldn't talk, and even if they did they knew nothing. They were signed up in a role that gave them little other than the opportunity to be caught. Whatever they could say would add up to nothing or be false and incriminate those who were not involved.

Raucous walked away, no one had tried to arrest him, no one could force him to stay. He told them where he was going, although they would have to be stupid not to guess the answer. He had made it there, in no rush as there was nothing to do but wait. The medics on the scene had been fast, but not worried, scared and cautious but not calling in a priest and praying to the gods as the only plausible way of saving her life.

Raucous had told the nurse at the desk who he was, had told them he would wait, had told them to tell him first, for him to know it all. And there he sat, the single man, with bruises and his own blood trickling down his back. He looked at his hands and he was shaking like a drunk slipping into a pub on a Sunday morning to quench his alcoholism in a way that wouldn't be a can of cider on a bench. There was an image to uphold, a way of doing things respectably. Raucous knew the rules and the etiquette, and he shook, and he knew why.

Time passed and the clock on the wall ticked and the drinks machine buzzed and hummed and periodically choked as if it too were taking a break. The couples left and others arrived. Most had eyes puffed with tears, until they too went. He sat alone, the evening dark, the single frosted window offering nothing more than the wall in which it sat.

The nurse came in, looked around the room through habit rather than stupidity. Raucous was the only one there. She stared at him, trying to judge, making calls on who and what he was.

"Is she Okay?" Raucous asked.

The nursed relaxed at the question, or at least the lack of venom in his words. She nodded and hit on a smile that had no humour. A practiced face they taught at college.

"She is doing ok. Nothing beyond repair. A couple of scars, for sure, but internally nothing that hasn't been put on the way to being fixed."

"Can I sit with her?" Raucous asked.

"On the way in, she said she wants you to be there when she comes round. We have set up a chair, there is a blanket. It might be a little while and I guess you'll choose to stay."

"I'd like that," Raucous told her.

He stood and the nurse led the way.

16

Too much time to think without debate, without another poking holes in your thoughts leads to ignorance and conclusions that don't hold up under logic. Raucous saw ghosts in it all and recognised them for what they were; wild ideas with no substance, based on experience and cynicism and doubt. But they could be true and he needed to know because he was alone. Inside, where he had spent too many years of his life to have grown in the way he should, solitude was accepted. He hadn't needed to run with a gang as there were none where he was. Small groups, without doubt, but nothing run, nothing organised. He was a loner even there, able to fight and hurt and be left alone. And he was. The top man, the guy who let peace reign or violence erupt didn't need the hassle, and Raucous played the game and stood as muscle whenever his space was threatened.

But here, outside, with free-range and weapons and a group of people beyond those limited to violent crime, he was lost without structure, without rules and without knowledge. He knew nothing of anyone, and had no recourse to a group with whom he could feel safe in numbers.

He watched Charlotte as she breathed. Her face was uncovered, no assistance to take in oxygen. She seemed at peace and machines whirred but he was not sure they were even connected to her.

She had held his hand, a smooth glide and touched and grasped and he had not known how to react. They had been walking, Raucous silent mostly, unsure of what to say or be or how to move. Charlotte had been quiet too, as she mostly was when calm. They had walked through a park in London, one of the many that take you across the city, and she had grabbed at his hand and made him stop.

"What are we doing?" she had asked.

And he thought he was hoping, hanging out being as much as he could be to get as much as he was allowed.

He had no answer and he knew Charlotte didn't expect one. He smiled and she watched his face.

But now he was there, watching this woman, looking frail for the first time, looked after and in need of care. He had brought this, had been the cause and catalyst to it all.

He reached out and touched her hand, one of her fingers clipped with a sensor to monitor heart rate. He left his hand there, leaning forward, uncomfortable with the stress on his back, but calm with the touch.

He sat and waited, in a room, alone in her presence, watching her face, listening to machines, thinking of nothing other than her letting him in, giving him something in her he had always thought out of reach.

Charlotte stirred, a groggy awakening, and Raucous held her hand as she opened her eyes and the memory of what brought her here came in slow and in detail.

She looked around the room, found Raucous with her eyes and smiled. Raucous squeezed her hand, hoping he was doing it the way she had to him.

"It's Okay," Raucous told her when her movements stopped. "Two scars, some damage, but you'll be good."

She nodded, looked away, stared at the door. She turned back to him.

"Are you going to kill them?"

Raucous didn't answer. Charlotte squeezed his hand.

"It is Okay," she said.

"This won't be enough," Raucous said. "They will come back for more."

"For you?"

"That's what I see."

She stared at him more, reading his face in the way she could, soaking in his emotions and making more sense of them than Raucous ever would.

"And then what?" Charlotte asked.

He knew what she meant, she thought he could never get out, never leave.

"I don't want to be George," Raucous said, speaking to himself more than her. "I want something else."

"Do you even know what that is?"

Raucous smiled like a kid trying to force happiness on hearing of a death.

"Beyond you? No."

Raucous wanted to tell her it would be easy, safe and quick, tell her everything he wanted to convince. But he couldn't lie and he didn't know. Arrogance is a friend when carried in a sense of reality.

He held her gaze without defiance, just a little kid looking for the acceptance from parents. Charlotte closed her eyes but they stayed shut for shorter than intended.

17

The door opened and a male nurse walked in. Locke and Simpson followed. An electronic notification had beeped and told those waiting Charlotte was awake. Raucous slid his hand from Charlotte's. Still with the idea that shows of emotion were for the weak when in public.

Raucous stood.

"Nice to see you awake, Charlotte," Locke said.

The nurse looked Charlotte over from up close. She lay compliant as he looked at screens and her face and held her forearm.

"You're doing Okay," the nurse said.

"You are going to say how lucky I've been, how I need to rest, heal, and then I'll be back to my best, right?" Charlotte told him.

The nurse was confident enough to smile and nod, and maybe that was why he was the one to come. Raucous standing tall and firm didn't seem to faze him. The presence of the police appeared to be something that didn't break his comfort.

The nurse smiled and looked around the room.

"I'll leave you to it," he said.

They all watched him leave, watched the spring-loaded door slow down and then slip into the frame with the squeak of rubber sliding against each other to form an imperfect seal.

Raucous waited, biting down on his own teeth, his jaw tensing and relaxing as if a dentist were asking him to grind on a filling.

"We've come to ask for information. Witness statement," Simpson said.

Raucous looked at Charlotte and she shrugged.

"You were there," Raucous told them. "Write your own statements."

"We were somewhat incapacitated," Locke said. "Unable to see exactly what was happening."

Raucous stepped around the bed that was between them.

"Convenient," he told them. "Hoods on heads, two trained people like you. Taken so easily. There but can't see a thing. Nothing to report if your eyes are covered, right?"

"They tried for you too."

"Only we fought back and swatted the kids away as they came."

Locke pointed at Charlotte.

"Didn't work out too well for her, did it."

Raucous moved quickly, Locke reacted but made the wrong moves. He tried to swat Raucous away with his outstretched right arm but the mass of Raucous moving forward brushed through. Raucous grabbed Locke's throat and marched him back against the wall, pushing him in and against through his neck.

Locke smiled as his face turned red. Simpson grabbed at Raucous but she could do nothing to move him.

"I don't have anything to know you are involved," Raucous said, moving his face close to Locke's. "But if I find you were involved in harming Charlotte, I'll cause you equal damage. You get that?"

"We weren't involved," Simpson said.

Raucous did not turn to her. He stared into the smiling eyes Locke was flashing.

"You set this in motion, you are stirring this up. Using me to draw people out. Nothing adds up and you are not even close enough to intelligent to play these games."

Locke smiled and nodded, pushing back on the hand around his neck. But not to break free, just to increase pressure, throw a sign that he wasn't scared.

"You are going to let me walk, leave me be for this assaulting an officer, because you need me. You think you are playing me. And maybe you are, maybe this is what you want. If you want the pieces that fall from what I am going to do, you clean that up."

"That is not what is happening, Raucous," Simpson said.

Raucous released his grip on Locke's throat. Locke slipped down a little but had enough sense to stay as upright as he could. He smiled, and rubbed at the red welts near his chest.

"What is happening is that I have two clowns coming for me and hurting those I care about. What I have is a pair of officers playing a game they are too raw to understand. And what I have is a mark on me."

"We can help you," Simpson said.

Raucous looked up as if there were a god that would listen.

"Help me? You are the cause of this. You are involved. Don't ask me to trust you."

"You think you operate at some higher level," Locke said. "You think you have all the ways to work a solution, seek revenge like you always do. Make it all square and even like a playground fallout."

"You know nothing," Raucous told him. "All you know is that you are new, you need to make a mark so you kick things up in the air like that little shit stirrer every school has, and then watch the fallout and step in at the last as some type of peacemaker. It's a tired routine and one that is going to get you hurt. You aren't good enough for the game."

Raucous turned to Simpson.

"How this works, and what you want, is to charge me up and let me go like a cartoon storm, spinning around causing chaos, smashing the place up looking to hurt, and you'll follow along with your badge and superior tones, making your arrests and claiming all the credit for a well-worked plan. But it isn't a plan, it's cowardice. You won't take risks, you just set me off against people who hate me because of you."

Simpson smiled, taking in every word. She paused and spoke.

"It started, all this, Charlotte, you and us, with those two deaths out in the country. That wasn't us, that was someone else. Whoever is responsible for that, there is where the blame lies. Everything else comes from that."

Raucous had nothing to say, there really is no point in empty words when faced with the facts you too hold as the truth. It went back to then, he was sure, that moment in time.

"So we'll be watching, following some when the need arises. And we'll do what we have to do. Whether you call that making a mark, or what I'd call doing my job," Simpson said. "Either way, the end is the same. And it is that which is important."

18

It took a day to put everything in order. Raucous made calls and gave responsibilities, some to people he did not trust but had no option other than to give them space. He told the truth in a way that seemed real but meant something else. He was going to back away, take time to figure out what came next, lay low, stay in the background. And they believed him. Charlotte was in danger, and Raucous had nothing in his life but her. They all knew, but most were unconvinced. Raucous hoped they all thought he would at least make an attempt.

As a young man, Raucous would have hunted down and killed. The revenge an easy one and the consequences known and accepted. He would have gone away just as he had, and served time, been the man and no one would call him a coward. It was the rules, the law of it all, the only way for it to be done. As an older man, as more sense had been earned, he knew that destroying his own life so he would be known as a killer was the dumbest move available. Going down for a double murder, with witnesses would leave him inside until old age.

But he knew he would kill, knew he had to balance the violence. He could not walk among anyone if they saw he had cowered away.

The Mountford estate sprawled and was one of five, all built up and crammed in to the smallest space available. Monuments on a massive scale of dull grey brick and white window frames. Communal spaces out front, where no one pure dared spend time, were patches of green framed by cracked concrete. Millions had been thrown at it over the decades from Europe and home, but it was cosmetic and wasted. Five estates, all joined, all linked, and all with criminals on peaceful terms. This was multi-generational gangland, specific groups for specific ages, from kids through to adult, and the names changed as tastes developed, all called crews or boys, but there was a blood-line through it, like the common Tudors and the drug selling Windsors, heirs to the throne on every corner. You could trace them all back to the time the huge, Eastern-European blocks-of-flats were put together without any thought to organic growth. No one lived here peacefully, no one lived here without fear.

Raucous knew enough to be quiet and unseen. It was not a place to walk and be noticed, it was not a place to demonstrate wealth. There were no deliveries, no pizza men nor private mail. Anyone attempting to provide a service would be stopped and stripped of assets. Empty flats, crumbling but officially occupied were storehouses for drugs, guns and contraband. Dealers openly sold in the daylight next to prominent monuments without fear. This wasn't a place Raucous knew, it wasn't a place where Raucous was known. He had size but it meant nothing to groups with weapons on their own land. Raucous here was a large nobody, a man of violence who didn't have enough to walk freely among them all. Every ethnicity, from British through to countries you couldn't spell, living and working together in illegality where culture meant much less than loyalty and affiliation.

The only modern shining building demonstrating wealth sat on the edge of the estates. It was once a building to interview the unemployed, became abandoned and occupied with squatters for fifteen years and used as a twenty-four hour concert hall for local musicians with gang connections and the place to off-load drugs to the sweating, violent masses.

Raucous had never been, but he knew some who had. Even the second era of love, with its fondness for MDMA hadn't brought calm, and now the music had veered fully to the violent. Raucous knew nothing and here he was nobody.

Now the building was official, a concert hall for the locals bought and paid for with regeneration funds that should have gone elsewhere. A large colourful façade of bright, primary colour squares that lit up and in random patterns, and attracted anyone who thought they could be edgy walking among the locals.

Raucous unlocked the door to the flat he had paid for in cash. The name he gave made up and the man he paid happy to be blind for the right amount. Locals had watched, seen the large man in cheap, worn hoodie and jeans, a loser, nod on the offer made. Word would pass and challenges set. Raucous paid money for the year, made sure the man understood it was a long-term deal. The first floor of a small block, a council flat the owner sublet. He had a view of a green and a road, but he had no knowledge, no real insight into where the action happened. But as the night set in, and he sat in the armchair in the front room that was also kitchen and bedroom, he saw the glow of the one expensive building, creating a halo of purple then yellow then red above the three-story habitable monstrosity at the far side of the courtyard.

His bed was small, with orange covers, looking like a large fish finger. He had brought a sleeping bag, a gun, a metal bar and knife. And as he laid back he thought about his lack of intelligence and the stupidity of his actions. He thought about messaging Charlotte, but his official phone was somewhere else, and contacting her from here would be a mistake. He had a burner, two numbers committed to memory, no plan and only a desire to remove the Darts from his life.

19

Raucous rose at six a.m. the light not arrived. He made himself tea, drinking from one of the three mugs he found in the cabinet above the sink. They held a quality of grey dirt, a ring of brown visible in the edges and cracks. He had thought before sleep, devised the plan for the day, as much as he could.

He was within an area of two football fields, three long, tall large brick buildings that without front doors and windows would look like large industrial warehouses for the steel industry. This was the Mounford Estate and it sat like the blocks of a game of Tetris played by a beginner with four others. They were all one with imagined boundaries and set names. Behind there was a large three floor carpark, designed to hold the residents vehicles, but no longer big enough to contain the explosion in cars, nor safe enough for anyone to leave overnight. A thief's playground and dumping ground for the stolen. It was closed, condemned and ready for development but the price of living here was too low for profit.

Raucous opened the curtains when natural light arrived. He was three cups into his wake-up routine and listening for anything to give him ideas on how the social system worked. The place was a replica of council estates across London; functional and thoughtless buildings to house as many poor as possible following regulations so accommodation was just the right side of squalor. The residents had done little to maintain, and the powers that be would rather let it run down and wash their hands of responsibility.

The people worked, but they worked poor. Any higher income and they would leave here to a place where walking a street at night didn't require dogs for protection or a death wish. Others ran drugs and the local economy was propped up by those using. The pubs of old with the Pearly kings and queens were now gone and replaced with the dens of other drugs and the sense of community had evolved into a bastardised celebration of hate.

Raucous heard voices, heard movement, the steps and stomps of feet. The cries of babies and young children. The shouts of adults, the coughs of lungs looking to inhale clean air, doors shutting, keys turning, and the barks of dogs. The sounds were different to those he heard every morning of when he was inside; the shouts of men, the keys, the locks and the heavy doors, but living here, the noises and sounds were a musical intro-theme to the life people led. Bird song and the crashing of blue waves would cause everyone here to stop in shock and tense for a violent change.

Raucous knew he would be watched, knew as someone only just arrived, his actions and looks would be monitored and any weaknesses noted. Saying hello to neighbours, smiling would all be seen as stupidity, as a man not knowing the rules.

Raucous had to set up a story, an explanation, show a routine and be a no one.

20

Raucous walked out carrying a bag. He was wearing a large, paint flecked hoodie with his head covered, and face in shade. He wore work trousers covered in plaster and paint, and work shoes that were months from the end of their career. He was carrying a holdall balled up in his right fist. It contained the gun and knife but looked like a man's lunch. He walked to the open space in front of the building. People looked in the way the inquisitive do, trying to hide their glances but reading anything they can see. A group of four kids in warm jackets and white trainers were stood waiting near a bus stop that was of little use as it was just a frame with no Perspex. They watched him, and Raucous kept his head down, stooping to look smaller, and hoping the baggy clothes hid his size.

He heard them talk and he saw from his peripheral vision they started to move. Raucous slowed his step as he wanted them to catch him in full view of the square.

"Hey, you," a voice shouted, and Raucous smiled.

Raucous kept walking as if he were wearing headphones and the world around him was there to provide a backdrop.

The voice shouted again calling Raucous by a swear word.

"Hey, big man," another voice shouted. "Who would you be?"

They were closer, Raucous could hear that much and sense their movements. There was nothing to think he was in immediate physical danger, they would be running were they intending to hurt. A fact-finding mission, a test of boundaries, a way of seeing what they could take and what Raucous would give.

They caught up with him, one boy walking past, making an exaggerated look up into the darkness the hood cast across the face of Raucous.

"Ugly fucker," he told his friends who laughed at the comic genius.

Raucous slowed some more but kept on moving forward. He felt one boy to his right and left, which meant one was behind, almost certainly directing. Raucous stopped but kept his head down.

"What's in the bag?" the boy in front asked.

Raucous took a large inhale of cold air. He looked at them all, squinting.

"My lunch," he said.

"Well, Mick," the guy in front said, "you need permission for things like that here."

Raucous smiled. Mick. They had got his name from the landlord already. He liked the name, even if it wasn't his. But the information had been conveyed in quick time.

"Surprised we know your name, Mick?" the boy to his right asked.

"I didn't realise my fame spread this far," Raucous told them. "But it kind of cuts down on introductions."

"You want to know who we are?" The boy in front asked.

Raucous shook his head slowly.

"Nope, I'm happy not knowing anyone. Happy to keep my head down, go do my shift work, come home with my beer and fall asleep. Beyond that, I don't really care. I'm not here to socialise."

"Why are you here?" the boy behind him asked.

Raucous didn't turn, although he moved his head to the side. He smiled.

"I'm here because I can't afford anywhere else. Soon as I can, I'm gone."

"You paid up for a year," the boy said.

"Figure it'll take about that long to get enough together to move on. Hopefully out of London."

"Why here?"

"I guess you go back to what you know. There is no one taking a financial gamble on me, no bank is lending me money, as I don't have a financial past. Cash in hand has its pitfalls, right? I grew up in Eltham, nothing there for me, nothing I can afford. So I am here, similar but different. Do my job, don't exist, and then move on."

The boy in front was looking past Raucous, looking at the boy behind, looking for some sign, an order or instruction.

"No family?" the boy asked.

"None that speak to me," Raucous said.

"A wife?"

"Had two, don't plan on having anymore. I don't have the money for it."

The boys laughed at this. This big man in front of them reduced to nothing, reduced to cash living in a place they defended but knew was the dregs. A man destroyed by females was no man at all.

"Enjoy your day," the boy behind him said.

"Unlikely," Raucous told them.

21

Raucous was cautious coming in, went slow and checked his door and lock for marks of break-ins. There were scratches on the brass but none he didn't know. He held the gun inside his bag as he entered his own house. He stopped and listened while trying to make customary noises. He stood in the small room between the front door and the front room, moving but alert to anything from the other side of the door. He opened the door slowly. He listened and walked through rooms looking for objects out of place, or movement. He saw nothing, everything as it was. He relaxed, and placed his bag down and stood for twenty seconds staring at his home.

Raucous picked up his phone from his bedroom. He charged it as he made tea and sat and thought. He hadn't been followed, he had used the underground, the crowds and the longest route to get home. If anyone followed he hadn't seen, and why would they? He was a large man with no prospects walking to work. A million men doing the same everyday for various reasons but all for the cash.

There were messages on his phone and he answered them. A check would show a flurry of activity in the morning. A man waking and getting in touch with those who needed his instruction. Charlotte hadn't messaged as they had agreed she wouldn't.

Raucous changed out of his work clothes and into jeans and hoodie, he had to walk around and be seen, show quiet, altered movements, like a man in hiding but pretending he wasn't. He walked the street and nodded hellos, but kept to himself and made his way to the hospital. He looked as he travelled on foot and on bus, and while he was no trained spy in the world of espionage, he knew what to look for, knew to double back and check for familiar faces and out of place cars. Nothing popped out but it was too early in the game. He kept an eye for group of youths showing their intent on hunting down, and grown adults in suits looking for him to lead them to arrests. He saw none.

It was the first days of a staged play and no audience had yet bought tickets to see.

The hospital needed investment, a coat of paint, some tender care. It looked like a building ready to retire, the inside a warren of blue linoleum and empty spaces that led to the room he wanted.

Charlotte looked white, thin and aged. He didn't tell her but she knew from his expression.

"Don't try and hide it, will you Raucous," she said as he sat down at her bedside. "I know I look bad, but make an effort."

"You look great," Raucous said, and he meant it.

"Compared to someone who isn't dead, I look fantastic."

She didn't move much, nor sit up. Her head resting on a stack of three pillows. She looked dehydrated, dried out skin with no fat stretched across her face. She looked as bad as when she came in, a drip with fluids in her arm, and her hands outside the covers and palm down.

"What are they telling you?" Raucous asked.

She smiled and bared teeth. She hated lies even if spun to promote happiness.

"I'm strong, I'm lucky, scars won't be too bad, You'll make a full recovery. All the usual."

Raucous knew they were words said in repetition here, but they had to hold truth.

"How long?" Raucous asked.

"A week before they will let me go."

"Drugs working?"

"Mostly."

Raucous accepted the news, leant back and reached out and held her hand. He knew she was staring at him.

"Has it started?" Charlotte asked.

Raucous smiled and nodded.

"Easy?" she asked.

"It's always easy to kill. Difficult part is not getting caught."

Raucous saw Charlotte slip into thought, maybe memories, maybe thinking of those lives she had taken.

"The police came back to talk," she said.

"Locke and Simpson?"

Charlotte nodded.

"What do you make of them?" Raucous asked.

"Kids."

"Too young to know better."

"Young enough to think we are dumb."

Raucous smiled at this and squeezed her hand.

"We are, but we know it. They just haven't figured out they are too."

"They kept asking about you. They don't seem to be able to find peace with who you are."

"A simple man with a simple mind," Raucous said.

Charlotte smiled.

"The country bumpkin from the city, all straw chewing simplicity. You aren't fooling everyone."

"Just enough of them for a peaceful life."

"It isn't simple though, is it, Raucous? Not simple at all."

22

Raucous knew without looking. He walked, avoiding darkness in his work clothes, his phone left beside the bed in his original home. The four kids watched him and smiled and nodded, and gave away the surprise. Raucous carried his bag in his right hand and beers in his left, the workman returning home after a day. His hood was up, his face hidden, but they knew it was him and he knew they were laughing.

The front door was closed but no longer locked. Raucous pushed the door with is right foot and it swung open revealing the room he was supposed to call home. The lights were on making it easy to see the mess they had left. The bed was turned, the orange covers spread out and covered in liquid. The smell Raucous recognised from nights in pubs of ill repute and urinals connected to nothing but the floor. His sleeping bag was among them, damper than the rest. The furniture remained untouched, the walls and floors clean. Everything that Raucous had brought, strewn and soiled. Raucous looked back at the door, the lock not broken, just open. A key had unlocked it, no one was wasting time on picking a Yale. He heard the four boys laugh, and he smiled to himself. They had him a weakling, a large man in large clothes destroyed by life with nowhere to go. A victim for life and one they would bully for amusement. Raucous closed the door, he shouted a swear word loud and long, hoping the anger he wanted to fake was heard throughout the estate. He heard the laughter of the boys outside, and their safe knowledge that he was never coming out to confront.

He switched off the light, pulled up the single chair, sat by the window, and looked out through the gap in the curtains at the boys stood milling outside.

23

They did nothing in secret, although they took precautions. The four boys had a system. A person approached, they talked, money was given, one boy went to a car, opened the boot, removed what was paid for and left it on the car. The person who paid walked by and picked up what was theirs. The money was shipped to a flat across the way. Never any drugs on their bodies, never any money in their hands. All out in the open, all easy to see, all easy to follow and film, yet they took these precautions the same. They were not hiding from police, they were hiding from rivals. The money was defended in a building, probably three men inside with weapons and a back entrance to move the money on further. The car a non-runner and out in the open but not on the road. Abandoned and dismantled on grass, no way to it in a vehicle as bollards blocked the roads, a pedestrian zone, and another abandoned car blocked the one road in. There was no way to organise a quick snatch and grab unless you came in on two-wheels. The deal surrounded by their own people. To try and take it would cause carnage and death. To arrest them would take five minutes surveillance, and a large armed team with vehicles to chase down the scooters they used to move around. No one tried, no one cared, no one needed the danger because no one here complained.

Raucous watched, the smell in his room becoming something that was there, something to accept. The mattress was dry, the whole scene as if he had been hazed at an American college. Nothing owned by the landlord was damaged beyond sheets, everything could be cleaned down. A childish introduction to the estate.

He watched the four of them as dusk moved into night. There were lights on lampposts, fifty percent of them working. Patches of light, one on the car, and one on the boys. Raucous thought about their age, thought about their life. They were late teens, moving into manhood, making a transition from the small gangs to those run by men. They wouldn't all make it in the roles they currently played. Their man of violence, the tallest and thickest set would be no match for any adult who had become an enforcer. They would need to adapt, change their style and those that couldn't would be harmed into changing their ways. They were on a cusp, moving toward twenty-one and the keys to a city that didn't want them there.

Raucous watched as the constant stream of people moving past, the boot opening, the drugs bought, the money shifted. He had no idea of the pricelist, or what they were selling. The people who came forward looked too healthy for anything hard, and maybe this was the hub, the central distribution point, the Amazon warehouse for the small sellers on the periphery. The bags and blocks looked too small to be significant, but large enough not to be for single use.

The people flowed, the boys rarely alone, and the money kept on coming and always moved to a ground-floor flat.

Phones were used, for what Raucous didn't know. The screens lit up, they showed them to each other, calls were made, texts sent, and all the while a constant stream of people flowed in and through. It was like watching a criminal convenience store with inexpensive booze for the disenchanted, only here the highs were illegal and cheaper.

Raucous had no intention of staying the night. Someone had a key, they had shown no respect and he was a victim until he made them think otherwise. He was going to walk out, fake a night-shift and head home. A night's surveillance not what he had wanted nor needed. He checked his watch and in thirty minutes midnight would be gone and activity was already heading down to nothing.

The noise was loud and scratching in the general silence and it meant something as the four boys altered behaviour. They looked and became quiet, watching the street from where the source came. Two lights beamed through, shaking side to side and bumping up and down as the scooters with custom exhausts of pops and explosions made their slow way to them. Two scooters designed in straight lines and sharp edges with red, whites and blacks streaked down their sides. A man on each with head and face covered in full, black helmets, face guards down and reflecting light. The four boys looked to each other as the scooters made their unsteady way across grass and mud to the bus stop. The boys were still, they glanced to each other. The scooters pulled up as close as could be without contact on their legs. The two men stepped off, the motors still bubbling over. They removed their helmets. Raucous tensed and stared. The Darts stood in the courtyard talking to the four boys.

Raucous couldn't hear but he didn't care, he had hoped they would appear, had hoped he would see them. And here they were, controlling their own land, talking down to the people who had come after them. The Mountford estate and the hierarchy of power.

Raucous watched them talk, and his heart pumped quick when one of the boys pointed his way and the Darts turned to look at where Raucous was sitting. He knew they couldn't see him, and he knew not to move. A flutter of curtains, a change in the still image of any kind would bring them over. Once in the past he would have invited them in, and maybe he would have got away free. But there were six of them, all armed, and he was in a closed space with no escape. There would be more of them too, all ready to march through the front door and take him on. He didn't like the chances of survival and the certainty of arrest.

The Darts asked something, the reply made them smile and they turned away. They walked to the car, one of the boys accompanying them, they looked into the boot, spoke some more, calm and quiet like a manager doing an inventory check. The boy removed two large bags, one empty and one half-full. The Darts spoke, nodded, happy and content with a good day's business providing what they sought.

The boys moved the bags to the flat across the way and the Darts followed. They all went in and Raucous watched and timed all of the Fifty-seven minutes they spent inside. Raucous thought of going to look through windows but there was no way of going unseen. A large lumbering man peeking through windows would have the locals out and ready to lynch.

He sat and watched a closed door and a window with a halo of light around its thick green curtains. He watched nothing for each and every second.

The door opened inward and the Darts left with two young men, two of the four Raucous couldn't tell but they sure looked the same. They carried large heavy rucksacks on their backs. Cash, Raucous thought, paper money, or plastic now, counted, wrapped and ready to be laundered in large bags and shipped to a central point. He watched the Darts load up their scooters, the two boys helping. He watched the Darts place helmets on, start their engines and slide off, the noise reverberating against the concrete and grey brick. He watched the two men linger and smoke, chatting about their day at whatever office they thought they owned. He watched them walk away in opposing directions, watching them vanish from the square. He sat and watched empty space with no movement but cats. He watched the flat opposite, the flat with the people, but no money although some drugs. It was the front reception to the business they were running only without the sign.

24

Minimum two, maximum four, Raucous thought. A flat on the ground floor, an office and storage space during the day but through the night a dormitory for the nominally employed. He'd heard of big businesses with the rich owners of billionaire fame providing beds for employees in high-rise office-blocks so you can jump straight into work on awakening. To Raucous it sounded like a voluntary prison to lock up your soul and give away life for the benefit of someone who doesn't even know you exist. He'd done it, as punishment, living by the rules set down, when lights went out, when you could wash, what you could and couldn't do and where and when you could do it. He couldn't understand why you would voluntarily enter into the situation. But he didn't understand the here and now either. Across the courtyard, in a small flat on the ground floor of a poorly constructed block of barely legal living space was a home to store, ship, and sell drugs. The people inside having decided on a career that provided nothing but quick cash and violence.

These people knew the Darts, had a connection, Raucous had seen that. It was a way in, a start, one that came earlier than expected. It would be an easy trap to wait inside and have them walk into their death. He could sit and watch their movements over days or weeks and see the flaws and calculate the time and place to attack. He could formulate a plan that would have him unconnected and the two boys dead.

He needed to look, he knew that but he knew he needed to be a nobody.

Raucous leaned down and pulled a can of lager from the cardboard box that contained six. He popped the ring pull and heard the buzz of gas, the fizz that played music to men who had sat down after a hard day's work. He poured some into his left palm and spread the liquid on his neck and clothes. He repeated the trick with his right hand. He smelt like a semi-drunk loser whose confidence was coming from the warm high of ethanol.

Raucous left the flat and walked away from the courtyard. He had counted how many flats along the drug den was on the opposite side. He walked out of the square, no noises, no movements, a cold silence as his breath bloomed in front of him. He could smell the booze on him, the stale air of someone looking to balance out a bad day with a temporary high. His hood was up, his head was down, and he shuffled away. The big man out with his work bag heading off to a shift, or to an all-night supermarket looking to slide from a high to unconscious.

Raucous looped around streets he didn't know but brought him back to the far side of the estate. He was behind the flats, another long strip of grass, kept short in the same way a young kid's hair was shaven to a single length by parents who cared little for looks but a lot for money spent at barbers. He counted the windows along, guessed at where the flat he wanted sat and saw the halo of light breaking around the edges of heavy curtains. A thin line ran down the middle, a crack through which to peek. Raucous gazed around, two-thirty a.m., no one moving, most sleeping and no worry of police to stop and search. His bag held a gun, a bar and a knife.

Raucous walked slowly, half a metre from the continuous wall of windows, every flat having a heavy backdoor, made of thick plastic rather than wood. One for each flat, one to bring you out onto this strip of green with a small road running through the middle separating it from the backs of a twin block on the opposite side. Maybe a planner's idea of play space for kids but the resident's idea of storage for bins and discarded bags of refuse.

Raucous slowed up to the window with light. The door next to it was new, thick, solid and, Raucous imagined, secured on the inside with serious locks. He walked to the window, the light inside bright enough to send streams of yellow out into the dark. He looked in at an angle into the room, making sure his face was not in full view. He could see only a small stretch, but it was enough.

One of the boys was crouched down, sat on his heels, smoking a hand-rolled cigarette. His back was to Raucous. The boy was looking up, bouncing slightly and speaking. The words Raucous couldn't pick out, but there was a drone as the young boy spoke. In front of him was a man, sat in a chair, not speaking, not because he had no words but because his mouth was covered tight in grey duct tape. He had short unwashed hair, a nose clogged with blood, swollen cheeks and cuts from blunt impact over and around his hazel eyes. He had the look of a man with genes from all over the world, skin that shone darkly. His wrists and elbows were taped to the armrest of a metal garden-chair and his ankles to the legs. His forearms were exposed as he was wearing a black T-shirt, which hid the blood stains a lot better than white. He was staring at the boy, breathing normally through his nose, looking bored. There were multiple red bumps all over his skin like he was the last remaining victim of smallpox.

Raucous watched, straining to hear, straining to see more through the gap. The young lad laughed, Raucous moved a little and the man in the chair rolled his eyes to the window and stared at Raucous.

Raucous didn't duck or try to hide, more movement and panic would bring more attention. But he looked at the man as if he was being challenged. The man stared back looking like he was done with the small lad in front and looking elsewhere to show the conversation was over. The lad smiled and stood, stepped forward and pushed the burning tip of his cigarette into the man's right hand. Raucous watched his eyes, watched him wait out the pain, not move or squirm, but sit still, staring at Raucous as Raucous watched the skin fizzle and the young lad laugh.

The man in the chair stared straight at Raucous.

The kid stood up straight, and the man looked away and at the boy in front of him. The kid pulled back his right fist and threw it fast, pulling up just before impact on the man's face. The man did not move. The boy laughed, rubbed the man's hair, turned right vanished from view and a door thumped closed.

Raucous waited, the man staring at him, and Raucous looking back. There was no more movement.

25

They stared at each other for a minute, no sounds coming, no more commotion, no more violence. The man quiet, still and watching.The window had two small panels at the top, both of them open. The main window was fixed, the airflow only coming from a six inch flap. It was too small to climb through, and could be moved out to specific distances according to the metal handle attached to its base. Raucous removed the bar from his bag, leaned up, prodded the bar through and pushed the curtain aside. The light in the room hit him fully and he was a clear sight to the man in the chair.

"How many?" Raucous mouthed.

The man held up two fingers, staring at Raucous all the time.

Raucous held up his gun and pointed to where the boys would be. The man nodded and held up one finger. Raucous removed a knife and he was sure the man smiled. The man nodded and held up two fingers.

The man was calm, had seen it all, was not shaking, not fighting, not trying to scream through the cover on his mouth. He was not a serial victim, not a man afraid of death. His chest was rising and falling at the rate of someone watching Sunday night TV.

Raucous stared and thought. He was in full view of the back windows of a whole estate. He looked at the man and the man indicted behind and to his right with a nod of his head. Raucous stared and the man made the same movement. Raucous moved the curtain further, more of the room revealed slowly and he saw it. There was a rudimentary hole smashed through the thin brickwork separating two flats. It was shaped vaguely like a doorway only too low, too narrow, and the edges like the teeth of a giant who needed braces. He could only imagine this was an escape route for times of trouble designed by an idiot. But it was a weakness, a way in.

Raucous stepped down from the window and the curtain fell back, but more open than before, more light shining out. Raucous looked back at the man, who watched him as if Raucous was the animal in a zoo. He looked to the next back door and window and saw a white plastic frame and a white plastic chunk of protection. The door one of those that had a triple lock built in, and the window double glazed, strong and near to unbreakable.

The guy hadn't asked, hadn't pleaded. He was still and waiting, accepting his position. Not a victim at all.

Raucous walked, pacing around the block of flats, looking at windows with curtains drawn and lights out. He walked around, back to the front doors, he walked along until he reached the flat he wanted. The door was made of wood, a lip at the bottom to help rain run off, the glass double glazed and frosted, but in four small semi-circular shapes. The letter box brass and the lock the same, at chest height and round like a pocket watch embedded in a flat shiny rectangle. Raucous jammed the thin end of the bar he carried into the frame between the door and wood at the height of the brass circle. Its two flat sides looking like the tongue of an oversized snake. He forced the bar into the smallest of gaps and heard wood creak and crack, and when it would not slide further, he pulled back, teeth gritted, leaning away as he tensed his back and arms. The pressure built, the creaks drawing out, nothing moving, all holding strong. Raucous pushed hard with his legs against the floor, adding all his muscle to the movement. A pop, and a smack as the door snapped open, the metal retainer in the frame clanking to the floor. Raucous stopped and listened, trying to hear voices, steps or shouts, but nothing came. He pushed the door but it jammed when three-inches open. A thick chain blocked its path as it tightened against its anchor on the door and on the wall.

Raucous swore.

The man had seen him.

He couldn't walk away.

He pulled the door to him so the chain sagged, he made a small loop in the chain in the tiny space he had to manipulate the metal links, he slid the bar through and started to wind the bar and shorten the chain as his foot held open the door. His foot held strong, the chain held too and Raucous twisted with strength, pushing this time with his left hand and pulling with his right. The door cracked, and his hands flew quickly as resistance vanished as the chain broke free of the screws holding it strong. Raucous lurched forward against the door, struggling to keep his feet, he stumbled into the corridor, stopped his forward momentum and listened, breathing shallow and quick but quiet. He heard nothing.

He turned and picked up his bag from outside, stepped back in and pushed the door shut, jamming it in place with the retainer and chain pressed up against its base. From outside, the damage caused would be seen if someone looked up close, but from a distance just another shut door in the night.

26

Raucous walked the corridor slow and controlled. The hole in the wall was at the end on his left, a doorway opposite open. There was light cascading out from the room with the man, enough to make out the beige walls and a patterned carpet not available since the nineteen eighties of brown slashes against cream. He walked to the end of the corridor, stopped short of the hole in the wall, he listened and heard nothing but the nasal breathing of the man in a slow rhythmic beat, he looked into the doorway opposite and saw a room full of boxes, a bedframe propped up on the far wall and an open pine wardrobe. A storage facility.

Raucous listened for movement and words and heard a vague hum of noise like the almost real conversations of a TV show, the accompanying music and sounds a vibration rather than notes. He pulled the knife from his bag, looked inside the room with the man and saw what he expected.

The man knew he was there, he nodded without looking, his back to Raucous, the dates of a tour written in small white letters on the rear of his black T-shirt. The door was closed but not shut, ajar by inches. Raucous stepped in through the hole in the wall, crouching down to fit through, paced slowly across the burgundy carpet to the door on the far side and listened. The sounds of actor's conversation low but audible, the orchestral backing sounding out to convey action. Raucous turned to the man, who was sat waiting, calm and not moving.

Raucous pointed out of the door, raised two fingers and the man nodded. Two men in another room. Raucous stepped across, knelt down to the right of the man and sliced through the tape holing his arm in place. The man continued to sit, his arm not moving at all. Raucous moved and sliced through the tape on the other arm and the man kept resting his hand on the chair. Raucous cut through the tape on each ankle and the man was free but he remained sat, the tape over his mouth still there and the man in no hurry to pull it loose.

The man stared at Raucous, sat in his chair, and he watched Raucous stand and step back. The man nodded, Raucous imagined a thanks, and the man got to his feet all slow and stretching like a newly awakened cat.

He was a few inches shorter than Raucous, about five ten, with the shoulders and physique of a man who preferred endurance over weight. Wiry and the T-shirt was not his as it hung baggy, hiding his chest and stomach, but his arms were muscled like a climber. The arms of a man of manual labour.

He hadn't removed the tape over his mouth.

The man walked to the small sideboard in the corner of the room. There was a thick glass ashtray on top overflowing with dead cigarettes. He picked it up and tipped the contents on the floor. He held the glass in his right hand by placing his fingers and thumb around its circular edge. He opened the door, stepped through and turned left.

Raucous shook his head but followed.

The man walked quickly but silently to the next door on his left, the door was open and light was shining through but not consistent, a flickering from light to dark, from multi-coloured to yellow, the kaleidoscope of images from a large screen TV.

The man stopped, put his arms to his side, standing just short of the doorway. He reached up with his left hand, dug his nails into his cheek, picking under the tape. He pulled and ripped the tape free, hair and skin coming with it. This sound the loudest in the flat.

The man stepped quickly into the room.

27

The man shouted, his voice deep and loud, an insult to the boys sat with game controllers in their hands. Raucous stood just inside the door, knife ready, body tensed, and he watched.

The two boys were sat on a small brown leather sofa, both had been hunched forward, pressing buttons and moving mini joysticks. The noises were not a TV show but a game where they pretended to be soldiers in a digital world populated by children around the globe all acting out fantasies with no danger of death.

The boy on the right of the sofa, the one to the left of the man, reacted first, dropping what he held and standing, reaching into his pocket but he was too slow. The man stepped forward and drove the glass ashtray into the boy's face. Teeth cracked, his nose bent and snapped, and a canyon of open flesh split across his forehead. The boy lost any connection to the here and now and dropped back, his neck bouncing on the edge of the sofa as he crumpled, his legs bent under him, his eyes open but seeing nothing. The boy to the right stood as his friend fell. He didn't reach for a weapon, he threw his open right hand attempting to push the man away, attempting an escape or search for distance. The man moved his shoulder forward and down like a boxer slipping a jab, his eyes always on the boy's face while his body dipped inches and the right hand went straight and over his shoulder. The man clenched his left fist, swung at the hips, pushing his left shoulder forward, his feet planted and the power coming up on through. He turned his wrist as his knuckles smashed the boy's chin, and the boy's head whipped right. The man reset in a smooth motion, shuffling his feet in unison to his right, setting them again, showing himself to be a southpaw. The boy hadn't dropped but his head was abuzz with panic and fear and adrenaline telling him to run and run fast. His head came back and the man threw a fast straight right, the one holding the ashtray with bits of the first boy's blood and skin stuck to its rim. The glass cracked against the boy's face the same as it had against the first and teeth snapped, his nose flattened and the deep cut went straight through his eyebrow. The boy dropped, falling back against the arm of the sofa, hitting it too high and flipping over the edge where he slid down to the floor, head down and feet up.

The man stood tall, away from his fighting crouch, and looked at them, dropping the ashtray to the floor, and he watched them, just as Raucous did. The man nodded his head and turned. There was a mini-fridge under the Large TV attached to the wall. The man looked at the TV and the game and the split screen and the two perspectives of soldiers on a roof. He heard the voices of real people chatting, asking what was happening, he saw the chat with messages from an unlimited number of people. He leaned forward to the console and pressed the power button and the image went black. He moved to the fridge, opened it, pulled out a pre-packaged supermarket sandwich, opened the wrapper and took a large bite as if it were the first food he had eaten in days.

With his mouth full and chewing he turned to Raucous.

"They really were the most inconsiderate hosts. Help yourself to what you want, it's all fresh."

28

"We should be going," Raucous said.

The man was chewing and looking at the two boys out cold, his back to Raucous but far enough away to have time to react. He knew what he was doing.

"No rush," he said. "These two babysit the night, no others come. Us rushing out would be seen and called in. We have all the time in the world. Best to slip out later, mingle with the masses. And besides, where would we go at this time? It's cold out."

The man turned to Raucous, looked him up and down and smiled.

"Now, you could leave, that would make sense, who are you, right? Well, you're Mick, the man across the road. But in the grand scheme of things, who are you?"

He smiled at this and opened the fridge, always keeping a space between him and Raucous.

"Nobody," Raucous told him.

"You'd think that, hope that really, wouldn't you? But a big man with a bag of tricks coming in here at the risk of death to save little old me?"

He took another sandwich from the fridge.

"You don't look like you need saving."

"That is where you are wrong, I needed saving and then some. I was waiting. Something happens or something doesn't. I survive or I don't. I got unlucky – or stupid – got caught, and then I got lucky because of big Mick and his good conscience. I'm Cooper, by the way."

"Mick," Raucous lied.

Raucous didn't hold out his hand and Cooper nodded but kept his hands on his sandwich.

"You don't look like a Mick," Cooper said.

"And yet I am," Raucous told him. "But, we are done. It is my time to go."

"That, as you very well know, would be a mistake," Cooper said.

"I'm not going to fight you."

Cooper relaxed his shoulders and smiled.

"Not what I meant, Mick. What I'm saying is you came over here for something more specific, certainly not as a saviour. You came her for some information, if I'm not wrong. Maybe just a quick recognisance this time. That turned bad, but you are after information all the same. Now, these two, if they aren't permanently damaged, have seen you, and know who you are, they did after, all piss all over your place today. But they do have the information you crave, the info you want. So we could sit and wait and see if they do come round, and ask some of those questions, you know? Besides, you can't live here anymore. Unless these two die because they know me, but they also now know you. It's a strange old world isn't it?"

Raucous smiled.

"And what information would that be?"

"The unusual kind, the Information I don't have, because if I did, I'd tell you, right? But I don't know your business, I can only guess, and I'm no monumental mind of genius, although in comparison to these two here, and if I may arrogantly say so, the majority, if not all, or their co-workers, I am on a whole other intellectual plain."

The man talked too much, Raucous thought, and he said more than the words themselves. He smiled at the games within the sentences, smiled at a man so confident in monologue.

"Arrogance has taken many men down."

Cooper nodded, drawing in air through his mouth filled with bread.

"It so nearly has me, look at me all there grumpy in my garden chair, used as a human ashtray – I thought my choice of weapon was quite a nice touch, poetic in a brutal way. But any way, I try to reel it in but when trying to hunt these little people down I do often get carried away and overestimate my own intelligence. It's the lack of competition I think."

Raucous had come in, saved the man, or at least released him to find his own path to death, and the two lads and this Cooper had seen him. The secrecy and surveillance all gone, the act of surprise no longer a weapon. Cooper didn't seem to be running, didn't seem to be scared, but then he didn't seem to be too firmly attached to reality.

"What's your plan?" Raucous asked.

"Good questions, always good questions. Sign of a bright mind. It seems a travesty you have fallen on such hard times, Mick. But the plan is to sit because soon a call will come and I will answer and talk. I will offer a compromise, one that each party can agree is mutually beneficial and then we can move forward."

"And how do you know this is going to happen?"

"Because it always happens. A call, a chat, a pep-talk or lover's whispers, I do not know. But every night a call comes in and checks are made. Tonight there is no one to answer but me."

Raucous stared at Cooper, nothing aggressive, not a call to fight, nor insult of intelligence, a stare to see if he could understand the man.

"Thirty minutes? Give-or-take a couple."

29

Cooper taped up the two lads and had them sat on the sofa. Their hands bound behind them, their ankles together, tape over their mouths. They were awake but not alert, concussed and in a throbbing migraine pain.

"You aren't looking great, lads," Cooper told them. "Some stitches needed and some proper TLC. I'm sure you have loved ones who'll care for you. Although whether they'll get the chance is a question for another time."

The two boys started to struggle and the one on the right tried to stand but Cooper kicked him with the sole of his foot and he bounced back down.

"It is Okay guys," Cooper said, soothing like a hippy with his hands palm down."I'm not going to kill you, I just don't have the anger and I suspect, the evidence of my guilt would be a little too overpowering even for the most unscrupulous of the legal profession. And, you know what? Seeing you here like this, I feel a certain level of sympathy. I doubt we'll meet again, and I am not sure you guys will make it to the morning, but I have been wrong before, multiple times. Many years ago."

Raucous stayed at a distance, by the door, edgy and uncomfortable.

"You think we need to stay and do this?" Raucous asked.

Cooper didn't turn, he threw his words at the two lads on the sofa.

"He's a little nervous," Cooper explained. "Probably his first time in a situation like this. It can get to you, you guys understand. Mick there was just coming over to have a drunken word with you – he really stinks of booze, probably spilt some on himself in all the angry excitement – about the toiletry problems you guys seem to have had on his bedding. Really not a nice welcome guys. And for whatever reason only he could explain, came in to rescue little old helpless me. Forever in his debt. "

Cooper turned to Raucous.

"Mick," he said, "There is always a reason to this. Stick around for the briefest of moments and maybe we could get these guys to speak, hear some words."

Cooper leaned into the boys like he was about to whisper a secret.

"I'm going to take your tape off your mouth, you'll maybe want to scream, but before you do think about the situation. Screams come from this flat on a regular basis, although I am very proud of the fact none were ever mine, so no one is calling anyone. And if you are too loud for my sensitive soul, and I am currently feeling very emotional, I'm going to slice a knife though your tongue, make it look like a snake's, you understand?"

Cooper ripped of the tape on their mouths. The boys inhaled hard and gritted teeth as the pain subsided.

"I'm not going to be so headmaster like and presumptuous as to demand an apology, that wouldn't ring true. However, here are some questions I'd really like you to answer. And if you could address them to Mick I would be much appreciative. So, here goes. How many boys have you coerced and groomed into transporting drugs from city to country in the last two years?"

The lad on the left spat out a swearword.

Cooper turned to Raucous.

"That is Gary," he told him. "He is the hard one. The bull lesbian of the pair. Very scary if you are younger than twelve and lack a brain or any physical strength."

He turned back to the boys.

"Tim?" he asked the other.

Tim looked to Gary for help and support.

"Oh, bless," Cooper said. "Touching really how much you admire him. However, I wasn't expecting an exact figure, a word along the lines of many, loads, hundreds, or something that equally means large would have sufficed." Cooper looked at his watch. "Time is moving on, so I tell you what, I'll speak for you both and you just jump in if and when I say something you must absolutely correct. Deal? Good."

Cooper turned back to Raucous.

"Mick, no need to pull up a chair, I'll make this as quick as possible and then we can scoot."

"The call?" Raucous asked.

Cooper looked at the two phones he had taken from the two boys.

"Yeah, having thought about that a little bit more, probably best not to be here when that happens. So we'll do this and then let's make a move, with the phones, and get as far away as possible so no one knows where we are."

Gary snorted a laugh.

"Funny Gary?" Cooper asked. "It's like you are thinking you have something on me. Pray tell."

Gary swore again.

"Very limited vocabulary has our Gary," Cooper explained to Raucous. "Anyway. Gary and Tim here have made their way up through the ranks, been members since they were groomed-"

"Groomed? Bullshit," Gary spat.

"Now that's the classic line from a victim of the process who just isn't ready to admit he is in fact a nobody and they are simply a tool for the older man who persuaded him into this way of life. Not exactly the classic Stockholm syndrome, more stupid idiot syndrome, eh, Tim? But him and his very close friend Gary worked their way up, sold a few friends down the river and used the same tactics used on them, all the presents and offers of a brotherhood, to get more young boys involved. Move drugs, move weapons, move furniture if there is money in it. Lots of boys. Quite a lot of them now dead or ruined, scrap."

"If you can't handle it, don't get involved," Gary spat.

Cooper laughed.

"You think you had a choice? You do, don't you. And there was me thinking you'd lost your innocence such a long time ago. You didn't and the kids you pull in don't have a choice either. Food, clothing, someone who they think will listen, that's all bluff. And they give you their debt in return. Sad really."

"County lines?" Raucous asked, and he wanted to know more, but he wanted to know why Cooper would think he needed the information.

"I guess that is the common language. Tim and Gary running a small section and a small group of young boys not old enough to be arrested and too numerous to follow. They take all the risks and get paid in phones. Everyone's a winner. I don't blame you guys, you are the same."

"Why would you think that interests me?" Raucous asked.

Cooper smiled.

"I used to read Sherlock Holmes, you know. Strange eh? Loved them, not so much the films. Black and white they were, mostly. But the stories? Loved them. Lots stuck with me. The idea of information being there to read. How people give themselves away. I'm not perfect, and my opinion is always changing. But you, I think, have a connection. Call it intuition."

Cooper smiled and turned back to the two lads on the sofa.

"So much more to say, and so much more to learn. Never stop learning boys. It is the elixir of life. Computer games not so much. But my watch tells me it is time to go so I will say goodbye."

Cooper placed tape over the two boy's mouths.

He rubbed Gary and Tim's hair in turn and they squinted their fury.

"Don't worry your pretty heads, fellas, we can call it quits."

30

Raucous removed the chain and metal block from the base of the door.

"Ready?" he asked.

Cooper nodded. Raucous had his hood up and Cooper had borrowed a black jacket from the boys tied up. He also had his hood up.

"Just keep walking straight, no hurry and no shifty looks. Side-by-side all the way over to the other side. Ready?" Cooper said.

Raucous nodded. Cooper held the phones, Raucous held his bag. Hands in pockets, Raucous opened the door with his foot and they stepped out into the dark and cold. They walked across the green square, frost settled already and the tarmac a crunch on the path. They walked quickly but without forced pace. Each had their heads down, but before they reached the far side and the edge of the block of flats, a phone buzzed away.

Cooper swore.

"Keep walking," he said. "We need to be out of view."

The phone kept buzzing but they didn't answer until behind the block of flats. Cooper pushed the screen on the phone and answered the call. The voice Raucous heard on the other end was loud, shouting and angry. Raucous could see Cooper was smiling as he listened, waiting for the voice to stop.

"You know what?" Cooper said into the phone once a pause was given for reply, "I simply don't care."

There was a break as the voice on the other end took in the words and tried to place the voice.

A word was said.

"Very good," Cooper told them. "It is indeed me. And I don't really want to reveal trade secrets so I won't go into an elaborate description of how, but suffice to say, Gary and Tim are not upto the job. But you knew that."

The voice started to shout again and Cooper pulled the phone away from his ear and made a pained expression to Raucous. Cooper placed the phone back to his ear.

"Listen, I don't need you to go and get the big boss man, I'm sure he is entertaining some want-to-be music star as we speak, but if you could simply pass on the message and my deal. Which is this, if he doesn't stop, and simply stick to the garbage producer career, then I'm going to chop him up. Got that? No need to write it down, it's a simple one. Goodbye."

Cooper closed the phone, he stepped around the block of flats and Raucous went with him. Cooper took the phone he had been speaking on and threw it like a world-war two grenade, straight-armed and powerful, the phone arcing and landing near the car in the centre of the green. The second phone he threw further, toward the door to the flat.

"Follow me," Cooper said.

Behind the flats were external steps up to the first floor. Cooper started to move up them.

"That is dumb," Raucous said.

Cooper stopped and turned.

"If we walk we'll be seen and hunted down very easily. You don't have a car, the boys said you use the underground – they like to know everything about the people here. So we are on foot, through the territory they control. If we had walked, the call wouldn't have been answered and there would be hundreds of kids out looking for us. We answered, and now they will be coming in here because they will want to know what's happened, and they'll think we are close by."

"We are."

"But the call won't have gone out to the wider public to keep an eye. So we keep our heads down."

"Guess work."

Cooper nodded agreement.

"Educated guess. Where would we go if we were running? Nowhere safe and nowhere quick is the answer. So follow."

Cooper walked the stairs and Raucous came after. He walked along a passageway, one side open to the air, the other a long wall of windows and doors. He stopped at a blue door, planted his feet, and pushed in with his shoulder. The doorframe creaked, and bent but held.

He tried again with the same result.

"You want a go?" Cooper asked.

Raucous set up in the same position and leaned in. The door popped open on his first push. The smell of mould and rot was overwhelming.

"You might want to cover your face," Cooper said. "Most of these flats are uninhabitable, not that this has stopped the council trying to put people in them."

There was no light, and no electricity. Raucous used the torch on his phone to light the way.

"You are going to have to turn that off," Cooper told him before he opened the final door.

Raucous complied and they walked into a room that was black, walls covered in thick mould.

"Cover your mouth," Cooper said.

He walked over to the curtains as did Raucous. Raucous held the material and felt the damp like they had been left outside in the rain.

Raucous looked to Cooper, asking what with a crinkle of his forehead. Cooper smiled.

"The pipes upstairs were stolen a long time ago, and what with no one in their right mind wanting to come here without an armed guard, the water pisses through. Forty-eight hours in this place and you'd have TB," Cooper told him.

They stood and watched the courtyard out front, the lamp shining down on the abandoned car and the bus-stop frame sat empty. Raucous waited, not asking why, having an idea at reasons and waiting all the same.

31

After five minutes they started arriving.

The first car they heard but did not see and Raucous assumed it was at the backdoor of Tim and Gary's flat.

"Maybe we won't get to see all the action," Cooper said.

"They'll be moving drugs," Raucous said.

"And weapons," Cooper added.

Raucous nodded staring out into the courtyard, watching nothing, but hearing motors, eyes alert to any shift in movement.

"Pretty fair assumption you'll grass them up," Raucous said.

"They don't know me, not exactly, but pretty fair. The police will come tomorrow though, give them time to clean up."

Cooper watched through the space he made in the curtain, waiting for people, waiting for something to see.

"I think they were worried I would set it on fire, but people live above. I don't know them, don't know if they are good or bad, and I don't get to risk their death over the destruction of a tiny amount of cocaine."

Raucous nodded and he saw the front door to the flat open. There were five men who walked out, all in black, all with hoods. Raucous squinted but couldn't see if the Darts were among them.

Cooper noticed his eyes and smiled.

"Looking for anyone in particular, Mick?" Cooper asked.

Raucous shook his head slowly.

"Just trying to remember faces."

Cooper kept smiling and nodding, watching the same group as Raucous.

"No one important yet," he said."Phone calls going round, need to know what police are doing. See if they have the time they need."

Cooper leaned forward, his forehead centimetres from the glass.

"Looks like they have only undone Gary and Tim's ankles."

Raucous looked and saw two of the five being pushed forward, their hands behind their backs.

"How did you know about this place?" Raucous asked.

"Could have been any of five. The whole floor is rotting. Surprised there are still doors on them."

"And the rest."

Cooper turned his gaze away from the action outside and looked at Raucous in the dark, the air thick.

"I scouted the place. Last time I was able to pop the door. Seems two days of being tied to a chair has weakened me somewhat. The door pops back, it's the frame that bends. There is not much living going on here, not much at all. I came to find out, made a misstep, got cocky – not for the first time – and got jumped. And then you turned up, and were I a god fearing man, I'd have said that was a sign. But I'm not and I take it as the luck I was owed."

More noises came from outside. Cars, Raucous thought, it sounded like two of them, big throaty engines going slow. But they were not seen as they too were behind the flats.

"Should have moved the other way," Cooper said.

"We should have kept walking."

All Raucous could see was they had trapped themselves in a space with no escape unseen. Cooper was back to watching the people outside.

"We wouldn't know what we are about to," he said, "and information is key, without it we use imagination and supposition, but the more info we have the better judgements we make, the better theories we can create to describe what we see. I paraphrase, but that is Sherlock for you."

"All I see is the need for a new flat."

Cooper smiled.

"I think you'll be just fine. You appear to be a man of many resources if too few words. A gun, a knife and a bar are not the usual tools of a plasterer. And neither is shift work. What is it that you do?"

Raucous stared and smiled himself. There was no answer to give.

"No point me saying you can trust me, but I have not shown that you can't," Cooper told him.

Raucous didn't trust anyone, certainly not a man who spoke and acted like Cooper. He'd met the like before and they all sprinted into their own death through the brilliance of their thinking.

"What are you to them?" Raucous asked.

"I'm an annoyance. The ghost of Christmas past. Someone they think they need not fear but so very much want to be quiet. I overstepped the mark they set down, and now I either run away or I face them down."

Raucous looked at him, up and down.

"You should run," he said.

"If longevity is the goal, then absolutely, run is best. But what wins out in your life? Old age or pride? Because I would put good money on you having led a life in which your pride has cost you freedom."

They listened to car engines, but they were moving away. Two engines gone.

"Moved the stuff," Raucous said.

"It will be back. This is a good spot. Very lucrative. Very safe. It is their own territory. Not a place for police."

They watched outside, the five men hanging around, Gary and Tim with hands behind their backs. Three men walked out of the front door to the flat. Three with hoods up like religious men from a time long gone. They needed candles to perfect the image. They each reached up and removed their hoods. Two were the Darts, and one other, in the middle, taller than them and paler of skin.

"Recognise them?" Cooper asked.

"The Darts. The middle I don't know."

"That's Franklin. See the gold crown on his sweatshirt? That is the brand of his record company. A cartoon crown in gold. Makes a lot of money. Or at least launders a lot of money through whatever they are calling that music. He was MarQuick's boy, but now MarQuick has gone, this fool has stepped up."

Raucous watched them, those three and not the others as they walked toward the group of five. Tim and Gary were forced down onto their knees. They looked up and words were exchanged with The Darts and Franklin looking from up on high.

Franklin reached to the back of his trousers and pulled a gun. The three men holding Gary and Tim fled fast in three directions. Tim tried to stand but fell face forward and Franklin aimed and pulled the trigger, the shot through the side of Tim's head and his body lost energy and movement in an instant, the crack of the shot ringing against the buildings. Gary was on his feet, his arms behind him, speaking and saying words, not running, not trying to go anywhere. His words were his strength. Franklin stepped forward and nodded, Gary stopped talking and Franklin lowered the gun. Gary bent forward slightly, breathing hard. Franklin looked to his right, one of the Darts said something, Gary straightened and shouted. Franklin raised the gun and fired from inches into Gary's face and Gary dropped straight down as his head flew back.

Franklin said something and he turned and walked into the flat while putting his gun into the back of his trousers. The three men who had run, came back and started to drag the bodies inside.

Cooper looked to Raucous.

"That is what you are dealing with, and that is who I plan to take down. Now you have many choices, but the main one is, are you going to hope that they think Mick was just a dumb guy in the wrong place or do you think they'll put the obvious together and realise that I was freed by a man named Raucous."

Raucous stared ready to fight, tense and floating in the con. Cooper held up his hands, palms out.

"You want the Darts for what they did to Mack but it wasn't them, it was Franklin, and I'd like the person who annihilates that certain asshole to be me."

32

Raucous stared at Cooper and Cooper held his gaze.

"Who are you?" Raucous asked.

"The reason I know you is we crossed paths fifteen years ago when I was young and you were king."

Raucous thought and tried to place him. Fifteen years was a long time but his life had been a series of segments in different buildings. Fifteen years ago put him in one of two places. The first made more sense.

"Dartmoor?"

Cooper nodded.

"I don't remember you," Raucous told him.

"And that means a lot to me because I don't want to be known. I was on remand, you were top man-"

"I've never run any prison."

"Not what I meant. You were the man, no one in their right mind aggrieved you, and for all my failings as a human being, and that list is long, being an idiot isn't one of them."

Raucous ran through his time on the moors, a peaceful spell where he was left alone mostly and demonstrated his violence infrequently. Cooper was not in his memories. He looked into Cooper's eyes.

"What is going on, and no bluster, no bullshit, just reality."

Cooper relaxed with the knowledge no aggression was coming.

"You are looking to balance out a wrong. One of your stable, or boys or family – I don't know which – got taken down. You know the reasons for that."

"Enlighten me," Raucous told him.

"Really?"

Raucous nodded.

"You weren't his dad. And Mack was involved. Most kids that pass through your place were, are or will be, you know that, it is the reason you are there."

"This is not telling me anything new."

"Mack was making a lot of money. Cool kid, I'll give you that. He had that thing, people listened. It's a skill, one that can be used and was. But he started to use it in ways that were not the company line."

Raucous stared more. He encouraged Cooper to speak with a swirling movement of his hand.

"There are two versions, and you'll prefer one, which is he was spreading discontent, talking to some about other ways to live, encouraging them to find other employment beyond moving drugs for gangs and a sense of belonging."

Raucous waited to hear the second. Cooper had stopped.

"The second?" Raucous asked.

"He was setting up a rival business, talking to the right people at the right times. Recruiting and stepping on the toes of MarQuick and Franklin and his crew. And the result was his death."

Either set of events was as plausible as the other. Raucous didn't know if he was being played. He had made the decision to be involved, to take steps he shouldn't without the information he needed. He had been the dumb one.

"What is it to you?" Raucous asked.

"Shouldn't be anything, nothing at all. I'm like you, no longer in the game. I don't take orders well, never have been one to agree to doing the bidding of someone considerably less intelligent than myself. Now you, you were happy to be the muscle for some people, and to be fair, you only really worked for the smart ones. Now there aren't any around and the kids have taken over."

"That's not a reason to be doing anything," Raucous told him.

"That's where you are wrong. I'm a guy, a bit younger than you, a bit of money that has never been taxed and never will be. Gary and Tim were very light on additions to my retirement fund. But you are looking to avenge a boy with whom, for whatever reason, felt a bond. Now I'm not saying that wasn't real and reciprocated, I'm not saying you were played. It is as good a reason as mine."

"You looking to avenge someone?"

"I'm looking to avenge the death of me."

Raucous looked at Cooper not understanding anything the man was saying.

"I was a kid, stereotypical shit for round here back in that day. Father and mother that hate each other but not quite as much as they hated me. No siblings. Yadda yadda yadda. So what? Grow up, get on with your life. You had it worse, I know that. But that's where I am. Nothing offered, no help, a little kid. So I join up, not the army, I wouldn't last a day there. The local gangs, and I learned, and I became useful and in return for that safety, I gave up me. Terrible isn't it?"

Cooper smiled, a story he had told and moulded to his audience over time.

"This is just a story," Raucous said. "It gets told a lot."

"And that is the crux of it, the story gets told a lot. And I am tired of watching it happen. Now I can't go back and take out the idiots that groomed me into being this sorry excuse for a human, I don't have that luxury, they are all, pretty much, god rest their souls, dead or pathetic old men in pubs listening to each other about how feared they are. This is the hardest pub in wherever. No, it isn't, it is just full of nasty old men. And I don't want to be one."

"You want to avenge the death of you?"

Cooper laughed.

"That is exactly what I am trying to do."

They heard the noises and saw the blue lights crashing through the edge of the damp curtains. Cooper looked as surprised as Raucous. They watched through the edges, trying to avoid any light shining on their faces. The courtyard filled with police, two armoured units on foot, their trucks behind the flats, men in black with large guns operating like the military which they all most likely had been. The courtyard became alive, lights shone through windows from the flats, people looked and people filmed, and the idea of a face peering through curtains became the norm. Raucous and Cooper watched some more.

The armoured police entered Gary and Tim's flat, there was loud communication, lights going on. Minutes passed with the police outside in a holding formation as people appeared from their flats to stare their hatred at the law.

Two men with semi-automatic weapons came out of the flat and spoke into mouthpieces on their shoulders. The activity stopped and they all waited, and Raucous didn't know for what until two suited figures came walking across the green in large black overcoats.

Raucous swore.

"That is Simpson and Locke," Raucous said, watching them stroll and talk like they were about to announce the solution to crime.

"I know," Cooper said. "Strange couple."

They watched them speak to the two armed men, nods and respect taken and given, they were escorted inside, lost to view and scrutiny.

Raucous watched the empty door for ten seconds and turned to Cooper.

"I think this the time to sneak out and away."

Cooper nodded.

"I have a feeling there will be people out searching for a Mick. I hope you covered yourself well enough. Mick will be a person of interest here."

"Mick doesn't exist."

Cooper smiled.

"But you do."

Raucous nodded and walked to the front door. They walked out, hoods up and heads bowed, hidden from the courtyard. They moved quickly, down the steps and away into the streets. There were others making the walk too, a few people who didn't want the scrutiny of answering questions on the door-to-door that was to come. Raucous and Cooper didn't speak as they drifted apart and walked in opposing directions. Neither looked back to see where the other had gone.

33

Raucous spotted him from the end of the road. There were limited spaces, all occupied by the usual suspects on a street where the law said you could park anywhere but local tradition gave each person a regular spot. The car was dark, bland and a saloon, not quite black and far from shiny, and just a little too powerful and a little too expensive to be ignored. There was one guy in front and Raucous couldn't get a perfect look, his vision was blurry at that distance, but it was police. A single one at that.

Raucous was coming back, still in his plasterer's uniform of work trousers and splashed hoodie. He needed back into his apartment but he would prefer to remain unseen. When young, and his gran locked him out so he'd stay at school, he could shimmy up a ladder in the back and slip through a window he had left open in the morning, but that was more than twenty years ago and when he was twenty percent smaller. They would know it was him when he rocked up to the entrance, but with his hood up, face hidden and a stoop, no photo could prove the fact. Raucous pulled the key from his pocket and walked the street, head down and making it clear he wanted no one to acknowledge his presence.

He unlocked the front door, walked the stairs, no one called and no one followed. He entered his flat, changed quickly, looked at his phone, saw the messages from Charlotte and sat and waited.

The bell rang within two minutes.

The guy in the car had been Locke, and now he was asking to be let in and Raucous buzzed him up, leaving the front door open but returning to the front room.

"Raucous?" Locke called.

"Come on in, take your shoes off and close the door," Raucous called back.

Raucous sat in his armchair in the corner of the room facing the doorway, there was a coffee table and a two-man sofa to his left. To the left of the door as Raucous looked was a low sideboard with an old TV on top. One of the large ones, the last of the boxes before flat screens.

"Can I sit?" Locke asked.

Raucous nodded and Locke sat on the very edge of the sofa.

Neither spoke as they tried to calm the room, waiting for tension and uncertainty to subside. It was his house, so Raucous spoke first.

"What is it you want?"

"I imagine Charlotte gave you a heads up, by message," Locke said.

"Maybe."

"Maybe," Locke repeated.

Locke opened a large brown A4 envelope and pulled out twenty photos, the top one was a mugshot and Raucous assumed the rest of the pile would be too.

"Can I show you these?" Locke asked.

Raucous nodded as he thought. He knew the variations on the trick Locke was playing. There were different things to do for different situations. Maybe three or four in would be a surprise photo, one that Raucous shouldn't know but from his reaction Locke could tell. Maybe a few photos in is a gruesome scene, an accidental placement of someone he knows all dead and shot-up. The magician's trick of forcing a card on a member of the audience was what Locke was playing. Raucous had plenty of giveaways.

Raucous would nod on each photo.

Locke placed them down one by one and Raucous moved his head as Locke watched for a reaction.

"Say stop if you recognise anyone," Locke said.

The photos were laid down and each one Raucous nodded his head but said nothing as Locke paused and placed the next. The third was no surprise so Raucous figured the fourth would be the reveal. Locke placed it down and a black and white photo of Cooper appeared, a younger Cooper but his mugshot all the same. Raucous nodded and Locke paused longer than the first three. Raucous looked up, forcing a quizzical look, asking with an eyebrow why he was waiting. Locke placed the next one and then the others down, in a way he hoped was the same as before but was faster, only just, but faster all the same.

Locke placed the last photo down.

"Nothing?" he asked.

Raucous took his time looking up, dragging the movement out like an old man getting out of bed.

"I'd say, and you know this, that I've crossed paths with most of those men. A few I don't recognise, although there is a vague recollection. All of the ones I recognise, I recognise because they did time in the same place I was doing time. I'd guess all of them have crossed my path over the years, but that is a lot of faces to remember. One of them is, however, dead."

"Just missing."

"Definitely dead."

"No body has ever been found."

"I believe his body no longer exists."

"Want to put that on record?"

"No, I do not."

They sat for longer, in silence as Locke picked up the photos, shuffling them and placing them in order. He put Cooper's on top and placed the pile on the coffee table.

"Do you have a recollection of this one?" Locke asked tapping Cooper's photo.

"Different generations by the looks of him. One of the ones I'd say I crossed paths with inside, but that would be a long time ago. I wouldn't put money on it. Why?"

"Person of interest is all," Locke said.

"I can't do your job for you. What's his name?"

Locke turned his head to the left as if clicking his neck.

"Nigel Cooper," Locke said. "Used to be an enforcer of sorts."

"Of sorts?"

"People vanished, or were killed, when he was about."

"Hopefully the right people," Raucous said.

Locke smiled and nodded.

"You'd hope so, wouldn't you?"

They sat in silence for another thirty seconds as Locke tapped the photos. Raucous waited, knowing a question was coming. It didn't take this long to formulate.

Locke stopped tapping and turned to Raucous.

"Why did Simpson come to you and tell you about Mack?" Locke asked.

Raucous had expected something more subtle, something better thought out.

"Your partner, ask her."

"I have. Got a good response. But what was your take on it?"

Raucous rubbed the back of his head. He knew the game, and thought of the positives obtained through sharing. There was nothing he could say that would bring anyone pain. Not if he stayed with the truth.

"It was good policing. She showed concern and respect and spoke to me directly when most would have sent someone else, or simply not bothered at all. I thanked her."

"She owe you?"

Raucous would have smiled but Locke was serious.

"Owe me? I don't even know her. She has involvement with some of the people who come to the gym. They are not all innocents. Building bridges is a skill. Gets overlooked."

"But you are a career criminal."

Raucous smiled because that was all he ever would be no matter what.

"I was a career prisoner. Got caught and then survived. I have worked for a few unlawful people, that isn't hidden. But I'm out, have been for a while. Your colleague was just doing the right thing. Not all altruistic, plenty of her own needs met, a police officer who actually gives a shit is a rarity. She appears to be one, and until she does something to make me think otherwise, that is the way it stays. I'm sure she knew that when she asked to meet me."

"So you trust her?" Locke asked.

Raucous couldn't understand the direction. The questions were not quite right because he was not the right person to ask.

"That is something else entirely. Her, you and anyone on your side would happily have me inside again. I am a name and bringing me down would make yours. Trust and respect are different concepts. She doesn't have both."

Locke stood and picked up his photos, slid them back into the envelope. He walked from the room and Raucous made no move to follow. He heard him put his shoes back on. Locke appeared at the door again.

"Information is key in everything. And the more I get about you, the more I realise I have no handle on you at all."

"No need to think deeply, Mr. Locke. I am exactly that two-dimensional character you all believe me to be."

Locke smiled like he knew he was being fooled.

34

Raucous walked the longer route. There were a few more minutes added but the main roads were mostly avoided and the quieter streets gave him more peace. He thought of Locke, the questions and the why, and the messages from Charlotte. He walked but was aware and he tensed as he heard the car slow and start to crawl next to him. Raucous didn't turn to look, he was no runner so he had to think of options. He saw the front of the car, silver and old in shape, a decade out of fashion, the scratches saying it had lived a life of poor parking. It was not a police car.

"Raucous," the voice said, and he recognised it and turned.

Cooper was sat in the front of a battered family Ford, silver, dirty on the wheels and the engine making a screech at low speed.

Raucous stopped and Cooper hit the brakes. The engine kept on running.

"Easier if you get in and then I explain."

Raucous stared into Cooper's eyes, shook his head slowly while smiling.

"Man you are difficult," Cooper said. "We need to move. The weak spot in your shitty plan broke. So now, what with you having not shown the respect they crave, Franklin is sending in the clowns. The violent clowns."

Raucous kept staring, not understanding why Cooper would talk so much, so badly and think Raucous would be afraid.

"What?" Raucous asked.

"The landlord you so kindly gave so much money to for a night's stay. They asked him who you were, he described, they showed a photo of you and he confirmed Mick is Raucous. Simple really."

"They were already after me," Raucous said.

But he knew this took it up a level. They had put Charlotte in hospital, maybe seen that as a balance, but he had stepped it up, and they had him for destroying the flat.

"They were never after you, not how they operate. They'll get to you eventually, physically, but right now they are after anything you love, and whether you have said that out loud to her or not, the whole world knows that is Charlotte."

Raucous stared at Cooper more and Cooper smiled and nodded like he knew he was passing through some type of visual security check.

"Raucous, they are going for Charlotte. In the hospital."

"And how do you know this?"

Cooper held up a phone.

"This. It is low-level, and not exactly top quality literature, or deep philosophy. It is barely legible English. But you are on a list. Identify and pass the word. You go anywhere near their territory and their electronic system is going to light up like a fire in your face."

"No intention of heading back in," Raucous told him.

"Which is why, if I can understand the awful spelling, lack of grammar and punctuation, they are going after Charlotte. Then, obviously, you. It is what they do."

"She is in hospital."

"A place I have entered in previous employment, walked freely through, sat down and had an interesting, if largely aggressive chat to people my previous employers wanted to keep under control. Charlotte is in a room, in a building whose doors are always open."

Raucous inhaled, not wanting to believe, but knowing the possibility was enough to move to action.

"When?" Raucous asked.

"Now."

"Why the warning?" Raucous asked.

"This might make us even, depends how it plays out. I owe you, and other factors too, which I won't go into. But important all the same. It isn't a trap."

Raucous walked around the car and got in. Put his seat belt on.

"An inspector Locke came and spoke to me this morning about you," Raucous said.

Cooper kept looking ahead, bending forward at the waist to give himself better vision of the road.

"I saw him," he said."Don't sweat it, he loves me."

Cooper indicated and pulled out into the street. No exaggerated acceleration, no speeding U-Turn of smoke and black streaks. A family car going nice and slow and calm on the way to visit an ill relative. Cooper sat back in his seat.

"Show you my mugshot among others, did he?" Cooper asked. "Always the same routine. He has nothing on me, as there is nothing to have. And I like him. One of the honest ones. Used to take down the crooks in the police. He is probably less popular among the force than you and I combined."

"Why is he after you?"

Cooper scrunched his face.

"He isn't. At least I hope he isn't. He just likes to know who knows me. I'm his litmus test. Turn your nose up, or ridicule or whatever reaction might come – fear might even be on that list – and it could give an insight into who you are. Obviously, if you have some info on my past misdeeds that might hold up in front of a judge, all the better. But there really isn't any of that around."

They drove for a minute, and Raucous eased as the route was the one to the hospital.

Raucous messaged Charlotte saying he was on his way and for her to be careful. He rang but she did not pick up.

"Who is coming?" Raucous asked.

"That I don't know. Not one of the regulars, not a street urchin, as Dickens might say. The level of conversation I have an ear to, are not particularly high up and as such know very little. I'm sure we'll find out."

35

Charlotte was sitting up when Raucous and Cooper entered her room. Raucous smiled at the improvement, whatever they were filling her with was working. Maybe she had replaced some of the lost blood. She looked frail, but the lighting was harsh, and she looked closer to alive than twenty-four hours before.

Raucous returned the smile Charlotte gave and sat next to her bed. He reached out and held her hand, squeezed. He thought the standard routine was to lean in and kiss but he didn't feel it was the right time, not with the audience.

"He came," Raucous said.

"I told you."

"I saw the messages."

"He ask you what I thought?"

Raucous nodded. She had told him he would come and ask of Simpson.

"He showed me about twenty photos of men who were in prison with me. Asked if I knew who they were."

"Did you?"

"I think I crossed paths with them all, but some are vague ideas, an assumption because they were in with the others. He seemed most interested in this guy."

Raucous pointed at Cooper.

"Nigel Cooper" Charlotte said. "How are you?"

"I'm good," Cooper replied.

Raucous watched them, back and forth, trying to look for clues.

"I was happy to hear you stepped away, found other ways to live," Charlotte said.

"Not as happy as me," Cooper told her.

"Are you back for me?" she asked.

Cooper shook his head

"You were never someone I'd hurt. It wouldn't be an order I'd carry out."

Charlotte turned to Raucous.

"Why is he here, and why the panic?"

Raucous looked to Cooper.

"There has been significant chatter about you this last hour," Cooper said. "And what seems to be a probable attempt to go a step further than the scarring of last time. Raucous here, kind of stirred a few things up last night, with, I admit, my own help. But as I have absolutely no one they could go after, they will be coming for me directly. You on the other hand are the nearest and dearest of Raucous and so are the one they will kill first. Had Raucous other people in his life, they too would be in trouble."

"Here?" Charlotte asked.

"That is the impression I got, yes."

Charlotte inhaled and then sighed. She scrunched her face and grimaced.

"What's the plan?" she asked.

"We hadn't got that far," Cooper said."We could fight here, but they might be armed and we are trapped in a room. No point giving away our advantage. We could try and head them off but we don't know who they are – it's not like they are going to come charging through. Which leaves us the option of copying the Godfather film and moving you to another part of the building and waiting to see who turns up."

"Can you walk?" Raucous asked.

"I managed to get to the toilet unaided last night, but it took a while."

They moved her from the bed, her hospital gown already replaced with a nightdress. She was slow and winced as she stood, and Raucous and Cooper took an elbow each.

"I doubt there are free rooms," Charlotte told them. "And don't even think of putting me in a cleaner's closet."

Cooper looked to Raucous.

"The waiting room is down the corridor a way," Raucous said. "There is a TV, and uncomfortable chairs. Gives us a view of the door."

As a plan it was awful, but it was the only thing they had.

They walked her slowly along the plastic flooring, she was strong enough to hold her weight, but she favoured her left side, pressure on her right made her straighten in pain.

They walked inside, the room empty, the TV on without sound, subtitles that were not quite correct nor in time with mouths constantly moving at the bottom of the screen.

"How long do I have to sit here?" Charlotte asked.

"Until they realise you've moved," Raucous told her. "You in pain?"

"I was stabbed, they nicked my liver, I lost loads of blood. The drugs are great but not perfect, the stitches feel open. So not as much as I could be but not as easy as I'd like."

Raucous watched her and understood the frustration she showed with being unable to defend herself.

"I'd leave you to fight them yourself," Raucous told her. "But I think you'd have less chance of breaking arms right now than otherwise."

Cooper stared at them and smiled.

"I'll wait in the room," Cooper said."Anyone comes in, you'll see and you come in after."

"If they are armed?" Raucous asked.

"Make sure you get there quick. I'm not carrying anything, and you don't have your special bag. You got anything?"

Raucous shook his head.

"Then the plan is to smash and then ask."

36

Raucous sat opposite Charlotte, the TV above his head. They didn't speak, Charlotte watching the floor rather than the screen. Raucous was looking down the corridor through the glass in the door, his hood up and his face covered with shade.

It was minutes before the silence broke.

"Where did you meet Cooper?" Charlotte asked.

Raucous was concentrating, trying to get ready, trying to think of what was happening.

"He was tied up in a flat and I untied him."

Charlotte paused, not asking for more information realising Raucous had little to give.

"How many did he kill?" she asked.

Raucous moved his head to the side.

"None, not directly."

Charlotte waited again, but looked up trying to see his face but only seeing darkness.

"He is a dangerous man," she told him.

Raucous knew he was, he had seen many without care but very few with a gambler's weighing of odds. Eventually everyone loses regardless of how much probability favours actions. Cooper thought, understood the possible outcomes and then tried to be on the better side. He operated on calculated chaos. His luck had held, his plans in-depth inside his head.

"He talks too much," Raucous said."Some of it interesting, more just sound to fill in the gaps."

"He worked for us for a time."

Raucous looked at her.

"You were inside," Charlotte said.

"In what capacity?" Raucous asked.

"Resolved problems. Highly intelligent risk taker. He won't do anything he doesn't want. But if you convince him, he'll do it."

"Easily persuaded?"

Charlotte didn't answer so Raucous looked up. She stared back and shook her head.

"He took on things he deems right, based on whatever system he has going in his head. Not too far from you. He will kill anyone if he thinks they have crossed some moral divide. He has been gone eight years."

Raucous knew that was a long time, he also knew that it wouldn't have been prison. Eight years off the scene is too long to then make a comeback for fun.

"I don't know what he is doing here, or why," Raucous told her. "I don't trust him, and maybe all this is a made-up joke. Who knows?"

Raucous put his head down as they came around the corner and Raucous sensed them look into the waiting room. His face was down, his features in shade, his phone was in his hand like he was playing some stupid game with shapes and colours when it was black with the time in white. He saw two sets of feet walking toward Charlotte's room. This was the third group, the first two had kept on walking through the double doors at the end and into a new ward. Raucous lifted his head to see who they were. The one on the left was wearing the plastic rubber shoes with holes, the strap across the Achilles keeping them from being modern clogs. The one to the right was wearing trainers. The man on the left was taller and wearing what essentially looked like plain, light green pyjamas, the one on the right was wearing blue. He was shorter and his left hand was holding the man in green's elbow.

They walked, not smooth, like two kids trying not to step together, a pause and a shuffle and foot placed down out of time. They stopped at Charlotte's door, the man in blue still holding the other's elbow. He spoke, the words inaudible to Raucous. The man in green nodded. They looked like a doctor and nurse confirming a plan before putting on smiles to pass on bad news. The green man pushed the door, stepped in first and was followed by the man in blue.

Raucous stood, nodded at Charlotte, the anger at being infirm all over her eyes, and he pushed through the door and stepped quickly to Charlotte's room, the large door just short of closing. He stopped it with his hand and heard Cooper's voice.

Raucous walked in.

The man in blue turned his head to see and Raucous smiled.

"They say they work here," Cooper said.

The man in green stepped to his left away from the man in blue, their connection at the elbow broken.

"What is it you do?" Raucous asked.

The man in green looked to the man in blue.

"I'm a doctor," the green man said. "I have worked here for five years. You can check that anywhere."

"We just came to check up on Charlotte," the man in blue said, his voice going for calm and reassurance. "Would you know where she is? She is not really in the right shape to be moving around."

"Why do you wear blue and he wears green?" Cooper asked.

The man in blue smiled, he looked to his friend in green.

"Would you like to explain?" he asked.

"It's just a choice. No uniform. Doctors and nurses. Used to be white, long time ago, now blue or green."

"So are you a doctor or a nurse?" Cooper asked the man in blue.

"I'm a doctor too," he said

"Doctor of sport?" Raucous said pointing at his trainers.

"Doctor of cancer," the man in blue said.

"Cancer?" Raucous asked as he stepped closer. "What ward would that be?"

"The cancer ward," the man in blue said.

Cooper was walking too, stepping closer. "Cancer ward? What's that in Latin terms? Is that Oncology or Pathology?"

The man in blue smiled.

"Fifty-fifty chance," Cooper told him as he stepped closer.

The man in blue pulled a knife from his cupped hand but Raucous saw it coming. He kicked at the back of the man's knees and the man fell forward. Cooper stamped down on the man's arm and Raucous swung his right foot and connected with power to the side of the man's head. The head didn't spin, it rocked to the side and the man dropped as if dead face first into the floor. Cooper reached down and picked up the knife. Cooper and Raucous turned together and the man in green was backing away with his hands out in front with his palms up.

"I'm a doctor. Oncology. That was the answer. Oncology."

"This guy?" Cooper asked pointing the knife at the unconscious man on the floor.

"They have me. I'm from Mountford. My family, they still live close. They know where. They threatened me today. They just wanted to talk, in private. Nothing more."

"What was the knife for, Doc?" Raucous asked.

"That was to make me get him in. That was for me."

Raucous walked across and pulled the ID badge from the front of his smock. The photo matched. The name said he was a Dr. Rollins. He rolled the man in blue over and pulled his ID. The photo didn't match. Raucous looked to Cooper.

Cooper shrugged.

"Call it in," Cooper said. "We can't kill them. Certainly not this one."

"They just wanted to scare her," the doctor said.

"Like they scared you?" Raucous asked. "That's just hope rather than fact. Who is this?"

"I don't know. I've never seen him before."

"Then why did you lead him up here in your away kit?" Cooper asked.

"He told me the name and address of my family. My sisters and mother. He put a knife to my throat. He told me where I'd grown up, who I knew. He told me he needed to just get to her and explain."

Cooper and Raucous stared at the Doctor.

They looked at him for thirty seconds, each one feeling the anxiety the doctor threw out in waves of shakes.

"I believe him," Cooper said, tapping the knife on the air in front of him.

Raucous nodded.

37

Raucous had made tea and was sat in his armchair, looking at nothing, thinking of Charlotte, thinking of what they were doing. The curtains were closed, the night moving on, Charlotte asleep and Raucous put down his cup, switched off the lights, walked quietly into the bedroom, stripped down to a t-shirt and boxers and slid as smoothly as he could into bed, next to Charlotte. He placed his head back on the pillow and listened to her breathing.

For three days Charlotte had slept, taken her medicine, something similar to what Raucous remembered as a banana flavour from childhood. Raucous had sat and waited for her to wake, cooked her food, chatted even though he knew she wasn't listening. The hospital had objected but Raucous had taken her anyway, to here, his flat. He checked in with doctors by phone, and followed instruction but it was nothing more than changes in temperature, loss of colour and a wound not healing when changing the dressing. What remained was just recovery, a waiting game as Charlotte's body fixed itself with the help of drugs.

Cooper had gone, walked away in silence as Raucous phoned the police. Raucous had not seen nor heard from him since. But he understood there was no reason for contact. Simpson and Locke asked questions about the other man because the doctor told them what happened. Raucous told them he thought he worked in the hospital. He feigned surprise that he didn't. But despite the police saying that Charlotte would be safe if she stayed, neither she nor Raucous believed them. The nurses said it would be best for her recovery, but Raucous pushed and they admitted she was free to leave. They gave instructions. Raucous got them a taxi to his flat.

Raucous drifted to sleep.

It was Charlotte who woke him. He had heard a crash, the sound of glass shattering but he had been slow to wake, unsure if it was a dream. Charlotte shook him as he sat up and the smell was strong, clear and filling his lungs. The heat was already beating through the door. He had left it, as was his habit, ajar, and the smoke and sounds of crackles came flowing through.

Raucous moved quickly, he stepped toward the door, opened it and a rush of boiling air smacked his face as flames whipped forward. He closed his eyes, and turned his head, but he knew his skin had been grilled free of moisture. He pushed the door closed, the wood and paint like the inside of an industrial oven, his hands burned, he shut the door with a bump of his covered shoulder.

He could smell the petrol.

He turned and Charlotte was standing next to the bed, a large t-shirt covering her body to her knees, black with some type of worn through design of a Disney princess. Raucous went to the curtains and pulled them open, his force ripping the top from its rings, the material falling to the floor. The window was ablaze from outside, the crash they heard, the noise that woke them, a Molotov cocktail aimed and thrown at the window. As he looked, he jumped back, startled as another hit the pane. A crash, a smash and the material ablaze setting fire to the petrol inside. A huge burst of flame on the other side and Raucous stepped forward again, looked down into the yard and saw flames licking, and growing and shimmying ever taller as rubbish, and rotten wood fuelled the fire as the petrol burned.

The room was hot, the air starting to scratch on his throat, his lungs starting to burn. He looked to the door, he turned to Charlotte.

"The mattress," she said. "Grab it."

She tried to haul it up, Raucous stepped forward and helped. They stood it up on its end, they walked to the door waiting to use it as a shield. Charlotte reached around and grabbed at the handle. She screamed, swore, pulled her hand away, the blister already formed.

Raucous looked around and grabbed a sheet, wrapped a corner around his palm, stepped across, reached for the handle, felt the burn through the material, pushed down, and pulled the door open. The crash of burning air whipped into the room, seeking out particles colder than they, filling the room in a moment with the heat from the burning source. Equilibrium arrived quickly, the bedroom a furnace equal in melting power to the rest of the flat. Raucous looked, the smoke had filled the room, the fire burning up walls, furniture from an age before safety, providing old wood to blow up flares to the size where they licked the ceiling. The flames had moved across the room, six internal sides of fire. The door on the far side open, the door into the corridor and the outside world locked and burned black, the carpet at its feet a simple patch of charcoal. The coats and shoes ablaze. The air filled with chemical fog and billowing grey-black smoke. The burn had started there. Raucous knew, petrol through the letterbox, under the door, outside the door. The floor was hot, and getting hotter, the fire below as well as here.

Raucous couldn't breathe.

"Get down low," Charlotte shouted, dragging Raucous by the shoulder.

Raucous was on all fours, Charlotte behind him, the carpet soft, the fibres resistant but not enough. Soft through coming close to a melting point. His armchair ablaze, the coffee table next to it recognisable but burning black. Raucous coughed, tried to inhale but couldn't pull in clean air. Charlotte pushed material over his face as if he were the victim to a killer using chloroform. She released her grip and he held the cloth to his face. An empty pillow case.

Raucous looked back, Charlotte's eyes wide, scared as were his, her mouth covered with the matching pattern. Some of the ceiling fell, a large sheet of burning paper. It fell on Raucous and his T-shirt caught fire, he felt his skin crackle, smelt the hair on his body singe. He screamed out in pain and rolled, the flames dying out but the heat never going. He looked to Charlotte and she was on her feet, crouching low, coughing, her hair on fire. He stood and wiped away the flames on her head with the pillow case in his hand. The room now only fuel, the fire beyond control. Raucous stood, took in no air and ran at the front door, seeing only a haze of black.

He couldn't smash through, he knew this. There was a chain, a metal chain that had soaked up energy. The flames were on him, the pain making him scream but as a means to fight, a means to force down the agony and make rational choices. He turned and Charlotte was at his shoulder. He grabbed the chain, he felt the shape burn into his skin as if he was branding a mark to show who owned him. The chain came free, his t-shirt ablaze. He turned and saw Charlotte patting at fire as it rose from the hem of her shirt. There was a Yale lock he needed to turn. He grabbed it with his thumb and index finger as he always did. The heat of the metal taking the skin from his bone and sticking it to whatever he touched.

The smoke around him, his eyes closed, the pain on his skin, the agony in his lungs. He had held his breath, he couldn't any longer. He inhaled, and particles and flames rushed down his throat. He screamed but heard nothing. He needed the oxygen, he needed something clean. He turned and saw Charlotte bent over retching or hiding, he didn't know. His head emptying of thought, of clarity. He started to drop.

He felt the clarity go, the high and rush of adrenaline ebb away, the quietness of a brain without thought. He smiled and he knew why, the peace of going. He reached back, felt for Charlotte's hand. He touched her and felt his last push.

He grabbed at the door, the burning metal of the lock sticking his hand to its surface. His skin the glue.

He turned, pulled the door in, the hot air rushed past him out into the corridor, flames licked past, looking for new sources of hell. The blast rocked him. He turned, his head light, his breathing not working. He tried to stand, knew he couldn't balance. Charlotte pushed him, hard and in his chest. He flew back, through the door, smacking against the wall on the opposite side. Charlotte smacked into him. He saw her face, the hair burned, the eyebrows gone, the skin red, welts rising already. The corridor was heating up, the flames grabbing at anything they could set on fire.

"Move," Charlotte said through a choke.

She pushed Raucous again, they slipped down the stairs, falling, unable to stand or stay upright. Like a drunk couple who were fighting their way out of domestic turmoil. They smacked up against the door to the street, the cold glass feeling like the most blissful high as Raucous laid his hands upon it. He smacked the button on the wall to release the lock. The door popped, opened, but inward. They stepped back, gave themselves space, staggered out into the street, saw the blue lights, saw the people, but all a blur as tears filled their eyes.

They staggered away, neither sure who was leading who, who was dragging who. They got to the far side, the noises of people and sirens difficult to hear over the cracks and pops and explosions from across the street. Raucous sat down, Charlotte sat next to him. They coughed and spat up black, Raucous rubbed his eyes, the pain cut through his mind. He couldn't see, not with sharp outlines, everything a blur. He looked up and saw the only home he had ever known, his own history, his family, what there was of it, gave him this and now he watched it burn. The fire engines started to explode water all over the building. Three engines and a dozen men, running in co-ordinated patterns. But they were trying to contain, not allow the fire to burn the street. What had been his was now a shell, something to be rebuilt over time as something else, something new, something that was not his.

The coffee shop below was popping and on fire too. The street was filling, people here to watch and pretend to help. Raucous looked at the street, at the people, he saw boys from his gym, he saw local people, he saw everyone he saw every day. He saw Locke and he saw Simpson, he saw people in cars, boys in hoods, too many and too blurred to identify. They all looked at him as he sat, red, burned, scolded, and black with carbon. He stayed sat, he put his arm around Charlotte, but he winced as his skin broke and cracked. And they stayed there, sat on a curb, watching his history burn, head against head as doctors arrived and they told them to separate and travel alone. The fire under control, embers burning but one section of the street, his own little section, a glowing shell.

They had come to do this, to take away everything, to try and kill or leave him without life. He looked at Charlotte, her burns, her pain. She knew, she knew him. There was no walking away.

38

"Are you meeting her?" Charlotte asked.

Raucous nodded.

They were in a small private cottage on the coast, paid in cash. Charlotte had given the number, Raucous had called. Information was key and he had none.

There are degrees of burns. First, second and third. Superficial, problematic and scarred for life. Their bodies were burned, the heat causing damage to everything. They had not been covered, they had not escaped quick, and their skin showed their fight. But they escaped in a way as to make nurses tell them they had been lucky. But Raucous knew that the luck was avoiding death, avoiding huge permanent disfigurement. They looked like they had been scraped by blades, and peeled by giants. But their damage was mostly second degree. Painful but not lasting, visible but fading. They were blistered, and cracked, and red. Creams to be spread to stop infection, cool water to relieve the pain, drugs to take edges from nerves that screamed at the attack on their protective layer.

Raucous knew they had been lucky.

Two weeks in, two weeks away from where he had grown up.

It had not been a warning, it had been an attempt. The destruction of his home, the untouchable palace of a local, known man. It was an insult, a measured statement to all that came to watch. They had wanted them dead, not just damaged. And with their lives they wanted to remove all traces of them.

The doctors gave them five weeks to recover. There would be patches that took longer, there would be visible reminders of being burned and testing cremation. But they would be hidden on bodies, and legs. Their faces and arms would recover, their hands would work again, and the blisters would fade, some small scars remain. They were too old to renew like the young.

They had two hand guns, and the house was on top of a hill with no trees to obscure views. If anyone approached they would need to be good to not be seen.

Raucous knew he was leaving her stranded, they had one hire car, a family Ford. But the meeting wasn't dangerous, no one knew they were here, and he would be back. A ninety minute drive to the outskirts of London, a meeting near Gatwick.

He needed to know, he needed to ask questions.

She was sat in the bar they had arranged by message. Raucous took his time getting there, circling around after parking up, looking for people he felt were not right, the wrong way of moving, standing too long in one spot. He was looking for observers and he was looking to see if he was followed. He walked streets he had looked at online, the map and intersections in his mind. A small busy centre in a fake rural outpost, a village swallowed up by a city a long time ago and on a flightpath so the tranquil life was through eyes and not ears. He saw nothing, even his paranoia brought no alarms. He entered the shop and she turned to look at him and she stood.

Raucous walked slowly, watching her and the room. There were three couples, all old, looking the part, all long since retired and all no danger. The staff were younger, two kids, one alternative cool because he had stretchers in his ears, and the girl tall, lanky and in glasses. In an American film, toward the end, someone would do a makeover by removing her spectacles and she would be a prom queen.

Simpson smiled and watched him walk to their table of old wood waxed clean. She was tall and wearing a grey trouser suit that was ironed into perfection, her hair tied up. She looked like an American lawyer.

They sat down, stared at each other a while, Simpson sipped her tea, looking over the edge of the mug.

"What is it you want?" she finally asked.

Raucous leaned in.

"You travelled pretty far to get here," he said. "No word of why. You want something too."

Simpson smiled, Raucous had seen this often. The reveal to a lack of stupidity always surprising people.

"Go on," Simpson said and picked up her tea.

"Locke came and saw me, asked a lot of questions. Almost all about you."

"He likes information. Thrives on it."

"But he wanted to know about me and you. Why you came to speak to me after Mack."

This made an impression, something for which she wasn't prepared. Her face tried to hide it but when in thought her expression went neutral.

Her eyes came back to the moment.

"Because it was the right thing to do," she said."I could run around and cause trouble at your level, but that just means more friction for me. I like a smooth day at work. Making low level enemies because I show no respect leaves me with low-level irritation all day."

Raucous knew this, it was an obvious tactic and one everyone saw and recognised but accepted as the kindness it pretended to be. There was little altruistic in anything anyone did. There was always an angle, a way to receive just as much as was given.

"Why do you think he asked?" Simpson said.

It was his time to think. He couldn't reason it out.

"I couldn't tell you. I got the impression he doesn't trust you. He wanted to see if there was anything between us, in terms of a working relationship. He didn't ask outright, he just wanted to see my reactions to phrases and ideas."

Simpson smiled and leaned back.

"Is there?"

Raucous smiled at this. He liked her, he didn't know why, but maybe he had been played. He was dumb enough sometimes to fall for sympathy tricks.

"Why doesn't Locke know what you are doing?" Raucous asked.

Simpson thought for a few seconds, Raucous thought she was weighing up options, which version of the truth to tell. She smiled and leaned in.

"Have you not looked this guy up?" she asked.

Raucous shook his head.

"Locke is the most hated policeman I've ever met. There isn't even an argument. He worked on uncovering the corrupt, and he was good at it. He has probably put more police away than I have criminals."

"So what is he doing here and with you?"

Simpson inhaled and looked around the room. It was amateur-dramatic level acting, but natural to her.

"There's an official story, which I think is a pretty simple and ineffective lie, and there is a more logical explanation, one which should make me angry, but ultimately, what would it matter? It isn't going to amount to anything."

She sipped on her tea some more, smiling at whatever words were running through her mind.

Raucous watched and waited, he knew she would have the need to explain.

"The official version, or cover story if you want, which I do, is that he got kicked out of internal investigation and bumped out here. He didn't want to quit because that would be a weakness, right? So he gets placed here, in what is, without question, one of the most corrupt areas of the country. McClintock heads things up and a dirtier policeman I have never met. Drugs, guns, knives, and killings on an endless loop, and no one but the low level picked up and put away. But a whole lot of people on the legal side making money and looking away, and doing a poor job on easy cases. The whole place is either inefficient or on the take. With McClintock, I'd say both. But you know this, you used to be a part of it."

Raucous listened, nodded because he knew the truth of her words. He wondered at what she was doing and made the decision she figured he had a connection with Locke and that he, Raucous would run and tell. There was the chance she wanted him to play both sides, gain info. But there was always the danger she and Locke were working him right now. He didn't have enough information to make any kind of confident bet.

"So he is down here to check and discover, and everyone knows?" Raucous asked.

"That's the way of it, yes. No one is stupid enough to see it any other way."

Raucous leaned back, saw the girl behind the counter watching him as if she had a magical power to stop intimidation through a dirty look.

"And he was stuck with you because you are the honest one, or because you are the leader of the corrupt?"

Simpson smiled again.

"It doesn't matter what I say. But for the record, he is with me because I was the only one who'd accept him. Just coincidental that I'm the only honest police in London. There is not a single officer here that would want to be associated with him."

It was Raucous who smiled this time.

"So why you, if you were the one choosing?"

"Because it's the difficult option. I'm a female in a masculine world, all toxic traits and idiotic banter. The women that make it do so because they are more alpha than the males. I'm not that. I don't plan to out-drink, out-swear, out-fight any of the Neanderthal idiots. But what I do want is for them, and me, to see who I am."

"Locke thinks you are bent."

"I believe he does."

"And there is nothing in that?"

Simpson held out her hands, a gesture of what can I do?

"I'm part of one of the most notoriously crooked sections of the force. I am promoted above my age. I deliberately make a choice to stand with him and spend my days working alongside. He is a suspicious young man, and he has seen and heard that I go and talk to people like you when bad things happen. I offered condolences and not threats. He'd be stupid to think otherwise."

"Then why do it?"

"Because I'm not part of the men-who-think-they-rule-the-world cartel in the station. Never will be because I don't want to. So I choose to be as disliked as him, but disliked by him too."

Raucous shook his head.

"It isn't dislike, he just doesn't trust you."

Simpson looked down at the table.

"For a man who wants everything to be clean, he carries a lot of dirt to get things done."

Raucous knew this wasn't a slip, this was a deliberate sentence, an accusation, one she threw out to see a reaction. All she got was Raucous not understanding.

"In what way?" he asked.

"It matters little," she said after a pause."He has taken everyone he wanted down. And hard. But he'll figure out soon enough that I am not one of his targets."

"Talking to me makes that a longer journey," Raucous said.

"Speaking to you gives me credibility. Shows you I understand, and shows all those boys that I am not one of the old school. That I do think, that I do understand-"

"And that you care?" Raucous added, smiling.

Simpson knew he was ridiculing her. Knew she had stepped over into fantasy.

"Not for each of you, but for the whole. Yeah, I do. It matters what happens. Not the money, not the promotion. I'm looking for peace."

"And if your colleagues push back."

"Locke is here, I believe, off the back of instruction from someone high up. There is no reason at all for him to be walking around, with me, investigating a nothing drug crime killing. MarQuick ran things, someone burned him alive. Now others have popped up. Too quickly in my mind. In this small part of London. No reason at all. So whatever he is here to do or discover, or cause, I want in on it."

Raucous waited, looking over her words, looking for tells in her sentence to point out lies. He saw none.

"He tell you anything?" Raucous asked.

"He is as cagey as you, only he does dumb a bit better. A lot of the lads think he is a bit special, in the negative sense."

Raucous knew the phrase, had been accused of the same, always by those people nowhere near as smart as they believe, those people walking around because they read a book and believe they understand every nuance when all they do is rabbit another man's ideas.

"Will you tell him we met?" Raucous asked.

"Will you?"

"I have no means to do that."

"If he asks I won't lie."

"And raise his suspicion more?"

"Everyone has patterns of behaviour. Suspicion arises from when they change. If I did something new or against my norm, then there would be alarms. But I'm not doing that. Locke is, he shouldn't be here, and he shouldn't be alone. That is not his regular way. I need to be the one with suspicion."

"It's a difficult way to be."

"It has served you well," she said.

39

Raucous circled back to where he parked. He watched and looked because he couldn't help his caution. He saw nothing, felt nothing until he spotted his car, parked in a small paid area on the edge. He was there, leaning back, looking at Raucous and waiting. Raucous tried not to break stride, but he faltered, the surprise, as it always is, unexpected.

"Having a nice day out?" Cooper asked when Raucous was close.

Raucous had pressed the fob on his key, and the lights had flashed and the door popped. Cooper slowly pushed himself to upright.

"I didn't spot you," Raucous said.

Cooper smiled at the compliment.

"There is an art to it," he said. "You can't let them know you are there. Rare that I get caught. And if the person isn't looking properly, it is easier."

Raucous took the insult, tried to figure where he went wrong. Knew he hadn't spotted the tail, and wondered if he was bugged.

"There is nothing electronic," Cooper said. "Just probability and logic. A few facts, a knock-on and then we meet. No one needs to feel bad about it, there is nothing to do other than get lucky, and you nearly did near the end there. I hadn't expected it. I had to make a move I didn't plan."

Raucous figured Cooper was massaging his hurt ego. He didn't need it, just like he never needed teachers to tell him he had done well when he had scored poorly in a test.

Cooper looked at him, stared in deeper to his face.

"You look like you have leprosy," he said.

Raucous smiled. The burns were better but he was flaking and peeling and scabbed.

"Anything you want?" he asked.

"You meet police on a frequent basis for someone who grew up disliking them," Cooper said.

His voice was light, no anger just curiosity.

"Looking for information."

"Aren't we all? I used to try and find out about the horses. And you know what? People just made up stuff I wanted to hear. Did you get any?"

Raucous thought about what he had heard, what she had told him. He had thought about the gaps in her talk, the parts he needed to fill in. He hadn't got there yet, he was waiting for the drive.

"Not too sure. A description, couldn't tell you if it was fact or being played. I don't know who she is."

Cooper paused now, squinting a smile, then flicking it off.

"You have something of a relationship for someone you don't know. But she is someone strange, I'll give her that." Cooper said. "She makes it easy to believe she is one of them and then she goes and does or says something that makes you think she is fooling you."

"Someone you know well?"

"Someone I need to know better." He paused and looked down at the floor. "What did she say?"

Raucous had no debt to return, no code he needed to follow. The information was his to keep, but this guy popped up, and he couldn't see the reason.

"Didn't want to know anything. She wanted to see what I had, and that looked like nothing from where I was."

"Maybe I'll see something in it."

Raucous thought he sounded like the police. A question they always used. He had never answered before, not honestly.

"She told me about Locke, about the hate they feel for him where he works."

Cooper's face lit up.

"No one likes a policeman who puts police away."

"She seems to."

Cooper's smile faded. The curious expression of a man watching a burlesque routine for the first time.

"Genuine?" Cooper asked.

"The way she said it, the way she talked, looks like she wants in on whatever he is here to do."

"Which is what?"

Raucous knew he had answered too quickly. It meant something beyond the base level of being spooked.

"On her word, bring someone down. Wouldn't know who."

Cooper looked at the ground again, scraped his shoe on the tarmac. He looked up.

"And why would you tell me?"

"Because I don't figure you. Don't see what you are or what you are doing. You haven't tried to scare me or use me, at least not that I can tell."

"That wouldn't be an easy thing."

Raucous believed he meant it.

"You know what I am going to do," Raucous said."You probably think you'd like to be involved. I'm not walking away. They will face me. And I think soon. But I'm not gambling like you. I need it all in my favour before I start, and speaking to you, and to them, and having as many conversations as I can with people who know is only going to make it easier."

Cooper looked at him, smiling but sad.

"Nothing ever goes how you think it will."

Everyone always had a version of the same idea, Raucous thought.

"But the decisions in the moment have to be based on knowledge, and right now I don't have enough."

Cooper paused again, laid his right hand on the car window.

"You think she is genuine?" he asked.

"I don't know what she is aiming for, but she isn't on the take. She isn't protecting anyone. She is odd, but only because she isn't like I thought she should be."

"Do you think Locke will figure that out?"

A question Raucous knew he couldn't answer. The void of information making it impossible.

"I don't know how smart or stupid he might be, but if he is the person she described, he isn't going to be trusting anyone."

Cooper smiled.

"I always had the feeling he couldn't put his life, even in part, to someone else."

"He'll be single forever."

"Just like you and me," Cooper said. "Even if we pretend otherwise."

Raucous wanted to argue, say he had someone, but he knew the point Cooper was making, understood the philosophy, and nodded along to the same theme of his life. Cooper was thinking too, Raucous could see that. Two men the wrong age to be doing anything, standing and thinking about their unsuitability for romance.

"How long you going to be walking around looking like Quasimodo?" Cooper asked.

Raucous smiled. A reference only the old would understand.

"A few weeks. So the doctor says. Not at all sure anyone could ever tell if I am back to how I was."

"Will you look more normal by the sixteenth?"

"I should."

"I have a way in. It'd be an easier night for me with a bit of muscle with intelligence. No hits, just recognisance. A way to see who and what is there."

40

"Sounds like you've made a friend," Charlotte said.

Her hair was stubbling back, make-up making her look further along recovery than Raucous. He felt like the lead in The Phantom of the Opera but no one had given him a mask.

They were walking along the coast, a cliff face down to a beach no one would ever use to sunbathe and a sea that stayed angry and ate up the rock with every crash. There had been houses here once, built before erosion was a study and they fell into the sea one by one over fifty years ago. The wind was choosing random directions and they stayed away from the edge like the sporadic signs ordered them to do.

"I think he is alone, wants help but won't ask. It is an invite to support but fluffed up by pretending it would interest me."

"But it does, even if you don't know what it is. Probably because you don't know."

Cooper had sent a message, asked about his recovery, wanting to know, without asking, if Raucous was a willing participant in whatever scheme he had set up.

"Do you trust him?" Charlotte asked once they had made it to the tallest part of the cliff face.

They looked out over the sea, and Raucous wanted to feel something, an affinity. He recognised the beauty, could see what made people come and look and walk and share their experience through photos. But for him, he was here because Charlotte seemed to find peace, or exhilaration, he could not yet be sure.

"Do you like all this?" Raucous asked, looking over the land and view.

Charlotte looked up at him, her arm linked through his with each having hands in gloves and inside pockets. The wool itched but his skin had healed enough to wear them.

"I should," she said. "I like the peace of it all, nice to see it a few times."

"Could you live here?" he asked.

Charlotte smiled and inhaled the clean air. She unhooked her arm form his.

"Could you?"

Raucous knew honesty was his only way with Charlotte. She read him, knew him and there was little point in faking truths to appease and say what she wanted to hear.

"No," he said."There isn't anything. It isn't anything at all."

"You like solitude."

Raucous smiled.

"I like finding solitude in the middle of the city. Here it's the only thing there is. Nothing happens."

"That's what people like."

"Not all of them."

They stared around, looked out over the water, Raucous could see little in focus. Maybe there were ships out there but what did he care? People working boats. People were working everywhere.

"I don't trust him, no." Raucous said. "I've seen people similar, and I think what he shows is him, but he has an edge of an act, like he needs to force what he once was on the person he is now."

Charlotte's smile faded away.

"He has killed," she said.

"So have you and I. I don't fear you."

There was always that disconnect, the ease to condemn people for deeds they too had carried out. There was an explanation for theirs, there always was, a reasoning and comfort in conclusions. But others didn't gain that level of empathy. They condemned without thinking through reasons.

"If I told you to walk away, would you?" Charlotte asked.

Raucous looked at her and smiled.

"I would, but we know you won't. Three times they have tried to kill you. You won't walk away from that. And just as you are healed so is the kid I shot in the gut." He turned to her. "But if you say you are done. I'll come with you."

They looked at each other, waiting.

"Do you think it's normal being this way?" Raucous asked.

"Normal for us, yeah. You can't walk away."

"Could you?"

She looked down, not wanting to say the truth.

"I tried, long time ago now. But I came back. I'm glad I did."

"To come here?"

Charlotte smiled and looked around, taking in the full panorama.

"I've seen Japanese palaces, Indonesian islands, and antipodean out-backs," she said. "And I can say with all my heart, they are, without doubt, better than a grassy cliff in the rain on the North Sea."

Raucous held her hand.

"Peaceful though, right?"

Charlotte squeezed, a sign telling him something in a language he could not quite grasp.

"I'm Okay, Raucous," she said. "I'm as healed as I am going to be."

"Can you fight?"

"That's the fear, isn't it? Putting yourself in that moment and finding it has gone, that you aren't able to do it anymore."

Raucous had carried this fear all his life, scared to come up against someone better, someone who could take him, someone who had no fear of him. He'd met some, those who felt nothing of danger, or at least never showed it, but they were all dumb. You had to feel scared, had to be wary otherwise you just thought you were invincible, unbeatable, unable to be harmed, and that led to destruction. To fear was to respect, and anyone can cause pain if they come from where you don't see them. He'd been stomped, but he came back, later if needed and balanced out the treatment, made a name for revenge. Then the only ones who came were those alone and with weapons, and none of those could put him down.

"It is the only way to be," Raucous said. "They are young, armed and without the belief that they can lose."

"And us?"

"We aren't young anymore."

"We act like we are."

Raucous thought this too, an old man acting like a young kid, like putting on the old clothes from the back of the wardrobe and heading down to see a band you liked when they too were fresh.

"What would grown ups do?" he asked.

Charlotte laughed, and Raucous didn't know if it was at him or because, but he liked it all the same.

"How would we know that?" she said.

41

"There are four crews running security. We are in none of them. We have the clothes, we have the look, and we have worked doors before. It's a big place, loud, bright and no one knows anyone else," Cooper said.

"We just walk in and hope everyone thinks we are with the other crew?" Raucous asked.

They had met as arranged by text. A small flat in what was once a tower block but was now student accommodation. There were too many floors to count and they were high up, the windows not opened because wind this high caused damage. Raucous looked out and down to see anything. Small cars, small people, and no noise.

"All bluff," Cooper said. "We just mingle and walk in, doing what security does. It's the weakness in their set up. Four crews, all in competition, all from the area, but employing outsiders. None of them have enough men but none of them can turn down the contracts. We are the faces from out of town, but we are wearing the right clothes, and we are doing and saying the right things."

"You want us to actually work?"

"It is the only way we'll blend. Walking security, looking out for illegal substances that are not being sold by the official sponsors of the night, namely Franklin, and Dart to Dart. We can roam, look and try and see."

"See what exactly?" Charlotte asked.

She was as healed as she was ever going to be she had said. Cooper needed a driver, a safety precaution if anything went south. A car ready, nearby for any runner that might occur.

"They know you," Raucous said. "And there is little chance of me not being recognised."

"Always that chance, but the local boys are at the local clubs. They aren't all here, at least the loose cannons aren't because they'd all start shooting and there are going to be wall-to-wall z-list celebs there. You're not-quite-top-level footballers, mediocre singers, producers of mildly competent music and an assortment of hangers on, gold-diggers and the general fame chasing weirdoes who see a closeness to money and crime as a confirmation of their lives."

"So why are we going in?"

"To look."

"For what?"

"Franklin is hosting a big party for all the second-tier famous. An album launch of some local boy made good. A big night that he'll believe will become synonymous with his brilliance in later years when he is the man. The mayor of London, the man that runs the city. Never happening, obviously, but in his mind that is the future. There are people there who can be pressured, there are definitely going to be moments of showing off, a look at this, or that, with both options being illegal."

"There is nothing we can do if there is," Raucous told him.

"We can film, we can photo and we can report."

"That is not why you are going," Charlotte said.

Cooper ignored her, he didn't need to convince anyone.

"And if there should be the occasion to possibly cause some damage, maybe permanent to Franklin and his boys, then all the better."

"So you are going in armed. With what?" Charlotte asked.

"A gun," cooper said and lifted his shirt to reveal a small pistol taped to the skin just below his ribs. "Only if there is a safe way, one in which I escape. I'm not into suicide missions, and my way out is with you two. Nothing funny."

Raucous nodded and looked to Charlotte. They had spoken on the way to the meet, and it were as if Cooper had heard. They figured he would be carrying, and they figured he would admit as much.

"We are carrying too," Charlotte said.

"Always best to get it out in the open. Pistols?"

Charlotte nodded.

"Couldn't tell you the make, model or manufacturer, but they work. Both fired, multiple times. Nothing jams."

"Shooting people is different from shooting targets," Cooper told her.

"Running a knife through someone's throat is different to stabbing a steak," Charlotte said.

Cooper smiled. Raucous wouldn't believe that Cooper had no idea that Charlotte had killed.

Charlotte drove, a hire car, near the top of the range, one used by professional drivers to pick up exclusive clients. A smooth, sleek saloon of German origin. Clean and shining. Back windows dark. The engine ran smooth, and the whole thing was registered to a man in Croydon who couldn't afford the price and knew nothing of the credit card in his name.

The throb of the night had yet to start, the bustle not ready. The streets were quiet because six o'clock was too early for anyone to arrive. It was the change of shift, the old timers after an afternoon session heading home to fall asleep on armchairs and sofas while staff turned over and cleaned the place for people to make a mess. There was movement but not to pack streets, only to make it to work or home.

The building shone brightly, a large multi-coloured monument to European investment funds. A sleek building of millions.

"You ever been inside?" Cooper asked.

Raucous and Charlotte shook their heads.

"Was a place back in the day. Anything illegal was inside, anyone hiding was in there too. It was a mess, the type only squatters can live in."

"Your scene?" Charlotte asked.

"Thought it could be, turned out not to be the case. The falseness of the people got me most. All living their dream, they'd tell you. But I didn't see anything I would feel as happiness. Pretty dark place all in all. It'll be interesting to see what they have done with the decor."

Charlotte pulled over and Cooper and Raucous stepped out. They had agreed to where Charlotte would park, and they carried a mobile for any contacts. Charlotte drove off without word.

Cooper and Raucous looked smart. The attire was elegant, not the black bomber jacket, Tesco school-trousers and ankle-high Doctor Martins of a drink-and-brawl pub. They had long black coats of expensive wool, black trousers made of material that had not been created from oil, and shoes light enough to feel like trainers while looking like Italian leather.

"Put this in your ear," Cooper said, handing over a white earpiece with a curled cable.

"Do they work?"

"Just for show. They will all have them. Put your finger to it when you talk, it'll make you look like one of them."

"Four crews, Royals, Smyths, Blanchard and Robertson. Anyone asks, pick one," Raucous said, repeating words said to him.

They walked around the back of the building where the catering doors were open. There was a large entrance for cars to the left. An exclusive carpark for those who merited acclaim. Vans were leaving, a small army of men and women in white, elegant and clean, and the ladies in little, but what there was indicated they were waiting staff.

They walked into the group.

"Who's in charge here?" Cooper asked the space in front of him. Three people used the hands that were holding cigarettes and pointed to a young man in a three-piece blue suit.

They walked to him.

"Could you show us your register of employees?" Cooper asked.

"What?" the man asked.

"A register of who you have working tonight."

"Is there a problem?"

"None at all. A safety check. It has been run a few times and we are here to do the final check before moving on upstairs. Nothing flash."

"It is emailed through."

"And that's great. But we need to check you know who they are and how many."

"I don't know that."

"Then how do you know these people are actually working for you?"

The man pressed his phone, typed something and then showed Cooper the screen.

"Here is the email." The man said.

"Yeah, I've seen that," Cooper told him, no aggression at all. "But we just need to double check. Annoying for you, annoying for us. But just the last check. It is cool."

The man shook his head but Raucous knew he had given up.

"Come with me," he said.

The man walked with Cooper and Raucous into the Kitchen. There were four security inside at the doors into the main building. Cooper caught them, and Raucous saw without looking. They kept their attention on the man in blue suit. He walked quickly to a table and opened a briefcase. He pulled out papers, the same he had shown them as an electronic attachment.

"These ok?" the man asked.

"You know they are, we know they are. But now the responsibility is ours, unfortunately. Any problems with your staff is now on us, not you. So thank you for that. And I hope you have a good evening."

Cooper spoke, louder than he normally would. They had attention and an audience and Raucous wanted to smile, but he kept his stern face. Cooper had just given them the best level of legitimacy they could gain in a simple confidence trick.

Raucous followed Cooper like Lennie to George in Of Mice and Men, a big lumbering fool with no ability to think for himself.

Cooper chose the door to the left as confidently as any man could. He nodded at the two security men, Blanchard written left of their chest on the black polo shirts they wore as a uniform. Through fashion alone Cooper and Raucous owned them. The two men from Blanchard's nodded and let them through.

The door led into a long corridor of brick, there were doors on the inner edge spaced three metres apart. They turned right and walked, the lights above them bright and the bulbs bare. They walked what appeared to be a straight line but Raucous could see the bend. They were walking the edge of a huge circle. A blue sign hung on the ceiling ahead of them with an arrow pointing left and up. The stairs were enough to climb to the top of a flat garage-roof.

The floor above had a lot of action. People were moving, an entrance opened and manned by six security. Cooper and Raucous kept on walking, taking in the building, the sights and layout. This floor had money. The glass was large and clean, the interior walls flat and white, the posters and pictures all large framed and performance shots of angry men and women hurling sounds into microphones and on into crowds. Most were black and white, others with random splashes of primary colours. Posters of concerts from past times in different places. There was space between the entrance and the inner room, a five metre walk past the outer shell into the inner area of live gigs and DJ sets. Cooper and Raucous kept walking, attempting a lap to see everything they could.

Half-way they had passed two more entrance doors, two more groups of security, and the people had started to come, early doors for those that wanted their place at the front, a place among the names and faces. There was a glass elevator shaft on the central wall. Raucous looked up as he walked and so did Cooper. It led up high, above the inner concert hall, to a walkway ten metres above. There were no stairs but there had to be somewhere Raucous thought. As they paced around they saw them, a diagonal steel staircase against the wall, curling around, and up to the same walkway above. Security stood at the foot.

They kept on walking, never talking, looking around, seeing it all.

They made a lap, had judged space and distance, seen only two ways down to the floor below, two ways up to the top and six ways into the building. They walked into the concert hall and the impact hit Raucous hard.

The lights flashed, the noise blurred into a wall of notes all seemingly hit at random times and at varying amplitudes each on the far side of loud. It wasn't strobes, but it was flashes, the room mostly blue, dark with glitter as the lights slapped surfaces. There were people and there were rooms. Raucous had expected a large empty space but saw rooms without windows and with thick doors. He looked up and saw the large balcony that ran all the way around the top edge, out and over the space they walked. There was no way up from the inside.

The rooms were filling, and the bars becoming busy, a stream of people onto the floor they walked. Raucous looked across the space and saw sectioned off areas of raised platforms, security acting as barriers. There was a hierarchy to it all, the taller the more important, the place to be up there under the ceiling, down here, near the speakers a place for anyone who could only aspire to being one of the bright criminal lights.

"I've seen enough," Cooper said.

Raucous could barely hear over the background blasting sounds of electronic noise and excited conversation of a thousand people and counting. The place would hold many more, the space between them all testified to that, but they were coming in, six doors open to the flow.

"Too loud," Raucous said as they stepped through the doors into the outer ring.

People were filing in, a constant stream. Early but they were all now coming.

Once past the doors and security, people had freedom to walk and roam and see and look for the place they deemed best to start their evening. The place was a hive, walking freely becoming difficult, a swerve, a planned route, an eye to see where people were coming. Raucous looked around, watching for anything, trying to find something he would like to see. There were people of all types walking and zipping through, some bumping. Each person dressed in a way they would call smart or cool or unique. It was a snapshot of the present day. It would age and everyone looking at photos would be able to guess the year. A modern spectrum of fashion all based on the past, and trying to be new.

Raucous saw them and held a finger to his fake earpiece. He spoke into his sleeve like it contained a microphone.

"Elevator," he said.

Cooper was good, he didn't look immediately, he pressed his finger to his ear and spoke in the same way.

The lift was to their right, the glass cabinet sliding down the glass tube, the wires and mechanics visible but never seen because everyone was watching the people inside.

"Who is it?" Cooper asked.

"Have a look, everyone else is."

And they were because that was the reason for the whole set-up.

Cooper looked, and while Raucous couldn't get defined edges when looking at distance, he saw enough to know it was Franklin, the Darts and two other men slowly moving down, staring out at the people, full enough to feel the reverence, spacious enough for the people to be able to part and have their cocaine messiah walk on through to receive awe and respect from grown-ups wanting near the infamy.

Raucous kept his head turned and Cooper looked at the crowd. They were security doing their job.

People quietened, those that saw, while some had no idea, and others who had drunk enough to want to be noticed. They spoke loudly but no one but those dumb enough to love them listened. Everyone who knew watched the glass elevator.

The lift hit the ground floor, the doors slid open, the two men Raucous didn't know walked out, Franklin next in his record-label hoodie, followed by the Darts. They didn't speak, they marched, Franklin smiling, the two men in front staring at the people they needed to move, a warning to leave space, while the Darts searched the crowd. Raucous watched, thinking himself invisible. He put his head down, and glanced to his left. Cooper was staring at the group as they walked. Cooper took a step forward and Raucous grabbed his arm to stop him going further.

Cooper looked down at the large hand wrapped around his bicep. The anger drifted away as he looked up to see Raucous.

"Momentary lapse," he said. "Almost lost it there."

"Plan?" Raucous asked.

"Leave or follow," Cooper smiled.

Raucous looked up, the Franklin's group would need to look back to see them. The hubbub was returning, gossip starting. They had seen the king of the building, they had been near the man.

Raucous stepped forward, following the group.

"Good choice," Cooper said.

42

The group stuck close to the inner curved wall, Franklin in the middle of a loose circle made of four. They had stopped looking around, and were marching, Franklin acknowledging hellos and shouts, the men in front not breaking character, mean faces all the way. The Darts walking like relaxed children. This all looked practised and a routine, Raucous thought.

Following was difficult as people stopped and thought only of the group of five men. They froze in place momentarily, and Raucous couldn't judge where spaces would be. They bumped people, who swore or moved, or stared. But they were two men, one large, looking like security and no one wanted conflict, no one wanted to lose their place in the building.

"They are going underground," Raucous said.

Cooper nodded.

The second entrance downstairs was the one they hadn't used. Three men stood at the doorway down, each man as large as Raucous, each with the same shaven head and frown. They could all be brothers. They all held their hands in front of themselves, not looking at people, only into space because no one would want any piece of them.

The group of five walked towards them, the three stepped aside, the group walked down the stairs and the three men stepped silently back into place. They were a human door, certainly armed, and had one job.

"We aren't getting through that," Raucous said. "Try the other way?"

Cooper nodded. Raucous could see his movements quicken. The addictive shakes of a man not hearing what he wants, like an animal trapped in a corner.

"We are here to see, not kill," Raucous said.

"Pretty good set up," Cooper told him as they walked faster. "Best cover anyone could have. Security everywhere, your own men at every conceivable point, all armed, and all perfectly acceptable."

"How often do these nights happen?"

"Often enough."

Raucous looked at as many people as he could and realised any of them could be anything. There was no uniform for the modern day crook. Drug runners, controllers, the heavy men, they all wore the same, or variations. There was no sharp suit for the top men, just clothes that were more expensive than the next without any discernible difference except the brand.

"If you are shifting something in then out, the chaos here would be great cover," Cooper said."A lot of movement, mostly innocent. You can't stop them all."

Raucous smiled at Cooper's thoughts. He sounded like he was thinking through an arrest, a way to bring it all down.

They were walking fast.

"I don't know if this is genius or stupidity," Cooper said. "Famous people everywhere, sycophants galore, cars and vans in and out. Everything and everyone watched. You could do anything here."

"We don't know that is happening," Raucous said.

"No, we don't. But if they wanted cover, this is perfect. How can you raid this place right now?"

Raucous looked around and saw the numbers and the confusion. A raid in this would be carnage and result in death. Too many people in on the game and no way of knowing who was who. There were weapons here, that much was clear. But the doors were checking faces not concealed guns and knives.

"Not changed much since the good old days of illegal squats and no-go zones," Cooper said. "They have just modernised the set-up. Prettier to look at. Same no-personality idiots swarming in to try and steal other people's cool and pretend it's their own," Cooper said, and Raucous could hear the contempt.

"Still want to look?" Raucous asked.

Cooper nodded.

"More than ever," he said.

43

They took the stairs down to the brick corridor underground. The sign still hung but there was activity now as if the space had become the walk way of a busy restaurant on a Saturday night. Waiters and waitresses, porters and security moving in space too small for the use. They walked the way they entered and pushed through the doors into the kitchen.

The man in the suit stopped and looked up. Cooper saw him.

"All good," Cooper shouted. "Running a check. Any problems?"

The man in the suit shook his head and got back to telling people what to pick up and where to go.

"He's running it," Raucous said.

Cooper nodded.

"Without a doubt."

Cooper turned to the man in the suit and stepped up close but kept his voice loud enough for security to hear.

"The meeting is on," Cooper said.

Raucous was intrigued by how Cooper played. He was a confidence trickster working in bluff.

"Anyone gone through?" Cooper asked, pointing at the doors with security.

The man in the suit shook his head. Cooper had his attention now, and Raucous tightened. There were many types of people, but the easy ones to fool were those who weren't scared. This guy was operating in a place where mistakes led to retribution from men and boys who wanted to impress with their level of revenge.

The man in the suit stood still.

"No one has gone through," he said. "No one has come out either."

"They will," Cooper told him.

The man in the suit stared at Cooper and pursed his lips. He turned his gaze to Raucous.

"Who are you?" he asked.

Cooper didn't miss a beat.

"Quality control. We haven't met because that would compromise what we do. You are an important man, central to much of what Franklin does. The Darts, as lovely as those boys can be, don't do subtle. We do. The muscle here is not as dumb as he looks."

The man in the suit stared at him more.

"You want to make the call, and I am surprised you didn't earlier when we first met. You can make it now, but there won't be an answer because the meeting is now. How do I know this? Because I am in on the details. Just like you. We need to check the corridor, send the message, and all is good."

"Why don't I know about this?"

"Without wanting to insult you, this is the weak link right here. If you are under the influence of someone, then it is an easy in. If you know nothing of us, then there is nothing you can do. However, in a short time, the meeting is over, we walk back through here, you make your call, and the traffic all starts again. Nice and easy."

Raucous wanted to speak but knew he had to remain silent. The large muscle to the smaller brains like it had been written so many times before.

"You are welcome to come with us, but that is not your role," Cooper said.

The man in the suit turned to the two men on the door and nodded. They stepped aside.

"See you soon," Cooper said.

They walked to the second doors, the ones they hadn't chosen first time. Two security had their hands in their jacket pockets. They were not ready to fight but Raucous assumed they were ready to shoot. The door they protected was more important than the other.

Raucous and Cooper walked toward them and both men shook their head, slowly and with meaning at the security.

Raucous smiled. The security looked to each other.

44

The other side of the kitchen was the same brick corridor, same bare lights, and the same number of doors, all closed, along its inside edge.

"He didn't buy all of that," Raucous said as they walked quickly.

"He looked too smart. He'll be thinking."

"I doubt he has met anyone dumb enough to come in as a pair and take on these people."

"Did you think he was in?"

"Looked that way to me. He was moving people, controlling security, not doing too much of the catering. He was wary of you. Maybe he figured the trick was something a paranoid drug runner would pull. I've been wrong plenty before, and maybe he is just a manager. But whatever it is, we are in. There isn't another way out."

The doors stopped and only a brick wall remained. They walked more, the bulbs glaring down. On the left, a double fire door with push bars to open stood shut. They walked up and past, looking down the corridor, seeing nothing but a long bright tunnel curving around. They stopped, looked at each other and nodded. They turned and walked to the fire doors.

They stayed silent, listening for anything, but the noises, despite being quiet yet repetitive were coming from everywhere. Thousands of feet, sound waves crashing and deflecting as people spoke above them. They could hear it all but nothing defined.

"Want to gamble?" Cooper asked, his voice low.

Raucous knew walking through was dumb, but coming this far, chasing ghosts but turning back was an insult to their own beliefs.

He nodded.

"How do you want to play it?" Raucous asked. "Straight up confident? Because if we walk in on Franklin and the Darts, we're done. They know us."

Cooper shook his head.

"They know you. Tim and Gary and a couple of hangers on saw me. They didn't have me as anyone but a thief. Got caught breaking in. Or, if truth be told, trying to leave quietly. I'm still a nobody. My name they might know, but they would never have seen me."

Raucous nodded, thinking of how he had made it through this far without death, and knowing that some of that was because he never made choices like this. Like two kids they had egged each other on further into difficulty, because neither wanted to be the first that cracked.

Cooper reached into his coat but Raucous reached out and pushed against Cooper's forearm.

"If we go in with guns out, we are telling everyone we are there to cause harm. It takes away one of our outs."

"And how many outs do you think we have?"

Raucous thought.

"If we are here to see, and your mouth keeps spouting lies like they are truth, more than if we stroll in trying to scare men with two little pistols."

Cooper smiled and took his hand out and it was empty.

"You want to go first?" Cooper asked.

Raucous smiled and shook his head.

45

They had made a good decision, but only enough to stop them being dead. Cooper had pushed the door slowly, waiting for the pop of the lock, to add weight to the edge and move to create enough space to walk through.

Cooper stepped through and Raucous followed and they saw.

Raucous didn't speak, trying to hold an impassive face, an expression that was bored with seeing all this again. He didn't look to Cooper as that would signify surprise. But in his head he swore. He had just bet his life on the skills he had but he felt like a boxer turning up to a fight to find he was supposed to wrestle. It was all wrong and they knew it. Bravado was gone. Raucous wanted an easy retreat, but turning and walking out was not an option.

Raucous heard the door pop back into place behind them as if they had stepped into a hermetically sealed room. He didn't move, the two men with automatic rifles were pointing barrels at them and staring. No one spoke.

Raucous looked around and saw where they were. An underground carpark, the size of a mansion's ground floor. Space enough to hold twenty cars, the floor smooth concrete with white lines but no vehicles parked in them. Ahead, toward the corridor that allowed access on the far side, about thirty metres from Raucous were two small vans, both white, and a large Bentley saloon with its boot open. But the cars and space were not his concern, it was the twenty men, fifteen of them in tracksuits but all carrying automatic rifles, and five in suits with nothing but small hand guns.

Franklin was in the middle, the five suits around him but at a distance. The two men who came down the elevator with him were moving boxes from the vans to the floor. None of the group looked their way.

Cooper looked at the man to their right, he put his index finger to his lips to signify silence. He stood tall, placed his hands in front of him and held them as if he was standing guard. Raucous smiled inside and copied the moves. Two men - two security – adding weight to the situation. The man stared as Cooper and Raucous looked ahead. He looked to his partner, they agreed in whatever way they had developed and lowered their guns.

46

Raucous kept his face angled down with his eyes rolled up to watch the action. It was blurred but not enough to be simple shapes moving on an undefined stage. There were words but he couldn't hear them as individual sounds. The sentences merging into one lyrical wave and the answers the same. There was no anger, no malice, just calm conversation between groups of men.

Raucous realised there were three groups, not two. The suits seemed in control, the ones leading. They appeared to rule the room, or at least acted like they did. Their faces were too far to have definition, but grey hair was visible on most. The tracksuits and sportswear were split in two, those to the left of the suits as Raucous looked, and those to the right. The Bentley, Raucous figured, was Franklin's. It looked blocky, like a sports car half-way through mechanical puberty on the way to an adult van. The big B on the back speaking of its quality and build.

The edges of the garage had men in pairs, spaced out, one group on each of the three doors, and two more at intervals between. Each man was carrying an assault rifle. Raucous had seen these before, seen them fired, knew that just one could mow everyone down if used with skill.

The entrance in had no guards because stationing someone there would be stupid. The set up was a three-way angle on the group in the far centre, and if all the men pulled triggers, the group would be unidentifiably dead.

Raucous wanted to look to Cooper but kept his head and body straight. He knew the two men near him were watching the action in the centre, he knew Cooper was too.

A van started and Raucous could not help but look up. The suits were climbing in, five men, like ushers at a wedding, getting into their transport to take them to wherever they needed. The engine started and they drove without waiting to warm the oil.

The men in the middle, ten of them, watched the back of the van leave, smoke and vapour pouring from the exhaust. The van headed up a slope. Raucous heard the engine idle, a pause of just over twenty seconds, a clanging noise as a door wound open, the engine revved again and the van grew quieter and then silent as it put space between them and there.

Franklin spoke to the five men in front of him, they nodded, and two of them picked up a box each from the floor, sliding them into the back of the van that remained. Raucous saw the movement of the man to his left. He raised his gun slightly, stepped forward, and rested his weight on his planted feet. The man to his right did the same.

Raucous looked to Cooper and mouthed a swear word. Cooper nodded, the men in the middle oblivious to the movement on the edge off the room. Raucous heard a clank as the door or gate or whatever blockade was at the end of the exit shut closed. Raucous looked up, The Darts still stood, still watched the five men pack up and jump into the van, two in front, three in back.

The van started as did the Bentley. Franklin driving the car in a large semi-circle away and around toward the wall where Raucous stood, rubber squeaking on the polished concrete.

Raucous didn't care for the Bentley, it was not his concern. The action was coming, but not next to him. He watched as the Darts walked to the front of the van and pulled their guns from the back of their tracksuit bottoms, aiming down barrels, holding their guns with two hands, pointing at the windscreen. The van lurched forward, accelerating, tyres screeching. The Darts fired but missed as they jumped away from the crush of the white van's grill. They fell to the floor but stood quickly, firing into the van as it sped toward the tunnel escape. Bullets hit, they thudded and left small holes in the side panels but the van kept moving, accelerating forward making it through the gap. The Darts fired again, aiming low, and the back right tyre burst, the van swerving and hitting brick, smashing up on the right wall, bouncing and hitting the left. The back doors opened and three men jumped out, handguns raised and firing indiscriminately as if their bullets could magically seek out targets. The Darts ducked, The Bentley pulled up, the door opened and Franklin shouted.

"Fucking get them."

The men around the edge of the room marched forward, guns raised, waiting for the Darts to clear space for an easy kill. They were aiming but not firing, their own men in the way. The easy option was for the Darts to scramble and head for cover, but they wanted the kill, they alone, and they marched forward, bullets from the men in the van whining around the room, smashing into walls high up as they ran up the slope, firing back at things they could not see. The driver's door opened, a man staggered out, blood on his face, a gun in his hand. One of the Darts walked up behind him, put his barrel to his head and fired. The other Dart looked through the passenger door and fired three times. He squealed in delight as he stared at what he had done.

Raucous looked at Cooper, saw him staring at Franklin, the carnage in the middle not for him. Franklin was metres away, hanging out the driver's door looking like an aged boy racer. The two men with Machine guns stayed in place, guarding the car and their boss. The man to the right spoke.

"You joining in or what?" he asked Cooper.

Raucous reacted before it happened. He saw what was coming and knew he had to move or be killed. Cooper pulled his gun from his jacket and pointed it at the man's face. He was giving him the briefest moment to back away. He gave the possibility to lay down the weapon, to eat his pride and vanish. Cooper wasn't being sneaky, he didn't set it up so he wouldn't see what was coming. Cooper stood in front, he had the drop but he had the lesser gun. The big guy with the rifle looked at the pistol and smiled. He raised his rifle and Cooper fired. The top of the man's head disintegrated, a fragmented scalping, his expression fixed in shock, and after a moment when gravity saw what it had to do, the rest of his body slipped down to the floor as if all his bones had gone.

Franklin turned, saw, jumped into the Bentley, shut the door and a click sounded as the doors locked. Franklin sat in his chair, crossed his arms, smiled and stared at Cooper.

Cooper turned, but Raucous already had his gun on the man.

"No time to choose. Drop and run, or die right here," Raucous said.

The man looked to Franklin in the Bentley, looked to Raucous and Cooper, but most importantly, he looked down at his colleague with half a head, and made a decision that would prolong his life short-term but would mean he could no longer be here again. He bent over and placed the gun on the floor, he turned and pushed against the doors through which Raucous had entered and ran.

Cooper turned to the car, reached out and tried the handle but nothing opened. He raised the gun to the glass.

"No point," Raucous said.

There were multiple gunshots from the other side of the room. The three men trapped but fighting back. The rapid fire of machine guns meant the Darts were no longer in the way.

"Why?" Cooper asked.

And he fired, his free hand palm out as if it would protect his body from fragments. The bullet did nothing but ricochet back leaving a scratch on the glass.

"Bullet proof," Raucous said. "No way he sits in there smiling like that if he thinks he is about to be shot."

They were stood, looking through the windscreen as if observing a leopard at the zoo. Franklin stared back, smirking and waiting.

"Why doesn't he drive?" Cooper asked and fired again with the same result.

"Because we are the dumb ones."

Raucous looked to the far side of the room, The Darts had seen, they were running, and firing, the bullets whizzing, most of them hitting the car, one or two above their heads, but then the impacts stopped. They needed to reload so they stopped their run and pulled spare magazines from their waist bands.

Franklin sat smiling through the thick heavy glass.

"We got to go," Raucous said.

Cooper stared at Franklin one last time.

Raucous and Cooper turned in unison, pushed through the doors, guns raised and ran.

47

Raucous grabbed Cooper's coat and pulled him left. The stairs led up to the main floor, the corridor Cooper was trying to run was too long and led to a kitchen, commotion and the man Raucous had let leave.

"We aren't getting out there," Raucous said.

Cooper was wide-eyed like a man in shock and anger but he nodded, understood the reason. They needed chaos. They couldn't run free alone. He slapped at the arm that held him, freeing himself, not wanting to be controlled. His face was splattered with blood, the blood of the man lay dead metres away. They took the stairs and heard the doors to the garage smash open. Raucous turned to look but the wall in the stairwell blocked his view. They took the stairs two at a time, and one of the three men guarding from the top turned and stared down. He spoke to his two colleagues who turned too, but Raucous and Cooper were at the top, pushing against them.

"Ambush," Raucous said. "Gone wrong in a big way."

It was dumb but all he had.

They were on the main floor, but blocked from moving. The crowds a packed unit, space ever contracting, ways through not popping into view. The three men had eyes on Cooper and his mask of red.

"Carnage," Raucous said.

The noise at the base of the stairwell rose, shouts, screams, and swearing.

"They're coming," Cooper told them.

The three men didn't move, Raucous heard steps, he pushed, the gun in his hand smashing against the nearest man's chest, staggering him back.

"Bomb," Cooper shouted. "There's a bomb."

People turned and saw this man in blood, the wide-eyes, the men stood with guns. The initial screams rippled out, those close, in their fashion of the day, pushed and jostled and ran without reason or a chosen direction. Their only goal was to move, fast and away from the five men they saw armed and screaming about terror. One of the men tried to grab Raucous but Raucous lashed out with his right foot against the man's knee, bending it back, making him stagger away then forward with the shift of balance. Raucous whipped the barrel of the gun against the man's face as he leaned in and the man's nose exploded pumping blood all the way down until the man's face slapped the floor, his body staying flat but his head bouncing up.

Cooper grabbed Raucous and pulled him into the masses. People screamed, pushed, kicked and fell. Those on the floor not able to rise as people trod on hands, walked over bodies and Cooper screamed bomb again.

They were moving now, bent over, guns in hand, being bumped and jostled, as crowds ran for exits. Many had headed for the stairs down to the basement. They had seen a door close and made their choice. A blockage to stop men running up. Raucous heard a shot, he stood up and looked to see a man falling back holding his chest, leaving space for the Darts to emerge. They scanned the room, on toes looking for a viewpoint. Raucous ducked down, Cooper had too.

"Get on Charlotte, we need an out," Cooper said.

The bodies were scattering, the word of bomb, the sound of guns, and the vision of the Darts with men and rifles sent the crowds crazy. They kept low like they were running for a helicopter in a Vietnam film while those around them stood up looking for escape and a route to the street.

"We need you close," Raucous said as Charlotte answered the phone.

Cooper was leading the way, Raucous grabbing Cooper's shoulder like he was a blind man.

"Don't know what you've done, but it is chaos out here," Charlotte said. "I can't get close. I'm where I said I'd be."

"Cooper," Raucous said.

"I heard."

They went through the double door out onto the steps, surrounded by panicked people, still low, still hiding but their human cover thinning out as they all spread into the space looking to move into streets they thought would provide protection.

"We got to run," Raucous shouted.

They were visible now, the people around them less than ten and moving further away. Raucous looked back and the Darts with four men walked out of the front doors, higher up they could scan the scene. They looked across, and forward and smiled when they saw them.

"Get to the alley," Raucous said.

They were on the right side of the building, Charlotte was two hundred metres away. They sprinted and heard the crack of gunfire. More screams rose from the thinning crowd and Cooper raced ahead, quicker than Raucous, flowing across tarmac. Cooper stopped, looked around, stepped back to Raucous coming forward, grabbed his coat and pulled in an attempt to increase speed. A crack fired out again, but Raucous felt nothing, no impact and Cooper kept moving. They hit the alley, wanting to stop, but forced themselves on. But Raucous knew they were slowing. The alley ended, another street cut across, and the alley restarted on the other side.

Raucous looked back and saw no one following, an empty way. They ran more, the adrenaline pumping but lungs and muscles reaching the end. They turned left and Charlotte's car was humming over, the lights on, and parked. Raucous and Cooper jumped in, both in back. Charlotte hit the accelerator, slow and smooth and they drove away.

48

"What did you do?" Charlotte asked when she had hit top speed for the road.

"Nothing. There was a deal and then a hit," Cooper said.

"The suits looked like police." Raucous told them.

Cooper turned, his face losing the edge of aggression, a relaxing of lines.

"They are. Three different areas. Big coverage. Wouldn't have thought they were the top guys. Important though. I recognised two. Big hitters. The other three I haven't really seen before."

Raucous turned his head left to look at Cooper. Cooper smiled.

"Information is everything. No point being smart if you know nothing," Cooper told him.

That made me dumb, Raucous thought.

"I know nothing," he said."But I know that was a planned hit. There was no falling out, no arguing. Those guys were marked to die. Everyone knew but them."

Cooper leaned forward, neither had put a seatbelt on, and held his head.

"That is the way of it," he said. "They represent a rival, of sorts. Not in any real sense, not now. Asked to come on board, probably, offered riches and then taken out. Simple, and dumb to fall for."

"But if you have police there," Raucous said to no one in particular.

"They should have known when the suits left."

"What happened?" Charlotte asked again.

"Franklin has police, guns, and an operation that looks like a small army," Raucous said.

"Just kids playing gangster games with a crowd whose loyalty is bought in cash," Cooper told them.

They drove in silence, Charlotte following speed limits and road signals, winding her way out of the area. But there were police cars with blues flashing, sirens blaring and they were all being dragged into the sphere of Franklin's place.

The streets were quiet, more people on foot than in cars. A darkness setting in and street lights coming dimly into life.

Cooper and Raucous sat back in the big comfortable back seats, staring at the ceiling, taking time to wind down.

Raucous sat thinking of nothing, breathing deep. Knowing he had been seen, knowing the Darts knew it was him. He had come in, killed, witnessed police and death and there was no way of coming out. Franklin had everything, and Raucous nothing. Men, law and an armoury. Raucous had just seen the power Franklin held, and he had walked in and invited them into a war. He didn't want to think, didn't need to run though consequences and theoretical futures. He needed to rest, and he needed to hide.

His peace wasn't found.

"Shit," Charlotte said, quietly but loud enough to be heard.

Raucous and Cooper knew and turned their heads, saw and grabbed their seatbelts, putting them in place.

Two cars had pulled out behind them, lights on full beam, the mirrors providing nothing but blindness. They weren't marked police.

"Do they know this is us?" Raucous asked.

"Don't think so. Just trawling, looking. Not many cars on the road, but we aren't speeding."

The cars slowed, full beams still glaring. One stayed behind, mirroring the car Charlotte drove. The other pulled forward, nice and smooth, coming up on their right, slowly moving up to the side.

Charlotte kept her face forward, until the light became too much and she turned to her right. The car had four men inside, two in front and two in back. It was a fair guess to assume the other car was the same. The man in the passenger seat held a phone to his ear, but stared into Charlotte's car all the time. He spoke, his mouth moved, words could not be understood. He placed the phone away, turned to the driver and nodded.

The car accelerated forward, pulling ahead by a few metres. The car behind, in communication with the first accelerated up closer.

Charlotte swore.

"They're pulling a move," Charlotte said. "If I don't react they are going to trap us in."

Raucous looked at Cooper, Cooper nodded. They pulled their guns, while keeping low.

"You ready?" Charlotte asked.

"Go for it," Raucous said.

The car in front was starting to slant across, blocking forward movement. It was a police manoeuvre but common sense. A car in front meant they had to slow and stop. They couldn't reverse because the car behind would come up close.

"Here we go," Charlotte said.

Raucous felt the power of the engine, he slid back as the car lurched forward and his own body wanted to stay at its own velocity. He felt the pressure as his shoulder dug into the soft cushions.

Charlotte had pretended to be following orders, was doing everything she should, but they left a gap big enough to drive through and she took it. She put her foot down, turned hard right, clipping the back of the car in front, the movement forward helped by the bump from the car behind. They whipped like they were in the dodgems and everyone was chasing them down. She turned a hard right, went through the gears fast but on time and their car sped away.

Raucous and Cooper sat up, looked into the cars, trying to find information, trying to see faces, but they could pick out nothing.

The engine roared but sounded smooth, a healthy rumble speaking of power and comfort. Raucous looked back, the two cars were accelerating and turning, their motors sounding every part their equal.

Raucous watched, trying to figure which way Charlotte would take them. They needed small roads, built up areas, and there was a chance they would lose.

His thoughts changed when he saw. He turned and looked to Cooper. Cooper swore, smashed his fist against the back of the passenger seat and their car filled with the glowing reflection of the blue flashing lights that the two cars had set in motion.

Charlotte shouted, swerving their car to the right, taking a small road she did not know.

She turned off their lights in hope of vanishing rather than certainty.

49

They flashed blue lights but made no sound. Two cars, Swedish made, black and heavy in power. They followed, single file because the space of the road dictated they must. Charlotte was in front in a mechanical game of tag. She accelerated, relying on street lamps to show the way, the engine humming, top gear and going straight.

The car bounced up and smashed down like turbulence on a cheap flight. Speed bumps, what were once dead policemen, laid across the road to prevent racing. The bottom of the car scraped out on the tarmac, the screech of metal splintering off.

There was another, and the same result, the car managing but it couldn't do it forever. Charlotte turned a hard right and the car held its front wheels but the back slid, Charlotte accelerating as she felt the back go too far and the car moved straight again.

Raucous looked back, the first of the police cars held up, reversing because it had misjudged the turn. The second blocked behind. Raucous saw Cooper tapping his phone.

"Next right," Cooper shouted.

"What?" Charlotte asked.

"Take the next right, ten metres."

Charlotte turned, the rubber tyres screeching, Raucous looked back and the police were back in chase.

"Second left," Cooper said.

"Where are we going?" Raucous asked as he bounced.

Charlotte turned, Raucous moved against the car's lean, Cooper pushing against the seatbelt, his mass flying forward. But he stared at his phone. The blue lights flashed bright through the glass.

"Go straight, have to cross two other roads. Don't brake, just go for it."

"Because you know there won't be other cars?" Charlotte shouted.

"If you slow, they'll catch us and ram us. Just head down and go," Cooper told her.

The conversation was bracketed with the noises of an engine and the rush of air smashing against the metallic body of a car built for long distance travel, a car to pick the mildly rich from an airport.

"After two?" Charlotte shouted.

Cooper looked at his phone.

"After that, I just have to hope the alleyways haven't changed too much in twenty years. This electronic map kind of says it's the same."

"That's your plan?" Raucous asked.

He was looking back and the police were there, holding at a distance, not close enough to hit and not far enough away to be lost.

They sped across two streets, no cars and no people to hit or swerve or kill. Empty streets of parked cars and ancient housing, terraces bookended with what would once have been the home for the supervisor.

"Now what?" Charlotte shouted.

Her eyes always on the road.

"Left," Cooper said.

The urgency in his voice made Charlotte turn the wheel fast. The back end slid out and around, Charlotte fought the spin, turning the wheel against the slide, accelerating hard to pull the front even. But the car was going sideways, it slid and hit parked cars. Their momentum shuddering to a stop. Alarms sounded, the car at a standstill but the engine still running. Raucous looked to the police, the first car, it's large grill with a blue light moving up and back across its top was bearing down, not braking, already hitting top speed. It needed to brake but it wasn't.

"Got to move," Raucous shouted.

Charlotte had the car in first gear, her foot down, the engine squealing, the big police car hammering straight at them, aiming for a full impact on the passenger door.

"Come on," Cooper said, staring at the lights getting bigger heading into him.

The car juddered, the tyres span, grip wouldn't come, forward movement, an edge rather than a sprint. The car rolled, picked its speed, Charlotte put it in second, the car jumped forward again, faster, moving, edging out of impact.

The police moved, tracking the target. Charlotte hit third, the car going fast.

The police car and its grill looking like teeth, ran straight, Raucous felt the impact but it was a clip, the car he was in moved but didn't spin. The police clipping and smashing into the parked cars, the brakes hit too late to stop.

"Go, go, go," Cooper shouted.

He hadn't seen the second police car, but they had seen the first. They hit their brakes, screeching slowing their forward momentum. Charlotte accelerated into unknown roads and Cooper sat forward, concentrating on the roads ahead.

"It bears right," Cooper said. "Follow it."

Charlotte did, at speed and locked into the road.

"Slow and then a right, really tight."

Raucous looked back, he couldn't see the police car although the blue flashes were lighting up houses.

"Slow down," Cooper said. "Turn left, should be an estate."

They turned and edged silently onto the small patch of grass surrounded by tower blocks.

"It is a warren back there," Cooper said. "We need to get gone."

He unbuckled as did Charlotte and Raucous.

They stood, waiting, Cooper not understanding.

"Keys," Raucous said.

"It's unlocked," Charlotte told him.

"We haven't got time," Cooper said. "We have to go."

Raucous smiled, he knew, had already decided.

"Our prints are all over it. They got me. You two not so much. They take identity from in there we are all going down."

Charlotte stared at him. Cooper nodded.

"We got to go," Cooper told her. "I'll lead you out."

Raucous nodded, Cooper pulled Charlotte's arm. She knew it was right but she looked back as Cooper pulled her away.

Raucous opened the boot, but he watched Charlotte and Cooper jog to the tower blocks and vanish behind them. He pulled out the jerry can of petrol, poured and splashed flammable liquid over the leather seats, over the steering wheel, over the clean floor. He stepped back from the fumes, not wanting to get overwhelmed and not wanting to set fire to the mist. He lit a rag, it burned bright from the damp fuel it contained and he threw it into the car.

The flames erupted, long tongues of fire immediately wrapping around the roof and encasing the seats. A whoosh sending his mind back to science lessons a lifetime ago. The heat beating out immediately, the air scorched, the fumes being erased through flame. He watched them burn, looked to where Cooper and Charlotte had been and saw an empty space. He smiled, he knew what he was doing, had a knowledge of what was to come.

He heard a male voice shouting his name.

"Raucous!"

So many times he had heard the shout, and it never meant anything but pain. In prison it meant he was taking a beating from guards, or was to defend himself with violence against someone who wanted his fame. At school it had been the beginnings of exclusion, from a lesson, from a building, from a week. Here it meant more, here his name meant revenge was coming but it was not his own. His smile faded, he stared into the burning car, all prints and DNA gone. He turned slowly and looked at them all.

50

He couldn't recognise faces because he had just seen blurs, but the suits and the grey made them the same men from Franklin's. They were all shapes and sizes like a small-town rugby team on the way to awards evening. Two tall, two short, two dumpy and two who were bang-on average, and all the girths between. Four of them were armed, carrying what looked like futuristic handguns of black design and silver barrels.

Raucous couldn't run, not fast enough to escape, and his pride wouldn't let him. He had never seen or heard of one man fighting off eight, no matter how good you were and how bad the group could be, the numbers and swarming made the win impossible. You could scare some away by destroying who came first, or annihilating the leader, but that was in a street fight over small grievances with puffed out chests. None of these was running away, none of them would leave a colleague to be hurt. Eight men, four armed, and all of them ready to fight as a group. If they queued and came one at a time, Raucous knew he'd win. But that only happened in films, and with people possessing powers normal folk did not. The karate films of bad dubbing and a token American actor where the little guy with not an ounce of fat takes down legions of goons with speed precision and power were only a script. Here Raucous had to decide.

If he fought and hurt, the punishment that was coming would be worse. They would reply with extreme violence to anything he did to cause damage to any of them. He could lie down and take his beating, hoping they would not kill. That was his only realistic goal, to be alive tomorrow.

Raucous smiled, he knew himself, knew he couldn't lie down, fake aggression then play dead for a group of men to kick and beat until their own ager faded. He knew to relax, to cover his face, to curl up but not tense. That would save him damage, save broken bones and snapped tendons.

He watched them walking toward him as if they were a street gang of mercenaries, they were fanned out, a slight semi-circle, their jackets left behind. Each wearing a waistcoat, shirt and trousers. The colours didn't match.

Raucous saw what four of them held and knew he was in for pain. But he knew Charlotte and Cooper were free.

He smiled to himself, maybe he would be the first to tell the story of defeating eight men alone.

51

Raucous charged and screamed, and he knew it was stupid and looked even worse, but he did it all the same. He wanted to run through the man in the middle, one of the tall ones with his slick greying hair and tweed clothes. He charged and bent over and drove up and through the man. He could hear the others swear, and Raucous knew he wasn't fast enough. The man hit the floor and Raucous turned, he saw the kick, and pushed at the shin aiming for his head with both hands, the force sending his knuckles into his face. He gripped with his fingers, pinching in, stood tall and then tensed with pain.

He heard the sizzle and crackle, felt the shock flow through his body from the impact on his neck all the way down to his feet. The pain beyond anything, every muscle in his body tensing as if wanting to explode. The pain left and he breathed deep, turning, trying to find the source. But the pain came again, into his back, the same crackle and fizz as the arc of electricity found contact with his flesh.

Raucous tensed as if shot, biting down on his teeth, screaming with pain. He swung his right arm wildly, hoping his forearm would smash anything. He spun and hit nothing and another fizz and crackle as a hand-held Taser drive stunned him. His right leg buckled as one of the men kicked the back of his knee. He dropped down, a Taser struck his neck, his right arm tense, the pain like his skin being peeled away. He reached out to grab, his eyes filled with tears. He felt a spray and burn as his vison filled with fire. Pepper in the face and into his mouth. He couldn't breathe. He reached out and grabbed at clothes, he pulled the person in, unable to see, unable to open his eyes. He stood, felt the electric pain in his neck, felt the push of the arc. He didn't let go, he tried to stand and the beating started. A kick, a punch, all with force, all to his head and neck. He released his grip, felt another electric shock that sent his back into spasm. Arching, he fell to the floor. He curled and covered himself as kicks, and spray and electricity flew in. He was awake, not wanting to pass into the unconscious world. The eight men around him, kicking, prodding, stamping and spraying. He could do nothing but lay there waiting for energy to ebb away and the next stage in what they had planned to come to pass. He drifted in and out of what seemed like a lucid dream. The pain coming and going and the ability to think limited to counting blows.

The violence slowed, the electrical shocks stopped, and Raucous lay on the floor, twitching, awake but unaware. He felt the hands search him, he felt the helplessness of being someone without defence. He wanted to try and move but couldn't find the energy, couldn't find motivation. He lay there, breathing, thinking of Charlotte, knowing she was free. He lay and heard them move, heard a car pull up, heard them speak, what about he didn't care. He imagined a discussion on whether to kill him or talk. He didn't open his eyes, the pain still there, the energy gone. He smiled, knowing he'd made a choice, knowing this was what should be.

He felt the hands on him, he felt the power that many people could bring to be. They lifted him effortlessly and without a struggle or fight, rolled him and pushed and Raucous slumped into the boot as if he were water and physical laws said he must fill the space. The boot was clamped down, the voices outside muffled. Raucous didn't know if it were dark or not as he squeezed his eyes closed.His breathing slowed, his head lolled to the side and he passed into the unconscious.

52

The only barrier to Raucous and the backseats was a thin board of carpet covered plastic. He reached up and felt it move. He smiled, his head and body hurting in time with the pump of his blood. The car was parked. Raucous opened his sore eyes and his neck creaked like old stairs. There was no light coming in and the boot was huge but then so was he and the space was all relative. His knees were bent up and he felt the clean fluff of an upholstered up-market SUV on his exposed skin.

The doors were open, he could feel the breeze, and he could hear two men speak.

"Franklin's is over-run. They are spouting news about terror or gangland hits. So we keep him safe and here is best."

"Is here safe?"

"Safest place we can be."

"They all know we are coming?"

"We have it covered."

The boot opened, artificial light broke through and Raucous squinted, his eyes sensitive to anything but black.

Two men in waistcoats peered in.

"Are you going to fight?" the man on the left asked.

He was holding the Taser but it was redundant.

Raucous wanted to pounce, show aggression, even out the beating they gave. But he had nothing but constant pain, a sharp scratch on every nerve in his body.

"Do we need the cattle prods again?" the man on the right asked.

Raucous didn't answer, not through fear but because he had nothing to say. It was not a genuine discourse, a jovial back and forth between peers. They held all the power and whatever they decided was the way it would go. He could fight, struggle, try to maim one or more, but to what end? He would receive punishment in return, punishment that would make the time to fight more difficult than it needed to be.

"I take that as a no," the man on the right said.

The two of them reached in and grabbed Raucous. Raucous didn't fight, he went with their physical lead and slid awkwardly over the raised lip of the back of the car. He stumbled out, grabbing at air. The two men laughed.

"If Charlotte could see you," the man on the right said.

Raucous didn't know what her thoughts would be, maybe finally see the waste he was when unable to draw on violence. He had nothing but the anger old wrecks carried into all-day drinking. The anger and memory of a body which could fight and now could only slow. He had nothing, his jaw hurting from the tense bites. He had no words and no way to fight back. His lungs drew in air on the back of bruises, his eyes blurred and watery like a child being told of their first pet's death, and his energy gone. He stumbled forward and he heard them laugh. The once great Raucous. There were four of them now, he could have taken four, he thought, and laughed at himself, the deluded man making excuses for his loss, making hypothetical scenarios in which none of this would have come to pass.

They pushed him through a side door and the look and smell hit him as all memories did. An old school police station yet to be sold off for flats and replaced further into the wilderness by a new, cheap, modern design. He was marched down steep narrow stairs with white walls scratched and streaked with grey like a giant dirty hand had dragged its unclean fingernails all the way to the bottom. The floor was linoleum and worn from the steps of heavy police shoes.

The only thing missing from memory were the shrieks and catcalls of drunks and Saturday football fighters. The place held an uncomfortable calm and silence.

The corridor at the bottom of the stairs had four heavy steel blue doors on each side. Each had a slider on front where a guard could open and look to see if anyone had caused self-harm. They walked Raucous down the middle, he could hear no one else, the cells empty. They opened a light blue door, it swung outwards and Raucous had to step around. He looked inside and smiled at familiarity. A concrete bench with a thin mattress on top. White walls scratched and smeared. A small window high up and set back, blocked by bars. A holding cell, not for long-term, simple safety rooms to let the drunk sober up and the aggressive cool down. They didn't need to push so they didn't. They didn't need to unlock cuffs because he wore none. His shoes and laces remained, as did his belt. They knew he posed no danger to himself and there would be no one else inside for him to kill.

Raucous took three steps in, and as automatic as driving home without thinking of roads, he turned, stood tall and watched the door slam closed, heard the key enter the lock and the mechanisms that held the door ratchet in to place .

He looked at the mattress, not more than a thick blanket, raised up on a slab like a sacrificial plinth, stepped over, sat down, lay back, reached over his head and used his forearms as pillows. Thousands of nights spent this way on softer beds but more aggressive walls. He closed his eyes, tears there for calming burns and not fear ran down his cheeks like the first night he ever spent inside.

53

He had his watch so knew the time. He guessed as he awoke and was wrong by an hour. Four a.m. and not three. The door swung out and light broke in, the bare neon strip in the corridor blaring a sticky kind of white into his cell.

Raucous sat up slowly, all from the waist like a military crunch. His right arm was numb from a lack of blood flow. His body creaked and cracked, ligaments running over bones and joints popping air. He looked across at the open doorway and saw the man he wanted to see. Franklin looked in, framed by the doorway, flanked by men in suits. They were among the eight that took him down, but different from the four that brought him here. He figured they were working a shift pattern which made it likely there were four on guard. He had expected the Darts, and maybe they were in the corridor, but he thought otherwise. The Darts would look, they would need to be at the front.

Franklin walked in, dressed in his expensive street clothes of branded hoodie, loose jeans and trainers harking back to the golden age of basketball. The clothes attempted to hide his age, but he was the modern equivalent of an old rock-star refusing to move on from the hedonistic lifestyle of their peak years. His face was older than Raucous expected, late thirties, a tinge of grey in his thick stubble and lines around his eyes that no one can avoid without surgery. His eyes were a glittering blue and his skin olive dark. He had a collection of genes from all over the world.

Raucous stared at him as he swung his legs off the concrete bed. He didn't stand because Franklin didn't deserve the respect. Raucous looked behind Franklin and saw four men in suits.

“They aren’t with me,” Franklin said, his voice North London but bent by public school.

It didn’t sound forced but learned.

“Normally I would bring them with me,” Franklin explained. “Always good to have loyal friends when entering the unknown. It’s my first time here too. But they are out looking for Charlotte and whoever her company may be.”

Raucous looked into Franklin’s eyes, a man short of six foot, with no physical size. His hands looked thin, his fingers long, not a man of labour.

“But I’m safe because I pay and were I to come to harm, Darts and boys would hunt them all down and kill them and any family. Fear is there, but I prefer employment. Money is good, and my word is that. I think you are the same, but whereas you once belonged to an organisation, you no longer do and can draw on nothing but past hopes and desires. Which is why I am here to talk.”

Franklin waited, expecting a response or a reaction. But Raucous sat and stared, waiting, not wanting nor needing to talk. Franklin wanted information and that was the only thing Raucous had. There was no reason to give it up.

The wait went on and Franklin nodded when the game dragged out.

“I am here to ask, politely, of the man you were with,” Franklin said.“I am under the impression he has been causing me harm on a regular basis these last few weeks. I’d like to know why.”

Raucous stared, no intention of talking. In America they called it taking the fifth, here he called it silence.

“Oh, come, come Mr. Raucous. My official friends can place him. We know his name, and some of his history. Recent years he seems to have been operating off the grid but now he is back. I’d like to know why and who he is with. He tends to pop up in places where bad things happen. I’d like to avoid that.”

Raucous looked at the police officers, wanting to see how their faces reacted to Franklin talking, spouting his truth about their role.

Franklin looked around at the police he was with. He smiled and they did in return. Raucous was alone.

"So you don't know the notorious Nigel Cooper? That is strange," Franklin said.

Raucous shrugged, staring into Franklin's eyes without pause.

"Dartmoor?" Franklin asked. "You were in the same place for six weeks. Fifteen years ago. By all accounts you would not have interacted beyond crossing on the walkways."

Raucous smiled because there were people who knew more about his life than he.

"Fifteen years? Long time," Raucous said.

Franklin relaxed, the first part complete. He needed Raucous to talk, any words, any sounds, but he needed there to be engagement.

"You caused me a lot of trouble this evening," Franklin said. "Congratulations on that. But you saw a lot of things you really didn't need to see. Cooper too. Because of that you are going to die. Probably not well. But I can give you my word I won't chase Charlotte if you were to, as my colleagues here would say, provide information that would lead to his capture."

Raucous thought of Charlotte and the way she was, the way she behaved, and what she would do. He smiled, hoping he would be someone she sought to avenge.

"She'll be chasing you."

Franklin smiled, showing teeth, all straight and white and maintained. A genetic inheritance rather than cosmetic spend.

"Her end will be this too."

Raucous stared at him, and Franklin stared back, no anger in his eyes, only curiosity and contempt.

"Why were you there tonight? I'm assuming you knew what was happening in advance, which perturbs me somewhat. It means there is a leak somewhere, or as is the modern concern, a way to listen in to communication. Both cause me trouble, someone to find and kill, or money to spend on encrypted networks. It would be futile to claim coincidence."

Raucous thought and tried to picture Cooper. If he had known his plan was poor, the execution wrong then the difficulty they made was all the more dumb because of it.

"Mathematics," Raucous said. "Probability, like dreaming of someone's death and then it happens."

Franklin smiled, nodded, waited for more.

"A big night made it easier to get in, made it easier for you to hide business. Two things coincide. Just the way of the world."

Franklin listened and nodded, but he looked unconvinced. He stared at Raucous but with a look that showed his mind was elsewhere, like a poker player thinking back to the moves of an opponent and the bets they made, looking for information in movements and choices. He smiled again and looked up.

"I have to leave, I didn't actually come to speak to you. Just seemed polite since I was passing through," he said."I had wanted to speak to you in person, see who and what you are. Turns out you are exactly as you should be. I thought I maybe would find something more. It isn't disappointment, it is surprise."

Franklin looked around the room, looked to the men he was with. Pulled a face like he had bitten into acid. He looked back to Raucous.

"Death row is a place you just wait, with nothing but the knowledge that your death is coming, but you just don't know exactly when. Horrible living with that over your head I would think."

54

Raucous had gone back to the concrete bed and lay back. There was no reason to sleep, there would be no peace. The cell was dark and he had heard movement outside, murmurs of words and conversations that ran short of debate.

Light started to break through the small window and the noise of cars on a nearby street splashed through the air. A constant stream of tyres on road.

The door unlocked and Raucous didn't move, he breathed out sharp through his nose, promised himself what he always had, no words, no quit. The door opened and four men walked in, not in suits of expensive tailors but the material of forensic investigation. Two carried cloth holdalls, in the corridor more people stood. Raucous couldn't count how many, but they were there as back up.

"Strip," the tallest of the men said.

Raucous rose, slid his legs off the bed, planted his feet on the floor and stared at them all. Two with Tasers, the other two dropping their bags to the floor.

Raucous bowed his head, rolled his eyes up, balled his fists and smiled. The two men with Tasers raised their weapons and fired. The darts flew out, the top one in a straight line for where they aimed and Raucous felt the impact in his neck and chest, the lower dart angled down and hit him in his thigh and hip. The electricity flowed and every muscle tensed, a shrieking pain but his voice wouldn't work, every line of his nervous system on overload. All his muscles tensing, pulling against each other, pulling tendons on bone. He couldn't hold balance, couldn't stay upright, couldn't move at all. He fell, but felt nothing of the impact, his body not bending nor bouncing, the crackle of electricity still running, his muscles still answering the message they sent, his body a convulsion mass, his legs shaking.

The electricity stopped. Raucous felt blood trickle from his mouth, his teeth biting cheek, his flesh torn. He tried to stand, couldn't move, couldn't think. The pain less, but a body that would not listen.

"Where is Cooper?" one man asked.

"Who is he working for?" another said.

Raucous couldn't see, couldn't focus but he could hear. He wanted to speak, tell them nothing but words of insult but his throat stuck on sounds, a gargle and nothing to articulate. He heard their laughter and felt two more darts enter his flesh.

His body tensed, his back arched until his spine fought back and could bend no further. He bit down hard, clenching teeth together, his hands rigid and fingers straight.

"We just want to know where Cooper is hiding," the tall man said.

He was calm, reassured, the promise in his voice easy to believe. But even if he had known, Raucous wouldn't tell.

"He has killed police," the man continued.

He crouched down next to Raucous, knees bent, up on his toes, an easy balance. Raucous wished he had faked the response to the shock, wished he could now pounce. It would lead to more pain, more beatings and likely death but he'd try and take a piece of this man with him, leave a scar. They say you are never truly dead until the last person forgets you. He would leave a mark so he would live on in the flesh this man would miss.

"Franklin's place was an annoyance, and I understand why Franklin is mad. But we want Cooper for real reasons. We want to know who he works for."

Raucous had control of his muscles again, but not in a way that would lead him to fight, only allow him to relax.

Raucous whispered a sound he knew was not a word.

"What?" the tall man asked.

Raucous rolled his eyes up into his head, leaving only white behind. He convulsed. The tall man leaned in, placed his hand under the neck of Raucous. Raucous made sounds that aped words. The tall man leaned in.

"We could end this now," the tall man whispered. "Just tell me."

Raucous made sounds again, peaceful noises, no aggression. The tall man leaned in, Raucous opened his eyes, wrapped his arms around the tall man's head, pulled him close, the man's face against his own. He bit, looking to take a piece of his ear but getting only tight skin on the edge of his cheek. He bit in hard and shook his head like an attack dog. The tall man screamed and pulled, but his skin wouldn't rip and his face stayed locked to Raucous. Raucous heard the shouts, the steps and felt the blows, kicks and punches to his exposed body as another dug fingers into his eyes and pulled at his head. He felt the electric shock and had no time to smile. He tensed, his jaw clamped hard, and he felt the skin split under his teeth.

The electric finished, his body stopped convulsing.

Raucous had nothing left, no energy but he tasted the metal of the tall man's blood. He released his bite, his eyes under pressure and he fell back on the floor. He laughed, eyes closed, waiting for the end.

55

They left him for the briefest, happiest moment as Raucous lay and laughed.

"We can't kill him," a voice said.

Raucous opened his eyes and saw the tall man pointing a gun. It was aimed into his face.

A man behind had grabbed the tall man's shoulder, trying to twist him away.

"We can't kill him, not here, and not without the Darts present. If they get Cooper, we swap this one out. They want him, we don't get to kill."

Raucous relaxed, the cut in the tall man's face would heal, leave a mark, maybe not the scar Raucous wanted, but he'd remember who put it there and people would ask. Raucous realised he had a reprieve, the briefest moment to survive. He was owned by the Darts, and if they found Cooper, death was coming. He knew it would be time spent in difficult pain. He pushed against the floor, every muscle he used burning in agony, his legs not working with the strength they normally held. He shook and twitched but made it to his feet. Four men in hazmat suits talking, ignoring him. A man in the corridor noticed, pointed to Raucous and they turned.

Raucous was stood as straight as he could manage, a fighter from the fifties beaten but not allowed to be counted out. He looked through the open door, saw the men, saw them all. One stood out, one not like the rest, one staring, not smiling, watching but not speaking. A female face in a crowd of masculine stupidity. Simpson looked into his eyes, gave no show of anything other than annoyed boredom.

Raucous stared at her and she held his gaze.

The tall man lashed out, hitting Raucous high on the head. He felt a kick in his abdomen, staggered back and he felt a kick that glanced off the side of his cheek. Raucous fell, face down, he tried to push himself up but had nothing, he pushed with one hand, rolled his weight to the left, looking to break the tipping point. His mass took control and he flipped onto his back, looking up at the ceiling, seeing blurred faces staring down. He smiled. He closed his eyes, waiting for more pain.

All he heard was the footsteps of men, the whip of his head as a heavy foot kicked his left cheek, he drifted out of the present and thought he heard the door pushed closed.

56

Raucous woke, face up, spread-eagled on the floor. He looked around without moving and noticed the room darker, the light fading and the sun having moved away from the window. He heard nothing, no noise from inside the cell and no noise from the corridor outside. He looked at his watch, which told him a time it was not. The hands didn't move, the mechanism stopped. Raucous smiled and sat up, his stomach tight and hurting. He got to his feet, and stretched, every muscle wanting to stay balled. He thought of a long time ago when he knew a woman who had bought a machine that attached pads to her body, and the pads to wires and the wires to a machine that sent electric impulses, the muscles contracting and loosening as she sat and watched TV. It seemed stupid then and even more so now.

He heard the steps in the corridor, and the key in the lock. He looked to the ceiling and saw the camera. They had watched and seen him move. They were coming now, for what he didn't know.

The door opened out and two men stood in sober grey suits and heavy black shoes. Two of the men from the eight that brought him here. The one on the left held handcuffs, the one on the right held a Taser. There were others in the corridor, Raucous heard them.

"We are moving you," the man with handcuffs said.

Raucous nodded.

"Are you not asking where?" the man with the Taser asked.

Raucous shrugged, it mattered nothing.

"How's your friend's face?" Raucous asked.

The two men looked at each other.

"We're taking you to see Franklin and the Darts," handcuff said.

Raucous knew they didn't have Charlotte, they would have said, gloated and tried to rile him with the things they would have done.

"I imagine, without our protection, your day will end badly," Taser said.

Raucous smiled.

"It started pretty poorly. No reason for it to end better," he said.

"Planning on struggling?" man with Taser asked.

"I haven't struggled since I've been here."

Raucous saw men edge into view on the side of the doorframe. They were all there and he hoped to see Simpson on his walk out.

He let them place cuffs on his wrists behind his back, let them pretend to be in charge and alpha males. He expected cheap shots when his hands were tied but they pulled no tricks. They asked him to walk, turn left and take the stairs. Raucous understood and stepped out into the corridor.

Like a line of honour three men stood each side of the corridor. The tall man with a chewed face was last on the left. The man who had placed handcuffs walked ahead, the Taser behind and each man stared at Raucous as he walked.

"Dead man walking," the tall man said, and his colleagues laughed the fake laugh of solidarity.

Raucous knew it was coming and he guessed at how. The tall man to his left, his head an inch higher than Raucous. The men stared and the tall man did too, and as Raucous was in front, the tall man dropped his head, looking to use the front of his skull as a ram against the eye-socket of Raucous. Raucous turned into it, forehead to forehead, thick bone onto thick bone. A thud like deer looking to dominate a rival, the tall man stepped back, hit the wall with his back, stayed upright, regained balance but was stopped from launching forward by the arm of the man next to him. Raucous felt the buzz, a brain fog but kept his step. The other men swung and hit whatever part of Raucous was closest. Raucous fell to his right knee, felt blows reign down, waiting for the initial fury to fade, stood, powered through some, rode with others and took the full force of none. They stopped quickly, there is only so much punishment to give and Raucous had reached a stage of boredom. Punches and kicks on top of the pain they had inflicted meant little to nothing. The next step was they take his life, and soon that would come. It was the way it needed to be. Raucous walked ahead, the six men stayed in the corridor. Raucous heard them laugh.

They walked the stairs, single file, Raucous in the middle.

"Fewer of you here today," Raucous said. "I thought I would get the full guard."

His jaw hurt and he sounded strange, a slow drawl where none had ever been.

No one answered, no one cared.

"You are going to die today," the man behind him said. "Do you understand that?"

57

Outside was dark, the night side of dusk. There were noises in the streets, cars going home, deliveries moving around. The background sounds of a city closing down. The van was sat in the small carpark. What had once been a space for marked police was now empty and holding a white, unmarked van. The man in front pressed a fob, the lights beeped, indicators flashed. He reached up to the door, placed a key inside an oversized steel lock and the backdoor popped open.

The man behind pushed Raucous forward, and Raucous stumbled without the ability to use his arms as balance. Inside was clean and empty, the van new and unused for any trade.

"Get in," the man with the Taser said.

Raucous paused, he didn't understand why. Something he heard, something moved, something he had felt before. He bowed his head and the man with the Taser pushed him and Raucous caught his knees on the bottom edge of the doors.

Raucous turned, the man with the Taser screamed, the other man's face contorted as he shook, rigid but for vibrations. Raucous saw two men, faces masked in the old school balaclavas of bank-robbers and SAS operatives. They were dressed in black, the only skin on show around their mouths and eyes. Gloved hands held Tasers, and the Tasers were being pressed into necks. The police hit the deck.

The masked men kicked and stamped, hitting shoulders and chests of the police on the ground. The shorter of the two, stabbed at each in turn, electric shock after electric shock, while the taller attached probes to the front of his weapon. He nodded, the shorter man stopped plunging electricity arcs into the two prone police. The taller fired into the chest of the man who had held a Taser. The electricity pulsed and crackled and the man's body bent and convulsed like a priest was ridding demons from his body. The shorter man attached a similar probe to his Taser and fired into the second man. The convulsions came as if there were a battle for the possession of his soul.

The shorter man walked to the door of the police station, he pulled a fist sized canister off his belt, he pulled a pin, opened the door, stepped in, threw the canister down the stairs, a flash and a bang happened in succession and smoke billowed out.

The man closed the door.

Raucous watched, a spectator to saviours or a new threat, he didn't know. The taller man reached down and searched for keys on the police, threatening electric shocks as they lay like a pair of lobotomised lunatics from the eighteenth century. He found them, put them in his own pocket and pushed Raucous toward the road. The shorter man stayed at the door, listening for movement, heard none and moved quickly across the tarmac.

They didn't stop, nor wait, a car pulled up, sleek, black and clean. It didn't screech, it pulled up slow, the taller opened the back door, the shorter climbed into the back, Raucous was pushed in, his arms still bound behind him. The taller slid in next to him. No words said, no indication given. The front seats occupied by two people, the one driving with a balaclava, the passenger someone Raucous had vowed to destroy.

58

Simpson looked scared. Her face not calm nor composed, she was trying to stay cool but twitches and looks gave her away. Raucous needed to know. He had nothing left, a new danger, more questions, more violence from people he had never known asking for information he had never held. A merry-go-round of idiots believing Raucous held the key to the question of life. The police in the holding rooms were nothing but criminals in suits with a protective layer of official promises to protect the innocent and uphold the law. Cooper had told him they came from different areas, a network of two-faced dealing to provide an ease to the flow of drugs from the city out into the wider country. There had always been connections, always a crossover between law and gangs, and Raucous had seen it all before. They were united now, expanding their trade and needing the police they held in pockets of cash to organise themselves, to create safe passage for all.

Simpson he could not understand. She had spoken to him and he had not seen the cracks in her lies.

The car kept moving, balaclavas on, a wise move because the streets were paved with cameras. Most of them, if not all, expensive with a quality worse than the very first camera phones. Endless hours of tape showing figures whose faces were indistinguishable from another. A grey blur of movement that caught nothing in detail. But their faces were covered except Simpson. That made no sense.

The two men were not holding Raucous, not pointing guns nor Tasers. They still held them but they were neutral, not crackling nor popping. They were not active. The driver was smooth, running corners and bang on speed limits. Fast for the area but not illegal. The driver indicated, entered a multi-storey carpark and wound the way up until the penultimate floor. Above was the roof space for those days when no other space was available.

The car slid into an empty spot on a floor with five other parked cars. If these people were good, Raucous thought, the cameras were already out of action, and two of those parked cars were theirs to drive away.

Raucous leaned forward, looking between the two seats in front. He looked to Simpson because she was the one who held the secrets. He looked at her hands, placed in her lap, her fingers entwined and her wrists together. They weren't going anywhere soon as they were joined in metal handcuffs.

Raucous looked to the driver. They removed their balaclavas en-masse as if silently instructed by a voice with a pitch too high for Raucous to hear.

"What is going on?" Raucous asked as he saw the driver's face.

Charlotte stared back at him, her hair ruffled from the wool. Raucous looked to his right and saw Cooper smiling back. He looked to his left and saw Locke.

"We are splitting in two. Raucous, you are with Charlotte and Cooper. I'm with my lovely partner, Simpson. Keys are in the glove compartment. CCTV is down, and we need to move," Locke said.

"Do I get the cuffs removed?" Simpson asked.

"She was there," Raucous said. "In the cells. She was there. With them."

"We know," Charlotte explained. "We didn't know if it was a set-up, her coming to us and telling us where you were. She said you were being treated pretty badly."

Raucous laughed.

"Are you one of them?" he asked Simpson.

Her eyes were wide, her words fast.

"They brought me in as a test. To see how I would react, to see if I was one of you."

"They will think you are now," Raucous told her.

"I'm not becoming them. I didn't know they were bringing me to see you. They set it up as something else. Something official. There was nothing I could do. I spoke to Locke as soon as it was safe."

Raucous turned to Locke.

"Do you buy any of this?"

"I don't trust anyone. Including everyone in this car. The motives I don't know, but if it was a set-up, they were lazy and stupid. If it was her doing the right thing then she has just put herself onto a small list of targets."

Simpson turned, her face in panic.

"They wanted to tie me in. They have film of me watching torture and doing nothing. They threatened me after, made it clear what was going to happen. If I spoke, they would know and I'd be dead. If I went to anyone, they would know, they have people everywhere and I'd be dead. I don't know if you have been brought in to find things out or you are one of their people. But I took the chance and gave the word. Now we are here. Take the handcuffs off."

Locke leaned forward and Simpson pushed her wrists to him. He turned the key and the cuffs fell away.

"Neither of you can lay low," Raucous said.

59

They meeting was in a holiday let in the country. Cars driving up a gravel lane to a house that was once a barn. Large panes of tinted glass had replaced the aged wooden door of old. Wooden beams from modern trees had been burned to look Georgian and were the obvious framework to a building that was advertised as vintage but was new for all but the smallest part.

Locke and Simpson arrived last, thirty minutes after Charlotte's car. The living room was one large space with a pool table, seating that didn't match in style, age nor colour, albeit each with splashes of red, yellow and blue. The place a combination of minimalist design that had given up on futuristic and opted for bohemian chic. A style layered onto furniture inherited from a Grandparent who had lived and died on a remote farm.

Raucous couldn't concentrate, his head was riding peaks and troughs of migraines without recourse to medicine. Nausea rode up and ebbed away without heartburn but with all the consequences of being caught with the shot you didn't see. He was sat alone on a two-man Chesterfield, which was covered with a quilt seemingly crocheted together for a primary school project. His heart raced, slowed, beat hard then whimpered.

"You okay?" Charlotte asked.

"Getting old," he said.

Raucous felt the sweat on his skin, the clammy nature of someone in need of beer. Charlotte had spoken, Cooper had answered but Raucous followed nothing. He focused on being conscious.

"They did you a lot of harm," Cooper said.

Cooper was on his feet, moving, agitated and not at peace.

"They did," Raucous told them.

There was a pause in conversation, Raucous was sure of this.

"Do you know why you are here?" Cooper asked.

"We're hiding," Raucous said.

There was another pause and Raucous spent it inhaling deeply through his nose.

"From who?" Charlotte asked.

Raucous thought, had the names ready to say but the sounds and letters drifted and mixed and came together out of order with other letters along for confusion. The room isn't spinning, Raucous thought, it is me who isn't still.

"What?" Charlotte asked.

Raucous looked at her, tried to hold eye contact but couldn't. His eyes rolled back, his eyeballs showing only white. He felt the slap against his cheek, figured it to be an immediate reaction as his hearing drifted in and out of working. He heard Charlotte repeat his name, heard her ask Cooper for help. He felt them gently lay him back, placing the right side of his face on the armrest. Someone draped the blanket over him as if he was a five-year-old boy at the end of exhaustion on the evening of his birthday party. Raucous didn't fight it, didn't feel the desire to force himself awake to hear voices of gossip and seriousness mingling together in a meeting between the five of them.

Raucous was aware of the movement around him, but he cared nothing. He was in a safe place, or as safe as he could ever hope to be when in company.

60

Raucous woke on the same two man Chesterfield he remembered. The blanket was covering him and one face turned upon hearing him move. Charlotte on her feet, all silent and waiting.

"How you feeling?" Charlotte asked.

Raucous didn't know the answer. He had spent many hours nursing the damage of violence. This was different, his heart seemed on edge, his head screamed at random times with no trigger.

"I'm okay," he lied.

He sat up and a sharp shock smacked his brain. He winced, but he made no noise.

"Where are the others?" he asked.

"Just me and you," Charlotte said. "They have gone. Didn't explain where or why, didn't ask for us to go along."

"Do you trust them?"

Charlotte smiled and shook her head.

"I don't trust anyone."

"Not even me?"

"That's different. We have history. We have something."

"Have they gone after Franklin?"

Charlotte shrugged.

"I don't know. It would be a poor move. Right now every alarm they have is going off. Their place raided, the police hit, you escaping. There will be panic."

"They have to cover themselves. Locke, Simpson and Cooper have things on them."

"We have things on them."

Raucous stood and felt his head swim and his nausea rise.

"You look bad, Raucous," Charlotte said.

"I don't feel good. My head is gone, my body hurts, my heart isn't doing what it should. I'm an old man."

"You're a man who has just had a day of torture."

Raucous nodded, but he knew he had gone over his limit. The stress test taken and gone too far. There were cracks right through him.

"Are you sitting this one out?" Charlotte asked.

"When are they moving on them?"

"I don't know. They have told me little. They came to see me when Simpson told them where you were and what was happening. They needed a driver, Cooper asked for me. They told me what I needed to know. I babysat Simpson with instructions to get out if it all went wrong. That's all I know. But you got out."

"They were moving me to Franklin's, about to be shot."

"You think Franklin can kill."

"I've seen him do it."

They waited, Raucous trying to claw back normality from sickness and Charlotte watching him looking for a time to step in.

"What's the connection between those three?" Raucous asked.

"You should ask them."

Raucous heard the noise of tyres on gravel and the hum of a diesel engine.

61

"You work together?" Raucous asked.

It seemed stupid, a contradiction in who they were and what they had been.

Cooper smiled. He was stood in the centre of the large room. No one was seated and everyone had space around them, an informal, badly defined circle.

"The pure cop with the criminal friend. It works. He doesn't trust me and that's fine. One day he will. I don't like corruption, don't like that they should be protecting but some are in on the take. My own history and beliefs. I was never a good gangster, wouldn't take orders without explanation. I was and am a liability they say. And I don't mind that, a liability is fine by me. I'm not on the side of good, I'm on my side, and I get to be naughty with people who deserve it. Just so happens Locke needs help. He can't do the dirty work so I do it. And I like it. Friends with benefits only without the nudity."

The three of them had come back, walked in and looked broken. Simpson more than the others. They had gone to see and come back with knowledge.

"And how do you propose we get out of this one?" Simpson asked.

She couldn't hold eye contact and looked at the floor.

"We could go all official," Cooper told her, the sarcasm not hidden at all. "You take your complaint and claims to the higher level. It is what Locke does mostly once I've had a play and people make mistakes. But what are you going to get? It won't work here."

"You won't get anything," Locke said. "We aren't investigating a single crooked policeman, we aren't talking about a small gang of bad ones, we are talking about a million-pound monthly turnover with every level involved in some way. Years of legal battles at best with you shipped out or desk bound and with no way to further your career. You'd be forced out. You know it gets hidden and blown away for us to be the condemned. You know that. Without Cooper's dirty tricks, I would have had nothing on most people I put away."

Cooper played the sidekick to the point of stealing the show.

"If we leave it here," he said,"push it to internal investigations and legal practices the outcome is nothing. It isn't tax evasion, it isn't smuggling. It is the facilitating of drug running. A blind eye on every turn and the goods get delivered and the kids are the criminals. And police who are in it for the thrill get paid and retire in the sun."

Simpson stared at the carpet, shaking her head.

"You made the choice to do the right thing. This is the right thing," Cooper told her.

There was a pause, nothing said, time given for people to think. If there was a way out, a solution, they needed to think now.

Simpson turned to Locke, her voice louder now.

"Get whoever it is that sent you down here on whatever mission to sniff out the bad ones, tell them, give them the information. They trust you. They sent you here for this."

Locke shook his head slowly.

"I wasn't sent here on any mission. I was sent here to force me out. They don't want me getting results, they don't want me finding out. Last time out I messed up. I went too far, tried to take down someone way too big to be brought down. I got shut down. They sent me here, to this absolute corrupt hell so I'd quit or something bad would happen to me. Those two choices are still open, but I like the second a lot less than the first."

"Are you afraid of these people?" Simpson asked.

"Has nothing to do with fear. I don't have the power or the backing to do anything. I speak, I get put on a desk on an island somewhere. Left to rot. I walk and who I am dies."

Charlotte had watched and listened and now she stepped forward.

"I want my payback," she said. "There are people involved that won't be touched. Franklin and the Darts aren't going to be taken down through a complaint about corruption. You are talking about your colleagues. I'm after others."

"That's what I am talking about," Cooper said, pointing. "Some people are just outside the net, and that means they escape and keep on doing what they do and that is destroying lives. I know this and I can't let that one go."

"I am not them," Simpson said.

"We know that," Locke told her. "But doesn't mean you can't use a bit of illegality to beat them. If you follow the rules but fight someone who has brought a gun, you'll lose every time. But at least you didn't resort to their level of cheating? That's not going to save you, and it won't stop them doing it again. The whole thing is rigged in their favour. I'm happy to cheat too. Brings good outcomes. Cooper taught me that."

"Good outcomes for who?" Simpson spat.

She was walking now, the energy of her thoughts replicated in her movements, quick steps, turning left and right, pausing but not being able to hold onto calm.

"For me," Cooper said. "For anyone who gets caught up with these people. And I know someone else will come along and take their place, and it all starts again, but if we do nothing it gets out of hand, and the whole thing becomes normalised and everyone just says, ah, well, that is the way it is, nothing we can do about that. Well, I can, and I do. And right here I will."

"You can't kill the police," Locke told him.

"But they aren't, are they? They are fake."

"The court won't see it that way."

"I don't care about the court. I care about what is right and what is wrong. I care about what I can do about it and right here and now I can do a lot."

Raucous stood, he waited for Simpson to look up.

"You went to see what was happening," he told her."You came back ashen faced. You know your career is shot if you don't stand up. Your life is gone, all those things you desired, planned for and wanted. Some you achieved. All gone because a group of men with nothing in common with what you think right push you out. I am the same. They will destroy you, and given the chance kill you and blame that on Cooper, or me, or someone like us. The rules are broken by them, but you think you can reach an equal footing through just being right. That isn't how it works, you'll end up destroyed."

"I can leave," Charlotte said. "Forget it all, forget they tried to kill me. I can leave and never come back, and live with the idea I am a coward."

"It is smart," Simpson told her.

"It is running away. And who would be next? And who was there before? Because I am not the first."

"Someone else always comes along," Simpson said to the room.

"Doesn't mean we have to accept what is here now," Raucous told her.

"I'm not breaking the law."

There was a pause because when someone believes, they can't be broken free with short words.

"You already have," Raucous said. "Here with us. You did the right thing, saved my life. You broke your code in that moment."

Simpson opened her arms wide.

"It was the right thing to do," she said.

"Sometimes the right thing to do is kill those who kill others," Raucous told her. "You can't do anything else. You have nothing. And they have all the power and influence that you think is neutral. It isn't, it is theirs."

Simpson turned to Locke, looked at him, pleading for support, to acknowledge she was the reason in the room. Locke stared back. She turned to Raucous.

"They nearly killed Charlotte and they wanted to kill you."

"Which is why I am going to kill them."

62

"I can't join in," Locke said. "I won't stop you, certainly won't condemn you all for it. But I can't be part of it."

"You never are, I do the dirty work," Cooper said."Not a criticism, just how labour gets divided. I would have been shocked had you agreed to be a gangster for the afternoon."

"Are you staying?" Locke asked him.

Cooper looked to Raucous and Charlotte and received no negatives.

"I believe I am," Cooper said. "I came here with you, because I owe you. For giving me my own shot at redemption. I knew the set up. Knew what was happening, had a good look for you and found Franklin, and the county lines and the use of kids. Hits a nerve, you know that. This isn't about corrupt police, this is about me and my beliefs. I got to do it. I can't walk away."

Locke smiled and he knew Raucous could see that as well as anyone. Everyone acting on their principles and everyone doing something different for different reasons.

"Which car are you taking?" Raucous asked.

"Whichever one you don't want," Simpson told him.

Raucous walked over to her, thought he should hold out his hand like a father congratulating a son he had never hugged.

"Thank you," he said. "I understand what you are doing, and why. That's cool. They are the same reasons I am doing what I am about to do. Just I don't trust the courts to make the right choices. Not with these people."

Simpson didn't speak, Locke stayed silent too. They walked out, not needing nor wanting to throw words of encouragement.

Raucous, Charlotte and Cooper waited in silence like they were at a crematorium until Simpson and Locke had driven far enough to be out of view. There were three of them in a room. They looked out the window at the green view.

"We are going to need weapons," Cooper said.

63

Cooper had raised an eyebrow when Raucous said the words. Surprise combined with unknowing, but he smiled it off and came along. But now they were there, at six a.m., light not quite over the horizon and Raucous wondered about the reaction. Cooper had been quiet on the drive into the city. Now he was silent.

They had parked up three streets distant, and walked in, looking for signs, looking for people who should not be there. They saw no one.

George's car lot was the same as always, a Portacabin, a small brick warehouse for the on-site mechanics and a large field covered in second hand cars. It was empty of activity, although the lights in the cabin were on.

"He is always in," Raucous said. "But this isn't right."

It wasn't, they had strolled up out front, nice and slow and obvious. George slept little and was on site most of his life. The mechanics were his greeting party but they were nowhere to be seen. There was no dancing of shadows in the Portacabin, no movement at all.

"It looks like a set up," Charlotte said.

"Maybe he just left the light on," Cooper suggested.

"The door is open," Raucous told them.

Raucous nodded, Cooper surveyed the surroundings.

"See anything?" Raucous asked.

Cooper shook his head.

Nothing was a bad sign, either good hiding or long since gone.

The three of them walked slowly up the steps to the Portacabin and the scaffold pole handrail.

Raucous entered first, Cooper watching if anyone was coming behind. Raucous stopped and swore, Charlotte looked and repeated his words. Cooper heard them, scanned the street once more and walked in.

"Don't touch anything," he said.

Raucous looked to the walls, he read the words. He thought of the mess whoever wrote this would be. His name, Raucous, daubed large on the far side of the office. The table and floor covered in splashes, the source of the ink sat back in his swivel chair, eyes open, skin white and dead. His throat slit, stabbed in the chest, litres of blood spurted out, and then flowed across his desk. George had died with knives. Someone had placed their hands in the mess and written Raucous across a wall. It looked like it had been done with the palm of someone's gloved hand.

George hadn't struggled, or at least it looked that way. Head back, throat open, arms at his side. His three-piece suit saturated in red making the blue material purple. Raucous stared at the old man, thought about the visit he made, thought about how he had been a man here for as long as Raucous knew.

"Any ideas?" Charlotte asked.

Raucous answered but stared at George. The old man, dead for a life he left years before.

"If it wasn't Franklin, it would have been the Dart boys with the help of the police. It obviously wasn't me. I'm not near dumb enough to scrawl my own name on the wall. But the police will want me for questions. Everyone knows he came to see me. And now here I am, my name written in blood like some crap serial killer making threats in childish acts."

"A man of interest, or will be when this is out there," Cooper said. "Which means, we need to move. This is a set up. Once this is called, everyone is looking for you."

Raucous swore again.

64

They heard the sirens as soon as they stepped out of the PortaCabin. Cars coming closer, but too many engines to be the first of the rush hour.

Raucous moved into the car lot, Cooper and Charlotte followed. They weaved through rows of cars, all parked up close, all jammed in, some clean, others stained by weather after weeks of being sat. They walked hunched, trying to make themselves small. When the sounds got louder they stopped and sank low behind a large SUV. They knew they needed to weave through, they knew they needed to make an escape. But they sat, backs to the car, the police in three cars with their illuminous markings, four others unmarked, black with blue grill lights.

Raucous looked over and squinted.

"Can't see them," he said.

Cooper looked.

"You know them," he told Raucous. "Four of the men in Franklin's carpark."

"The tall one?" Raucous asked.

Cooper nodded.

"How's his face?"

"Seen better days."

They sat and waited, not wanting to move, not wanting to give the police something to watch, something to chase down.

Raucous looked to Charlotte.

"Did you know they'd go after George?" she asked.

Raucous shook his head.

Cooper turned to them, his face that of an arrogant student surprised his peers can't answer the most basic question.

"How much don't you know?"

Raucous turned to Cooper, not understanding a single thing.

"He was Saint's man," Cooper said. "A long time ago. His minder, his protection, I imagine at some point his friend."

"This much I do know."

"You ever look into Saint, and who and what he did?"

Raucous shook his head.

"He was a pretty poor crook," Cooper said. "A grass if you ask me, no way a man that stupid stays free without offering information over. But that is just a thought, no proof, just gut to back that up."

Raucous nodded, not understanding where this was going.

"He loved women," Cooper went on. "Always did. Any, not one to turn any female down. Resulted in a lot of offspring. A lot. His genes will be in all future generations around here."

"What has this got to do with anything?" Raucous asked.

Cooper stared at him, trying to figure out if Raucous was messing with him.

"Franklin is his one of his sons, the oldest from what I understand. Darts are too, and so was Mack. They are all related. Half-siblings, and whatever. A really shallow gene pool."

Raucous stared at him and he saw Cooper smile, the delight in being able to share his superior knowledge.

"It's ok to do the smash and grab tactics, Raucous, but you have to find out the information first. You can't just assume you are right. You have to know. Without that there is no reason to be doing this."

Raucous looked at him and shook his head. This little guy who held all the knowledge he had wanted. He had never asked, assumed too much and guessed at too little. He needed his help.

"What about the police? Who are they?" Charlotte asked.

Cooper smiled again and pulled out his phone. He pressed in a four digit code. He opened his gallery, swiped down and opened a file. He showed Raucous and Charlotte his screen, and started to swipe slowly.

There were more than twenty shots of men, black and white, no colour at all and Raucous recognised them all.

"Which one did you bite?" Cooper asked.

Raucous touched the screen and swiped so previous photos came back. He stopped on the man staring into space as if he were modelling spring and summer wear.

"This one," Raucous said, pointing.

"You chose right. McClintock. A self-proclaimed hard man. The reason he didn't go into organised crime is because he is weak and a coward. He had a choice many years ago. Involve himself with street thugs or pretend to go straight and be the outsider in the middle of posh. He chose the latter. He is a weak policeman of power, but would have been dead as a crook."

"That's him there?"

Cooper nodded.

Raucous sat back and inhaled long, slow and deep. He rubbed his face.

"This is all a set-up," he said. "Franklin makes the hit, McClintock gets called in. I'm enemy number one. Armed and potentially dangerous."

"And you get shot as soon as you appear."

"I think you'd die in custody," Charlotte said. "You look like a man on edge, look like you've cracked. Spreading your name on the wall like that. I think you'd almost certainly commit suicide while inside after someone made an error and didn't spot the shoelace you smuggled in. A real tragedy, not being able to find out your motives and reasons and what conspiracy theory you would start inventing."

Raucous knew it made sense, knew the idea was as close to what they planned as could be. The details of the set-up mattered little, the end, his death and silence was the outcome they were chasing.

"We are still going to need guns," Charlotte said. "Three pistols against the armoury you say they have is not going to work."

65

They watched them from the car.

They had snaked out of the car lot, not looking back, not standing tall. They had found the back, jumped the wire fence, and walked around to where they had parked.

"Who do I follow?" Charlotte asked.

"McClintock," Cooper said. "He'll be the designated lead. He'll be their mistake. He is the weak spot."

"He'll be on guard," Raucous said.

"It doesn't matter, he is too arrogant and too stupid to think we would come to him."

They waited and watched, the activity and the forensic team with their tent, the street cordoned off, workers turning up and being arrested. Mechanics pushing back, big men not taking kindly to their boss being dead and the police having no respect or manners. McClintock stood away from it all, mostly on his phone, messaging and smiling.

They watched him and no one else, watched him talk to uniforms and white suited people, watched him order people and make demands. They saw people roll their eyes, ignore or walk away. A man talking with the idea he has respect to people who kept the fact they had none hidden behind ridicule.

"They are coming for me," Raucous said. "Neither of you."

Charlotte and Cooper paid no attention and didn't answer. They knew what he was saying and paid it no significance. Raucous knew he had to give them a way out.

"I'd describe it," Charlotte finally said, "as you coming after them."

Cooper smiled and turned from the passenger seat to watch the back where Raucous sat.

"Thanks for the easy route out," he said. "But I'm after Franklin, and it is easier for that to succeed with you. Admittedly, this is something that makes the day difficult. Everyone is going to be looking for you. But if we use it right, it could be a positive."

"How do you figure that?"

"They will expect you to be caught or to hide. They are flushing you out. Public enemy number one and all that. You'll be on telegraph poles and the side of milk cartons in America. That type of thing. Logical to put your head down."

"There is nothing to put me there," Raucous said.

"There is that," Cooper answered. "Which doesn't make sense. I figure they just want you in custody and then they can kill you."

66

They drove away, taking turns slowly, having no direction but only distance to aim for.

"What's the move?" Cooper asked.

Raucous had been sat, not watching the streets but lost in his head. They were trying to get him identified and followed, they were trying to get him to break cover, make a mistake and lead everyone to Cooper and Charlotte and whatever hideout they presumed they had. Raucous thought about the hate he felt for McClintock and his crew, the pain he suffered and the idea that they were coming for him. They knew he wouldn't grass, wouldn't speak to police, wouldn't cooperate. It would mean talking down criminals and showing the connections they had. He would go down and being an informer would mean he was marked and attacks would be financed by gangs and rewards posted for scars or the loss of sight. He knew that even if it were the right thing to do to bring down those he loathed, it would mean a lifetime of fear as he rotted away in the segregated section of whatever prison they deemed fit to hold him. A lifetime in isolation to protect him from those who had a grievance because Raucous would have broken the code. He was marked, by the police, which was something he couldn't beat. He had limited time, he knew that. A short moment in his free life to act and kill and gain his revenge.

"Could you ask Locke where McClintock lives?" Raucous said.

Cooper turned around slowly. Charlotte swore quietly.

"No need, I know."

67

They drove the road, a long loop, an island of twenty houses, ten behind ten, with gardens backing onto each other in the middle. There were fifty houses around the outside on the opposite part of the road. What had once been social housing, now privately owned and worth millions. Each were semi-detached, all had a small front garden that had to the last been paved over for parking space. They were all square boxes of uniform design and a couple still had the red step outside. McClintock had number twenty-six on the outside of the island. The house didn't stand out, it was the same as all the others, the only difference in income could be seen in the cars left outside.

They drove past and out of the street.

"I need to look," Raucous said.

Charlotte looked to Cooper, they knew. But they wouldn't argue.

Charlotte pulled over.

"You don't need to Raucous," Charlotte said.

Raucous smiled and reached for the door.

"Careful for cameras," Charlotte warned.

Raucous nodded.

"If you see anything, tell me," Raucous told them holding up his phone.

He was hoping and he knew they had him pegged for the same. He wanted McClintock, and he wanted him here. They would wait, at least Charlotte would and he had no reason to believe Cooper was different.

He walked the street behind, along a straight road the Romans would be proud to call their own. The houses were tall, all converted to flats, what once were the rich places to live were now the home to students who cared little for upkeep. The council houses behind had become the place to live. London worked in reverse at times. There was an alleyway with steps up and a dog left bend, then one to the right like an S drawn in straight lines. He walked it and popped out onto McClintock's street two doors down. He walked as casual as he could, knowing there would be neighbours watching, people bored with their lives on the look-out and that he was too big a man to go unnoticed. He tried for confident steps, hoping he looked like nothing but a man not worried about being seen. There was no gate, just an opening onto a paved car-space, the side of the house a long corridor sided by brick and a wooden fence grey from age and bleaching to death.

At the back was a conservatory, one with the funny roof he remembered someone calling an orangery. Names all to do with uses. He looked inside and saw a summer sofa and weights that were never used. On the back wall was a backdoor, locked shut. The windows were closed, no openings to be seen. Raucous stepped back, a small white dog jumped up and pawed the window. No barking, no yaps, but a tongue out and scratching at the glass. Raucous looked inside, the floor with a pool of urine. A lap dog trapped in a glass room wanting nothing but connection.

Raucous looked through the back window and saw a kitchen lifted directly from brochures, the classical current look of wooden surfaces, a kitchen island and pastel schemes. The kitchen everyone wanted and those that could afford already had. McClintock had the house of a single man, which he was. Cooper had told him so. No wife, no kids, no family and no taste.

Raucous walked to the shed, the door closed and held tight with a padlock. Raucous pulled on it but it was solid. He pulled again, forcing as much as he could but nothing moved. He walked around to the side where there was a small single pane window. He looked in and saw a lawnmower and the dismantled frame of a double wooden bed. Middle-class boredom writ large in bland suburban lives.

He knew what he was doing, he knew he wasn't really looking for evidence or a stash of weapons. He was waiting, like his teenage self used to wait in places where women hung out. He was wanting McClintock to come back, he wanted the danger, the confrontation, the chance to look him down. It was childish and dumb pretending to be making a move to gain information when all he wanted was to hurt.

Raucous looked into the conservatory again and the dog jumped up, pushing on the glass and flipping back again and again. It wasn't the dog Raucous would guess was McClintock's. He stared as the dog played for attention, jumping, circling, scratching. White curls and pink paws and a tongue that lolled without muscle.

The phone in his pocket vibrated.

"What?" Raucous asked.

"McClintock is coming," Charlotte said.

"Alone?"

"Seems that way."

Raucous had an easy way out. He couldn't walk and risk being seen, but he could wait, hide and then walk when McClintock was inside. He would go in through the front door, coming out back made no sense. But there was the risk.

Raucous knew what he was doing on the lower level, making a bet with himself, setting up possibilities, wanting but not wanting. He wanted this man, this McClintock. He owed him, and whatever it was that scratched away, he needed to balance out the torture.

Raucous thought and made the bet. He waited at the back of the house. If McClintock went in front, he would walk away. If he came out back, he would take him down. The choice would be for chance but he knew he was stacking odds where they shouldn't be.

His phone vibrated again. A message.

"Get out."

Raucous heard the car pull up, a series of slow moves forward and slow moves back as McClintock edged into the space, off the pavement and all on his land. The door popped open and was slammed shut, a beep and crack and locks clicked into place. Raucous drew in breath and held it. He smiled, the buzz of possibilities. The possibility of violence. He heard the key in the front door lock, the door open and then close. Raucous smiled, he should go, walk away. But he waited. Held his place.

He listened for noises, anything at all that would give him an excuse to attack. He knew what he was doing and he knew it was all dumb. He waited, a minute passed. He had to go. The back door opened, a dog ran out, sprinting around the corner, jumping up on his leg. He reached down and patted its head, the dog's tail wagging in the stump it was.

He heard McClintock swear, he heard the dog's name, Fizzy. The dog heard too and it ran back to where it had come. Raucous edged along the side of the house, looked through the conservatory glass, saw McClintock on his knees using kitchen roll to soak up urine. The door was open, the dog was dancing around happy with its freedom, circling and bouncing, McClintock's back to the door. Raucous walked quickly, two steps to the open door, two steps in. McClintock turned, saw, started to stand and Raucous drove his right elbow into McClintock's face. He dropped quickly and backwards, his hands up and rigid on his chest, his fingers making frozen claws as he lay unconscious. The dog bounced in and licked his owner's face.

68

Raucous dragged McClintock into the kitchen, sliding across vinyl floors, over the ridge to the door and onto ceramic tiles. McClintock was breathing, nice and deep, not quite back to the real world. Raucous looked through kitchen drawers and cupboards and found black gaffer tape. He rolled McClintock over onto his face, pinned his arms back as McClintock started to grumble, and bound his wrists. McClintock was coming back into the now slowly, his eyes open, blinking, looking around, needing to remember. Raucous moved quick and bound his ankles. He grabbed McClintock by the collar and pulled him up and pushed him back so he was sat, legs out on the floor, his back resting against the cupboard under the farmhouse sink. McClintock started to make noises as if words were coming. Raucous bit off a strip of tape and placed it firmly over McClintock's mouth. He waited until McClintock was as fully in the conversation as he could be.

"Hello," Raucous said as McClintock's eyes widened. "We need to talk, but I am just going to have a quick check. I'll be back shortly. Think about what you need to tell me."

Raucous picked up the car keys from the work surface, and walked through the rooms in the house. He called Charlotte.

"All good," he said when she answered off the first ring. "Under control. Give me a heads up if anyone comes through."

He switched off the phone not wanting to hear her thoughts or opinions on what he was doing. He knew it was dumb, a risk going too far.

The house revealed nothing other than McClintock employed a cleaner or he was the tidiest single man in London. It was a show home, nothing personal, nothing that made the place anything but stereotypically and fashionably bland. The art was mass produced nothing.

Raucous stepped out of the front door, beeped the car open, sat in the passenger seat and searched the glove box. He found nothing but papers detailing services and new parts. He opened the boot and saw a large military green holdall, leaned in and unzipped.

Raucous swore. Two black assault rifles, four modern handguns with magazines that slid in and two Tasers. He zipped the bag up, took it, locked the car, walked back into the house and shut the door behind him. In the kitchen the dog was jumping up on McClintock's legs.

Raucous texted.

"Have guns."

The blue ticks appeared meaning charlotte had seen.

McClintock had tried to move, edging toward a small square door that covered a space under the stairs. Raucous smiled and realised McClintock really was stupid. Raucous opened the door and saw money, bricks of money held together with elastic bands.

"That is a lot of cash," Raucous said.

McClintock struggled on the floor as if he were a fish flopped at the bottom of a boat.

"I'm not interested in the money," Raucous told him. "I don't need it and won't take it. Those guns though, I am interested in those."

Raucous picked McClintock up by the collar and threw him back into a sitting position. He ripped the tape off McClintock's mouth.

"You thought about what you want to say?" Raucous asked.

McClintock swore, and tried to spit. Raucous placed his large right palm over McClintock's face and pushed forward. The thud as McClintock's head hit wood made the dog stop dancing.

"That's okay," Raucous said. "We need to go through that stage. It's ok, the lack of respect I have for you won't ever change. No need for any of it."

"You do realise you are dead, right?" McClintock asked.

Raucous inhaled and smiled. He loved the classics.

"You'd be surprised at how many people have told me that, all the way back to when I was a teen. I'm still alive. Always the empty threat."

McClintock held eyes with Raucous but he twitched his vision to the left, and Raucous turned to see. He was looking at a clock on the wall, checking the time, not wanting anyone to know he was doing so.

"I'm not going to be long," Raucous said. "Just need a few answers."

"I'm not telling you anything."

Raucous smiled.

"I hoped that would be the way of it."

Raucous unzipped the bag and pulled out a Taser. He held it in his hands and rolled it around. He smiled as McClintock tried to move again.

"You can't crawl faster than I can walk, so there is no need to keep trying. These things, I assure you, hurt."

Raucous looked at the Taser and saw it had no attachment, it was ready to drive into whoever was there and have the snap of pain explode locally.

McClintock's eyes widened, Raucous figured McClintock had seen Raucous last out the shocks and think he could too, but the doubt crept in. Raucous pressed a button and jammed the live electrical arc into the base of McClintock's neck. McClintock screamed, Raucous released, realised he should have covered the man's mouth.

"Hurts, doesn't it?" Raucous said.

McClintock was drawing in air as if this would numb the pain. Raucous ripped a piece of tape and moved to cover McClintock's mouth. McClintock stared back. Raucous stuck the tape on.

"You'll have to nod if you feel like telling me anything," Raucous said.

McClintock looked at the time on the wall.

"You think you can last?" Raucous asked and jammed the electric probe into McClintock's neck, aiming for and hitting his adam's apple.

McClintock screamed, but no real sound came. Raucous released the pressure and McClintock tried to inhale, sucking in tape rather than air.

"Want to talk?" Raucous asked.

McClintock nodded and Raucous ripped off the tape. He looked at his phone, saw no messages or calls and placed it on the floor next to McClintock.

"What's going on? Why the scene for George. No one is going to believe I wrote my name in blood on that wall."

McClintock snorted, an attempt at a laugh.

"Your DNA is all over it, and in the next day or two, whenever a couple of killings happen, your DNA is going to be in that too. We got your blood, spit, skin and hair to spread around murder scenes for the foreseeable future. You'll be forensically tied into everything."

Raucous smiled but he knew the danger. DNA on the scene, his own, taken from when he was in the cell. A drop of blood, his saliva, his bodyhair, and with his record an easy connection to make. A gangland killing, and Raucous has a past of revenge.

"So whatever you think you can achieve, you can't," McClintock said."You are now the man everyone wants to take down. All of this, it is nothing. You kill me then they will keep you alive and hurt you every single minute."

"And if I speak when caught."

"Speak to who? You'll speak to us. And that is all. Whatever you say won't be believed right upto your inevitable suicide. You couldn't handle another stretch without freedom."

Raucous nodded, he liked the idea and wondered about how many prisoners, those that always defended their innocence, had been done in the same way. Science takes centre stage, how the samples got to be there never considered. Blood links you to the scene, you are guilty.

"What has Franklin got on you?"

McClintock looked to the time again, a brief movement of his eyes, a check. Raucous looked at his watch: three minutes to the hour.

"Nothing," McClintock said. "A pathetic man like that has nothing on me. A means to an end. Crazy, but not enough to be a danger as of yet. MarQuick controlled him, but he has gone. Franklin won't last. But he has a network, one that works and one he inherited mostly. A lot of money and people get killed but not as many as before, and the ones we want gone get to go. You know how it all works. You are part of it."

You can never escape, Raucous thought, not fully, not here. That was who he had been and who he was being now.

"So you take the money, manage the crime to your liking, and destroy lives."

"You think you can save people? You know you can't. You are just setting up a situation that you think will help you repay the debts of your past. You save no one. It is an inevitable future for them all, the collateral, that is what we look after. No one beyond those choosing to get in are killed. That's part of it. The ones not playing are safer that way."

Raucous had heard it all, the old timers saying they only killed their own, and the new breed saying they only fought those who deserved it. It was all a lie as if there were physical laws protecting those who hadn't signed up. It was a nonsense, a fallacy he had once bought into. A code of honour to which no one he ever knew paid heed.

"You control it all, let them make their money, destroy lives and you manage the edges for cash."

McClintock smiled and nodded.

"Franklin runs it, his men police it, and I control the crack-down. He steps out of line he is gone."

Raucous smiled at the man's idiocy.

"If you step out of line he takes you out."

"He doesn't have the brains nor the balls to do that. The man is weak. Just like you."

Raucous stared at him, another disappointment of a man, someone he didn't believe, trust nor respect. Someone he would have once fought and maimed for the difference of opinion. He smiled.

"You going to kill me now?" McClintock asked. "Because your only way out of this is through having me on your side. I control it. Me. You need people to back off, I call it. You need evidence to vanish, I do that. You need that idiot Franklin and the dumb Darts to leave you be, I do it. You need me alive and you need me on side."

Raucous stared at him more, the silence was always a ploy that worked. McClintock needed him engaged, needed conversation. Raucous thought as quickly as he could, figuring options and futures and there was truth in what McClintock said.

The phone on the floor buzzed and moved.

Raucous leaned down, the screen already alight, the message on a drop down. Short and sweet. Incoming call. He pressed the green button.

"Company. Four of them. Police. One car. Get out now."

Raucous nodded, McClintock watched as Raucous delved into the bag. McClintock panicked, predicted his death. He started talking.

"No need, Raucous," he said. "We are good. I can call it off. Only I can call it off."

Raucous found what he was looking for, attached it, turned to McClintock and fired the Taser darts into his chest. McClintock buckled, rising up from his seated position, heels on the floor and his head against the cabinet. He slid down, rigid, then relaxed. Raucous placed tape over his mouth, wound more around his head, hoping the time to take it off would give him space to leave. He picked up the bag, heard a car pull up outside. He swore. The dog went running to the front door, jumped up and scratched at its surface. He heard a voice say Fizzy. Raucous walked out of the conservatory, looked around for people. He heard them chatting and laughing at the front of the house. He walked with the holdall, back across the garden, climbed the six-foot wooden fence, jumped down into the garden, all flat green grass of a mythical England. He walked quickly, not caring to be spotted through the gap between houses.

He figured he had less than a minute, he figured, at the end of it all, he needed McClintock alive.

"I'm coming out on the main road," he said into his phone.

69

"An old one but it works," Cooper said.

Raucous had told them of his DNA and samples being spread.

"That doesn't leave us much," Charlotte added.

She was concentrating on the road, looking in the mirror to try and guess at the contents of the holdall. Raucous saw her.

"Two automatic rifles, four handguns and no spare ammunition. Two Tasers, one recently used."

Cooper laughed.

"How did McClintock face that?" Cooper asked through a smile.

"I don't know," Raucous said. "He was talking but the way he was looking at the clock I'd say he was stalling for time. He knew they were coming. There was a meeting, there were guns. There was a plan. I don't believe it was for me."

Cooper's smile faded. He looked at his phone, searched through apps, typed in words.

"He say anything about Locke?" he asked.

"Just asked if he was in with me. I said no."

Cooper nodded and looked at his phone again. He paused, wanting to do something but not quite making the decision. He stared at the screen, messages open on an app that boasted of encryption. He stared and thought and made a move, typing in words and pressing send.

"To Locke?" Raucous asked.

Cooper nodded.

"He is a smart guy, weird but smart. I get the feeling he knows they are coming for him. Simpson I do not like."

Raucous couldn't figure the bond, the relationship.

"What is it you two have?" he asked.

Cooper's smile faded.

"A mutual debt," he said. "Like you two but without the romantic edge. He saved me, I saved him – the order of that debateable. I was going for suicide by provocation. He was going for an arrest. We crossed paths, got lucky and I have nothing else to do other than be me, and that means when I owe someone, I stick around till it is paid back. I owe Locke in a big way. What's the deal with you two?"

"Same," Charlotte said from the front.

Raucous smiled, he knew she didn't want to hear his bumbling attempts at explanation, knew he didn't have the emotional vocabulary. She was protecting him from harm.

Cooper smiled, looking at his phone.

"He got it?" Raucous asked.

Cooper shook his head and said, "Nothing I can do about that."

Charlotte slowed, pulled into a residential street, crawled along until a parking area with space appeared on the left, she indicated and turned in, found a spot beside a van that hid them from the road. She turned.

"What's the plan?" she asked. "Because we are doing nothing."

70

Raucous sat and heard and listened and knew. Charlotte was trying to talk her way to a resolution while Cooper waited knowing he was only ever doing one thing. The details may change, the ideas alter, but the actions and their outcomes were always unchanged.

Raucous knew this too and spoke.

"We already decided we were not running. My set up changes nothing other than the consequence. McClintock is a nobody. His end is coming. People that dumb don't last. We put the hit on the Darts and Franklin and work with what happens after."

Raucous knew escape from murder scenes was easy, physically walking away was what everyone did. Only the dumbest or those that kill in moments when out of control stayed where the blood was flowing. But science made placing you in the scene as easy as if there were film. Everyone's phone told companies where they were and at what time to an exact place and moment in time. If your phone was there then so were you. If your DNA was there then you were too. The first step in catching any fool was to check their digital records and then test for their physical presence. A couple of ticks and the guilt was confirmed. Raucous knew this, knew how stupid people could be. But he had always been someone who knew how stupid he was and took precautions to mitigate the poor odds he held.

He would be given the time to serve for any killing McCLintock wanted. Franklin and the Darts would be added to a list.

Cooper and Charlotte were watching him, waiting for his words.

"I'd rather go down for something I did. Franklin and the Darts deserve to die. I'll take the hit for them. We won't get caught but I'll get framed. That leaves you two with freedom."

Raucous knew they could say nothing because Raucous was already a guilty man with a lottery ticket possibility of walking away free on whatever path he took.

"I'm getting put away for something if I do nothing," he said. "If I do something then maybe there is a chance information pops up that gives me a road out. I don't want back inside because this time it would be for life. But I can't run and hide, not forever."

Charlotte watched him, he could feel it and see in his peripheral vision. Cooper nodded, accepted it all. He knew, understood and had no emotional connection to blur the logic of thought. Cooper accepted the facts.

"The easiest way is to wait," Cooper said."We watch and when they walk free from the building they are in, we walk up, bullet in the head, and walk away. We don't need to announce to the world that we killed them, I don't need the fame nor the kudos of being that man. I just need to know that I did it. That is enough for me. If they don't ever find the bodies or never know the whys and who, that's great with me."

They waited, all thinking, all trying to plan a future and see possible outcomes but none of them would have Raucous a free man. It was the only ending they couldn't avoid. For it to be any other way they needed extra.

"It is Okay," Raucous said.

Charotte looked at him wanting to smile but finding nothing. "Maybe something comes up," she said.

Raucous didn't need to say that none of them knew what that could be.

Cooper spoke again.

"We have guns, we have patience, we know where they will eventually be or already are. They can't be holed up forever. The Darts live as a pair, and Franklin has them as guards. We just have to wait till they all come out, follow them, and we walk up and shoot."

"Simple plan," Raucous said.

"Ones that always go wrong," Charlotte added.

71

They sat and watched and waited. The building was locked down, no activity and no external security. The night of terror had taken the licence away, there were no nights planned and none allowed. It was a modern vault of emptiness. But as Cooper said, Franklin lived there. It was his fortress, a bastion of power in an area he believed he ruled. There was no movement outside, no trucks arriving or going. Every entrance shut and bolted. The night in full darkness. There was no way in that wouldn't require force or luck. Franklin in the penthouse looking down and no way of reaching the top without death.

They didn't know how long.

"This could be days," Charlotte said.

Raucous and Cooper nodded.

"Could be minutes too," Cooper told them.

They sat in silence, the cold coming in because windows were open at the top to release the moisture their breath produced. They watched the building's underground garage entrance. Nothing moved and they saw no people.

"They look locked down," Charlotte said. "No security, just locked doors."

"Too quiet," Raucous said.

Cooper checked his phone as he had every few minutes since he sent the message to Locke.

"Anything?" Raucous asked and Cooper shook his head.

"Normal?" Raucous asked.

Cooper shook his head again.

Raucous knew he was thinking of McClintock, knew he was trying to figure out if Locke had been taken down.

Raucous stared at Cooper, waiting for Cooper to realise and look. It took ten seconds.

"There is nothing I can do," Cooper said. "I don't know where he is."

"We don't know where anyone is," Charlotte said. "We could be watching an empty building."

"Franklin is in there," Cooper said. "That's his safe place."

The lights on the road made them all slouch back in their seats. Two cars were rolling slowly toward them. Both had their headlights on, and both were moving way below the thirty limit. There was no way to make out the model or plate of either car as the lights shone forward and out. The only thing they recognised was dark colours. They watched from their parked position in a small road looking across from the entrance. The cars slowed more, turned left and stopped. Their engines running, the low purr a constant sound in the empty night.

"Recognise them?" Charlotte asked Cooper.

Cooper nodded.

"The second one is McClintock's," Raucous said.

"The first is the car that brought his friends to his house," Charlotte told him.

Light wasn't shining directly on them, but the glow of two headlights made making out who was inside an impossibility. They heard the clunk of a heavy door mechanism shudder into action and the screech of metal scrapping metal. They watched the entrance edge open as it slid from right to left, the metal groaning against the mechanism all the way. The door smashed into its safety rail and stopped its movement.

Raucous thought, hoping he would stop, knew he needed to talk himself out of possibilities.

The cars moved into gear, and rolled forward on pristine tarmac. They moved forward in unison, arcing left, the first vanishing down a slope, the second vanishing immediately after.

They watched, heard the mechanism start to clank again.

Raucous looked to Cooper, who smiled and nodded.

"Twenty seconds at most," Cooper said.

Charlotte looked back, "You are kidding me," she said.

Raucous grabbed the holdall, opened the door, stepped out and started to run. He heard Cooper coming after him. He listened for Charlotte, could pick out no noise and headed for the closing door.

72

A risk and a gamble was all good but not without limits and always without stupidity. Never lose your head when looking to bet big. The door was closing, the gap narrowing but not enough for panic to set in. Raucous had to be smart, he was going to make the gap but he knew he could not predict who was on the other side. He could be running into them all, alone and with all the weapons he wanted zipped up in a canvas bag.

Raucous slowed, and felt and saw Cooper run past. He watched as Cooper slowed too, walking the last of the way, stepping through the gap, no light shining, only darkness. Raucous thought of the cameras that must be filming. He thought of everything that should go wrong, about choosing the right time to take risks, about how his bets had failed when young and how he tried to be smarter as an adult. He was failing here, he knew that. Thinking was the last thing he needed, he told himself, he just had to act.

Cooper was across the threshold, inside the building, the other side of the door when it would be closed. Cooper looked back, like a child on a mission looking to see if his friends were still in on the dare. Raucous walked forward, stepped over the metal runner that showed where the door slid closed. He crouched down low as Copper had done. They crouched like little kids playing in the sand, waiting for the door to slam closed, waiting to be trapped, waiting for there to be no other choice but to move forward.

They felt the door edge to its final position, they braced themselves for the crash and the lock. Raucous turned, heard the breath, heard the step, looked right and up and saw Charlotte step through, crouch down and look at him. He wanted to smile and got a quarter of the way there. Charlotte shook her head, the anger he loved clear in her eyes. The door smashed shut, the engine stopped pushing, minimal light from outside gone, the area dark but not black. There was no sound close, but a low hum of activity pushed up from the bottom of the long slope and a shallow glow of light crawled their way.

73

Cooper placed his right index finger against his lips, a redundant gesture as no one had plans on talking. They looked around as they acclimatised their eyes to the dark and strained to hear the reason for the low vibrations in the air.

They were at the top of a corridor built for cars. There was no walkway, only two brick walls up to the ceiling, a square tunnel that led only forward and down. There was nowhere to hide and no obstacle to provide barrier. Cooper crouched, putting his face to the floor, pressing his right cheek against smooth concrete and staring ahead. The car park was two metres downhill and their feet would come into view. He sat up, shook his head and Raucous didn't understand the meaning. Cooper edged forward, crouching low, his head as close to the ground as he could manage. He waved them to follow and they did.

The floor sloped down gently, levelling out onto the carpark floor of polished cement. There were four cars, the Bentley one of them, scratches where bullets had hit, a tyre deflated and glass that had shattered but not broke. It was parked to the left as soon as the corridor opened out into a large rectangle. The far side the two cars were parked, and eight policemen in suits lingered.

There were strip lights that lit the far end while the side where they were walking slowly had nothing but darkness. Cooper held up his hand. They stopped and waited trying to breathe quietly and make no noise.

Cooper looked and moved, quick quiet steps until he was behind the Bentley. Raucous could see him and Cooper had a view across the open space. Raucous watched and waited, Charlotte to his right, the holdall in his left hand. Cooper looked over the bonnet of the Bentley, turned to Raucous and waved him in.

Raucous walked in a crouch, Charlotte behind in the same awkward style. They reached the car and sat down. They were all-in, Raucous knew that. The way out closed, the mechanism to open it unknown, the way forward a hive of police, unknown number of security and the Penthouse with Franklin and the Darts. Thinking made him realise the stupidity of thoughtless decisions. He had put them all within a maze of violence and they had no way out but to smash face first into whatever they had waiting.

The noise of the conversation on the far side was loud and it sounded like all eight men were giving thoughts and talking people down. Too many voices for contentment and too loud to confirm calm. The light reached where they were but they hid in shade. Cooper was watching from low down on the edge. Raucous watched him for any sign of communication.

Cooper swore low and quiet. Raucous turned and raised up so he could see over the bonnet. Raucous saw what Cooper had, Charlotte was watching too, a parody of three kids hiding out behind a fence and watching through a window.

Raucous saw her step out of the car, elegant and calm. He couldn't see her face as well as others but he imagined she smiled. Cooper swore again. Simpson was talking to the eight men, gesturing with her hands which would only make sense if you heard the words. The other eight voices were talking too as if each of them needed to have a point of view heard in the heat of debate.

Raucous couldn't speak because he didn't want to be heard. A sea of concrete between them and the police and no way to bridge it without announcing their arrival and getting violent replies. They watched in fascination rather than anger, nine people, all paid to uphold law, standing and chatting in the basement of a gangster's house.

Their voices grew louder and Raucous picked out McClintock and smiled. A man trying to claw back credibility through verbal bullying of those who think him a fool.

A man opened the boot of the second car, he leaned in and Raucous expected weapons or drugs or both. But he saw quickly what it was and reached out and grabbed Cooper, holding him tight, not letting him move. Raucous looked at Charlotte and her face told him fear.

Cooper pulled forward but couldn't move. He turned and stared at Raucous and found Charlotte staring too.

They pulled Locke from the back of the car, crumpled, wrists tied in front of him and a face that lumped and shone red. He was pushed to the floor and the nine people on their feet stood and stared as Locke tried to stand. McClintock walked up and kicked Locke in the ribs, making Locke leave the floor and come down onto his chest.

Cooper surged and Raucous held tight, the shirt he was wearing stretched and pulled.

"Think," Raucous said quietly. "We can't get to him so we can't save him."

Cooper released a little of his pull. He turned and sat back not wanting to watch, not wanting to make a mistake of uncontrolled rage. He swore again. Raucous kept looking. He watched Simpson talk, in the centre of them all, hands moving, arms up and down. She seemed to be speaking directly to McClintock, who looked around. Raucous thought it was for support, maybe he was being challenged. It was a guess, and a hope.

There was a pause, a sudden silence like someone had blasphemed in a Sunday sermon. Raucous squinted harder, had faces come into focus then drift away as his eyes relaxed. McClintock stepped forward, Simpson looked into his eyes and didn't flinch as McClintock drove his forehead into her face. She dropped straight down, her legs buckling but not bending back. Her head cracked against the concrete and McClintock stopped forward and kicked her ribs, looked at his audience, shouted an obscenity and then punted her face. Two of his colleagues pulled him off, held him back as he struggled to attack an unconscious woman.

Voices raised again, swearing and shouting. A group of men without a leader.

Charlotte unzipped the bag, exposing the guns.

Cooper and Raucous reached in.

74

They stayed crouched, hidden from view, listening to the voices slow down and calm. Cooper on alert, anger rising, his face set into a fighter staring down an opponent. The men talked quietly, footsteps paced further away. A door opened and then slid closed. Raucous recognised the sound as the double doors. They waited for minutes, Raucous counting in packets of sixty. He got to five. He turned to look at Charlotte and Cooper.

They heard no more voices. Cooper looked again, over the car, he crouched back down and held up two fingers. Two men. Raucous mouthed Simpson, and Cooper nodded. Raucous mouthed Locke. Cooper shook his head. They were holding weapons, Cooper an automatic rifle, Charlotte the same and Raucous held two handguns.

Charlotte had looked at the scene where Simpson lay. She placed her gun on the ground and crawled to the opposite end of the car, past Raucous and Cooper. She crouched, rose to standing and walked slowly away at a diagonal, trying for quiet, seeing how close she could get before being seen. Raucous hoped he understood the silent plan. Cooper looked at him, eyes wide. Raucous placed a hand on his shoulder, a peace offering but also making sure he stayed out of view.

75

Raucous couldn't see, didn't dare rise to watch what happened. Two men, Simpson on the floor and Charlotte tiptoeing toward them. She needed them to see her soon, she wasn't going to rush them, she was taking a gamble, needing outcomes to happen that were far from certain. Coughing or making a deliberate sound would just make the trap easier to see. It needed to be organic, to make them take time to see what was happening.

Cooper moved and Raucous held him by the shoulder. Raucous shook his head. Cooper needed to trust. Raucous didn't like the unknown but it had to be what Charlotte was planning. There was no other way. She was three metres ahead and still no noise from the men. Charlotte fell, hitting the concrete. Raucous could hear that much. A man's voice sounded, the words lost but the noise annoyance and shock. There were two men and whatever decision they made would lead to the outcome Raucous chased.

He waited to hear footsteps, thinking there would be only one but hoping there would be two. They spoke quickly to each other, organising or explaining. There were no walkie-talkies of instant chatter, only phones that would be unanswered or on silent. He listened out for the steps, heard two pairs of feet walking slowly and smiled.

Charlotte was out of sight, she had fallen and would be laying still. Cooper stared at Raucous, looking for instruction, trying to discover if his thoughts were right. Raucous raised an index finger to his lips. The steps kept coming and a voice kept asking, "Who are you? Can you hear me?"

Raucous couldn't see, but if the two police weren't dumb they would have guns pulled, pointing at Charlotte, if they were smart or trained, they would be scanning the room. Raucous took them for smart, it made it safer.

76

Timing was everything, he needed to act as if choreographed in practice rooms. The footsteps were close to Charlotte, they stopped, a male voice asked, "Who are you?"

Raucous looked to Cooper and nodded. Be ready. Cooper nodded back and smiled. The gambler's pleasure.

Charlotte made her move and Raucous rose to his feet in time with Cooper. Up, visible and guns pointed at police heads. They turned to see who was there.

Charlotte drove the Taser up into the fist man's groin, and he screamed, dropping his gun. The second man saw Cooper and Raucous, looked at his colleague on the floor, saw the two guns raised, pointing at his head. Raucous nodded, looked at the man's gun and looked down at the floor and the man understood but didn't want to cave. He made an attempt at making a choice although they all knew he was only going one way. He acted enough, knew he risked all by dragging it out further and placed his weapon down on to concrete with his thumb and index finger.

The first man rolled over, curled up like a sleeping infant as Charlotte got to her feet. Raucous pulled the man up by the collar and dragged him toward the car. The second man followed as a volunteer. The boot was open, there was space inside for one comfortable so Raucous lifted the first man up and bundled him in. He looked at the second man, looked at the boot of the first car and then the boot of the second. He gave a choice. The man reached into his pocket nice and slow, Cooper covering him with a gun, and beeped the locks open. Raucous indicated with a nod for the man to get in and he did and Cooper slammed the boot closed.

They looked at each other, Charlotte, Raucous and Cooper, not knowing what to say or what to do. But noise made them act

Simpson stirred, groggy and mumbled. She tried to stand but failed like a boxer not accepting their opponent had separated their senses from their body. Her face was already swollen, coming up, flattening wrinkles and she held her ribs. "Thank you," she said, but the words were all slurred and she winced as her mouth moved. Her jaw would reset but right now it was broken and hanging half out of the joint.

McClintock hit women hard.

77

Simpson couldn't speak without pain, a wince and an inhale on every other word. But she needed to talk, they all knew that. They waited as her head cleared enough for coherent words, alert to the possibility of the police return. Cooper had eyes on the door, they all stayed silent waiting to hear noises they knew were danger.

Simpson saw Raucous watching her, a gun in his hand, loose at his side but tense enough to be ready to shoot.

"I'm not with them," she said. "They picked me up, lied, got me here."

"How?" Cooper asked, turning his glance to her.

She shrugged, telling them she was a fool.

"And Locke?" Charlotte asked.

"I don't know. They had him. I saw him out of the car. Didn't know he was there."

She rasped and winced, and pulled in air through a mouth she didn't want to open.

"They got a plan?" Raucous asked.

Simpson went to smile but it turned into pain. She pointed at him.

"You," Simpson said. "They want all of you. Dead. Locke too. Me as well now."

"Do they know we are coming?" Cooper asked.

Simpson shrugged. She didn't know. But they would need to be stupid to imagine they would run.

"They planned on drawing you in," she rasped. "Just not this soon."

Charlotte looked at the two men, Cooper and Raucous, thought about their minds working, about the violence they were preparing themselves to do. She could see it in them, the rage they brought when attack was the only option for moving forward. She saw Raucous fight it, saw him look to her. She smiled because she knew it meant he felt.

"They will have men with guns, or boys at least," she said."The loyal idiots who think this is a game."

Cooper and Raucous stared and thought and smiled and knew. An unknown number of fools to shoot through to reach the men they wanted.

"Not many," Simpson said. "McClintock won't want witnesses."

They stared at each other, knowing the only action they wanted to take was to walk through them all and mow them down.

"Phone in the police," Simpson said.

Raucous looked to Cooper and smiled. Cooper shook his head. Charlotte watched them play the game of most masculine in the room. They didn't realise it was her.

Cooper's face fell, he reached back and grabbed his phone from his pocket. He held the screen up close like an old man whose eyes are shot. He stared at the screen and swore.

"A message. From Locke's number. Directly to me. He would have had to tell them. It isn't saved anywhere."

"They got him to talk?" Simpson asked.

"No need to try. If he needs help, which, let's face it, he does, then the only out he has is me."

Cooper read the message.

"Says they want to meet. Me, Raucous and Charlotte. A talk. We could bargain for Locke. They have Simpson."

Cooper smiled before reading out the last words.

"They want us here within the hour."

Charlotte spoke quickly.

"Any way of tracking your phone?"

"No internet on this. None of those apps that spy on you. Old school. Text or phone. Probably some way but none I know."

Charlotte looked around the carpark.

"He has the police, that's eight, the Darts, and himself. Possible he has others around, but a skeleton security staff for nights like these. No one in their right mind is breaking in here. CCTV?"

Raucous shook his head.

"They don't film. Too much illegal activity. Just guards. The building is soundproof too."

"Where will they be?" Charlotte asked.

"Penthouse. Stairs or lift. Glass. Difficult to do it unseen."

"If we make it up without noise, we can do it. If it gets to be a gunfight, we need to get out," Charlotte said, and she knew she was becoming the biggest fool of them all.

78

They left Simpson with a gun taken from the police in the trunks. They didn't leave her a phone, and made sure there were none in the cars. They didn't want police swarming in, they didn't know who would come and who to trust. Simpson wasn't going anywhere soon, and if she staggered out, she could only come in the direction they were using. This was theirs, and they needed to claim the deaths as their own. No legal talks, no deal making, a simple sentence of death for any crime they chose to admit.

Raucous had pushed through the double doors into the corridor with a precision in movement that made him slow. The corridor was empty, no noise of footsteps and only Cooper and Charlotte for company. Raucous pointed to the right, indicating the sign that showed the steps up to the ground floor. Cooper smiled and nodded, Raucous hoped it was a thought of when they were here before. They edged along the corridor alert to noise, looking for cameras but seeing none. Cooper stopped them and edged his eyes around the corner, looking up the steps. He turned back and motioned them forward. They walked slowly, one step at a time, watching the light at the top grow brighter and closer. They heard nothing but their attempts at muting footfall and breathing slow.

Cooper reached the top, peered around, held up his palm to stop Raucous and Charlotte. He stepped back, looked at them and shook his head. He held up two fingers, and pointed at his rifle and shook his index finger. Two men, no guns.

Cooper looked again and motioned Raucous and Charlotte out, they followed on tiptoe, and saw the men, or boys, or teens, or whatever they were. Child security, street kids in sportswear but there for respect and the eyes that technology wouldn't replace. Their faces were hidden as they stood side-on to the stairs. They weren't talking but they weren't alert, they were bored, or tired or stupid. Charlotte moved with grace and quiet, Raucous moved at her side, the air they beat forward or a shadow or sound made the boys turn, they had time to grunt as the one to the right had a stock rammed into his face as Charlotte didn't break stride to blow his nose and knock him out. The second kid had a little more, but the outcome was the same, Raucous walking forward, swinging his forearm and taking the kid out with his elbow.

Charlotte and Raucous stood over them, listening, trying to hear anything that would make them hide. Raucous looked down and knew there was no dragging them from view. They wouldn't wake quick enough to sound alarms, but they would come back to the living. They had been standing at the entrance to the central room, in front of shut double doors. The stairway up was visible, the glass elevator too. Raucous looked up and saw no light nor movement, but he heard no sound from inside.

He pointed at the double doors. Charlotte smiled and Cooper nodded, those slow movements of a man convinced. They looked at their weapons, made sure they were ready. They walked to the door as a trio and Raucous leaned his weight and pushed, aiming to leave a gap big enough to look through.

79

Raucous saw what he wanted, smiled at the scene, turned his head, nodded and waved them through. They were quiet, no barging in shouting orders and making everyone hit the floor. They fanned out, Cooper left, Charlotte right and Raucous taking the middle.

Raucous raised his gun, holding it in two hands pointing forward. His knees bent not through training but through watching others. To mimic was a way of learning. He saw to his right and left, Cooper and Charlotte with rifles raised, covering what was in front. He looked at the room, remembered the last time here, the noise and the lights, the people and the screams. Now it was empty of movement like a warehouse storing movie sets. Raucous watched the people in front, saw who he thought he needed to see. Franklin saw them. The police and McClintock saw them and they could do nothing but freeze.

Eight police in suits, Franklin and four of his boys. There were no automatic rifles, and no visible guns. They were holding, Raucous knew that, guns in underarm holsters or tucked in the back of joggers, or lying on the ground, but they were all out of quick reach and semi-automatic rifles had a design that could kill before any of them could touch their triggers.

"You'll be thinking we won't shoot," Raucous said. "Somewhere in your brain. But think calmly now. You know me, know the people I've killed. You know that I am pegged for murders, a life sentence, and a few extra won't do me harm. Cooper wants you dead, probably wants you to make a move, to lift those guns from where they are hidden and fire."

Cooper smiled and nodded, his gun moving along the group, back and forth, not shaking, just aiming and looking and nodding.

"Where's Locke?" Cooper asked.

There was no reply and the four youths looked to Franklin.

"Is he dead?" Cooper asked.

Franklin looked into Cooper's eyes.

"Not yet, but soon," he told him.

Franklin pointed at a small room, a stripper's private spot where money exchanged and one-on-one shows took place. The door was closed. Raucous stepped over, motioning people to move away and give him space, each of the people trying to stay far from the aim of the two rifles stroking their moves.

Raucous pushed the door, light broke in and Locke was sat on a chair, breathing through his nose with his head forward, unable to topple because he was taped to a wooden chair, the line across his chest, his mouth open but filled with blood. He looked up and smiled, his teeth chipped, his lips swollen and his eyes almost shut.

Raucous nodded, Locke smiled again and moved his head slowly up and down.

"You can go," Raucous said to the four young men in sports clothes. "Your choice, everyone has a choice. You made a couple and you are here. I've made more and arrived after. It's all good. This doesn't have to be an end. You can walk away."

He spoke and wanted to believe there was a chance they would move, take the offer of freedom in exchange for a new direction. Each of them looked to Franklin who didn't even offer them recognition. Franklin would only look at Raucous. There was no anger, not that Raucous could see, only spite and the ability to stop himself from charging an attack.

The room was silent, men staring trying to figure out escapes or words to use to gain an edge, looking for exits and imagining strategies to find healthy freedom. The routes were simple but here and now an impossibility without damage or death.

No one spoke. Raucous, Cooper and Charlotte were holding the room with the power they held in their hands. No one moved from where they stood but heads were turning, looking, faces trying to seek assurance from men, or orders, or an idea of what was next.

Raucous knew he didn't need to speak, knew they needed to wait for someone on the other side to seek conversation and a way forward and out of the loss they were in. A phone buzzed, not a ringtone to embarrass but a vibration. Raucous watched Franklin smile.

"I'm just going to look at the number," Franklin said.

"Don't do it," Raucous said.

"Just going to look," Franklin told him, not stopping his movement. "No need to shoot over a phone."

Cooper pointed his gun closer, tensing up as Franklin reached to his pocket. Raucous knew Cooper wanted the excuse to fire, the fallout of running and chaos not something he cared about beyond Franklin's death.

Franklin pulled the phone from his pocket, looked at the screen, didn't press a thing. He smiled and put his phone back into his pocket. He looked around the room they were in, a huge space of pop-up bars and mini retreats for the private nights of celebrities and stars and gangsters and fools to spend their money and make their connections through being seen. Everyone chasing any type of fame.

Franklin's smile remained and he returned his gaze to Raucous, stared into his eyes and started to look up.

Raucous knew, figured it quick from the look but way too late from the set-up. Raucous swore, started to move, needing to be in a new space, move from the one he was in. He shouted to Charlotte and Cooper to go. Franklin's smile went.

"Do it," Franklin shouted.

And the shots rained down.

The crowd spread, pulling guns, looking for cover and firing off whatever they could. Raucous looked up and saw the Darts, each bare-chested and each leaning over the balcony high overhead. They each held two pistols and were firing like they had been caught up in a Wild West saloon shoot-out. They would need chance and luck to hit anyone but the carnage the shots caused had broken their momentary reign.

"What the hell are they doing here?" McClintock shouted.

"Saving us," Franklin said.

Raucous watched them run like an angry couple, bickering but escaping. Raucous aimed and fired off two shots that missed and he had no idea where the bullets went. Everyone had pulled or found their guns and dived to cover, hoping the fools up high wouldn't shoot them dead with the random aim of drunks.

Raucous saw Charlotte hit the ground, diving forward, the edge of a pop-up bar made of balsa wood and chipboard providing cover from sight but none from bullets. She placed her back against the bar, her rifle in her hands, listening and watching, ready to shoot, aware she had limited ammunition. Cooper had mimicked on the other side and Raucous was closer to him.

The noise died, firing stopped and the cackle laugh of the Darts flooded down. One of them shouted, which of them didn't matter, an interchangeable two of mindless choices.

"You hanging out there, McClintock?" Raucous called.

They knew where he was, his voice was only confirming what they saw, not singling him out as the target's centre.

"You blew it," McClintock shouted back. "No need for the speech where you tell me you'll take some of us with you. You aren't taking anyone."

"I don't need to take you, Franklin has that one planned."

"Not going for it, Raucous," McClintock shouted back.

Raucous had no time to process words, he needed to go with thoughts he was half-forming in his mind.

"Darts seemed to surprise you," Raucous said.

The Darts laughed from up on top and Raucous braced for the inevitable shot. It came, the bang, the whizz and crack as the bullet hit concrete.

"Franklin would have told you they were elsewhere, and we know why that is. You told me when I passed by your house."

"I didn't tell you shit," McClintock said. "I was stringing you along to bide time till my boys turned up."

"That's not how it went. You know that."

"Weak, Raucous. Weak and stupid."

Raucous pulled his phone from his pocket, the screen intact, the electronics working well. He was listening, he looked left and right and saw Cooper and Charlotte ready to move, ready to fire, each of them listening for movement and looking for signs they needed to attack.

"A whole lot of it sounds true to me. You weren't too kind about Franklin, you hate the Dart boys. You were none too positive on your own crew."

"Wasting time, Raucous," McClintock shouted back. "No one is buying that. I was there. I told you nothing."

Raucous turned the speaker up on his phone and played the audio. McClintock's voice, cracking, begging, and talking. It was the start of their conversation, no details and nothing McClintock said about anyone important, just chatter of a man who knew he was about to face pain.

Raucous pressed pause.

"I got it all, McClintock. Everything you said. The way you told me Franklin was at the end of his time, that you had his replacement ready."

"Bullshit," McClintock shouted.

"Want to hear it Franklin?" Raucous shouted.

He looked to Charlotte and Cooper, they nodded, they were ready. They had nothing but chance and hope to find a way out. They needed chaos and confusion. Twelve on three in a straight-up shoot-out left no other outcome but death.

Cooper motioned up to the balcony and to his left. Charlotte motioned to the area to her right. Raucous nodded, he had centre.

McClintock was talking fast and low, throwing words and talking the situation down. His voice raising, ever increasing in volume.

"That stuff on your phone?" Franklin asked.

Raucous smiled.

"All of it," he said. "McClintock is playing you. But you know that. Him and his boys are not being straight. They have you on the edge of being removed. Them Dart boys are too crazy, too unpredictable, and as McClintock said, you are just too dumb to sort that out."

Raucous slide the pointer along the blue line on the screen and let the audio run. There was a scream, McClintock taking electricity. There was a pant, an inhale and McClintock started talking down the man he was hiding with.

"They are here to take you out Franklin. Think about it, you know it. You can't trust them. They are here to ruin you."

Cooper was smiling, Charlotte serious, waiting both to move.

"You can't hide from it McClintock, I got it all on tape. Soon as that electricity went in you, the words came out."

"Bullshit," McClintock shouted, drowning out the audio.

Raucous couldn't see but he heard and pictured movement in his head. A gun firing, McClintock shouting, bullets hitting wood and concrete and walls. Raucous looked to his left and right and nodded. They tensed, muscles balled up, ready to explode, listening for the opportunity, the time to go. They waited, hearing McClintock firing and shouting but no one else joining the theme. The noise stopped, no more words, no more shots and Raucous waited one more second.

They rose, aiming into spaces they had picked out moments before, three of them, Raucous, Charlotte and Cooper, firing, moving, walking away, zigzagging back toward the door. McClintock saw, stared, fired an empty chamber, looked at his gun and dove to the floor. A bullet hit him, a shot to left side, Cooper or the Darts was impossible to say, his arm or chest Raucous couldn't tell, but McClintock span and dropped.

"Get them," Franklin shouted.

As they moved in bursts, firing out a retreat of general aim and single shots or flashes of fire, Raucous saw the young boys with assorted handguns follow the orders of their lead and move and take pot shots, not aiming, not knowing, believing the gun did all the work. Two dropped, shot in the chest, by who he didn't know. The bullets pinging around the room, most from in front and some from above. Cooper shot up, and a rain of glass splashed down as protective barriers shattered and fell from the walkway above.

They reached the door, Raucous turning to push, his back to the action, the door hit with bullets, he crouched down low, pushing through and feeling the air change and a wind come in. Cooper and Charlotte pushed through behind him, out in the circular hall, the doors sucking closed, a brief quiet, a short look, a knowledge that movement was needed but no one had a place to run.

They backed away from the door, pointing guns at chest high, and edged toward the outside wall where large doors of shatterproof glass and aluminium frames stood locked for protection and a barrier to the outside world.

The door pushed open, two of Franklin's boys came out, pistols up, fingers not ready to pull on triggers.

"Drop them and go," Raucous said, and the two just stared as if they had the upper hand.

The one on the left sneered and Cooper shot, a thigh exploded, not a scratch but deep penetration, through muscle and flesh and shattering bone. The leg flew back, the boy's face flew forward. He fired again but the gun was aiming down. He fell with a slap as his face hit the ground, his gun spun away and Raucous walked over, picked it up and put it in his waist band.

The second boy was running, his face forward but his right hand back, sprinting away, looking to make it around the curve to where he couldn't be seen. Cooper raised his rifle and fired, the boy fell, sliding forward, his left buttock pouring blood, his hand back, the gun still pointing but flat on the ground. Raucous walked over as Cooper and Charlotte kept their weapons on the door. He reached down and picked up the gun. The boy screaming, the blood pumping out. Cooper had hit him three times, a quick, accurate burst, buttock, back and hamstring.

"It was your choice, kid," Raucous said. "Nothing I can help you with now."

The boy screamed more, and anyone close to the door would hear the pain and have to be real sure to walk through and out into the space.

Charlotte was crouched by the door, no holes pushed through, no dents seen. The bullets that had hit were lodged on the other side, soundproof meant bullet proof. She listened, concentrating, trying to hear over the two boy's screams. She shook her head, they looked around, they were in open space, nowhere to hide. Logic told them to run.

81

Without speaking they edged away toward the external exit. Guns at the door, the two boys screaming making listening for movement difficult, like being the last group inside a museum with two tired kids crying for home.

"We can't just wait," Charlotte said. "We out?"

Cooper shook his head.

"I'm not leaving Locke," he said.

They looked at each other, the doors to the outside air metres away, glass they couldn't break, but doors that could be forced but no time to count.

They heard before they saw, footsteps trying for quiet but only weakly, left and right, flanked and the curve of the wall hiding whoever was coming. Raucous looked both ways on repeat, not moving forward nor back, Cooper and Charlotte the same.

"I have no idea how many bullets this thing holds," Charlotte said. "Single shots so far, but I don't know how long that lasts."

Cooper was the same. One rifle, one magazine and no knowledge. They could point and fire, push the switch to single and remove the safety. Pointing and shooting was easy too. But they weren't military, they had no spares and no idea how long they last. Raucous had four guns, no idea how many bullets and no spare magazines. Knowledge and experience was always better. Right now they had too little to make good calls.

The first whizz zinged by, the air scratching at ears as a bullet flew by and hit the outside window. The glass fractured but didn't explode, a large circle of white in lines streaming out from the impact centre.

"Fuck," Raucous said.

They raised their guns as they bent into a crouch, turning and aiming, flanked and being set as targets in a cross-fire. Another whizz and the first of the police in suits was visible to their left. Raucous moved, making a decision for himself and hoping it would be for them all. He walked forward to the door into the central room, gun raised, out of sight of the groups coming from either side. He didn't fire, he knew he had to hold on to ammunition. Nothing to waste, nothing to shoot without thought and leave themselves defenceless. He pushed up to the door, his right shoulder leaning and touching. He pushed, crouched low, the door swung open, he tried to picture the rooms, the bars and the cover, made a choice before seeing, chose the place he would hide, to his left, low down, that room for strippers and secret deals. He pushed through not knowing if Cooper and Charlotte were behind, hoping he had made the right call.

82

The room had changed, not in lay-out or content but in senses. The lights were off, the room dark, the glow of blue and flashes of colour as if a concert were about to begin. Music blared, electronic and loud, a voice repeating the same line and then cutting to distortion. The air reverberated, the walls vibrating to a bass that carried its energy in big power waves. Back in his youth Raucous hated these nights. But here there were no sweaty masses, pulling faces and moving as a one like a school of cod. But the noise and the lights were as strong now as then, and Raucous winced at the present as well as the past.

Charlotte dropped down next to him, Cooper to his right. To hear they had to shout.

"We have to take them all," Charlotte said, her voice barely carrying half-a-metre. "Put them all down."

Cooper nodded, Raucous too. Raucous looked up to the balcony and saw nothing but the flashing lights above. He heard nothing but music, saw nothing but light explosions. Hated the scene, the sounds and the people. But he knew it was the same for everyone.

"Seven of them, plus McClintock, Darts and Franklin," Raucous shouted.

Cooper stayed quiet, smiling, eyes wider than before. No one spoke, told him a word, they let him build and hit his point of concentration. Cooper nodded, he had understood.

The door opened, a gun barrel came through, then a hand and an arm, and then a face. It looked to the right, when left would have been the way to go. He turned his head scanning with his eyes rather than his gun, he saw the three of them crouched down, saw the three guns. He had a choice, back away, retreat and rethink, but arrogance or panic hit him and he chose the other option, tried to pull his aim on Charlotte. Three guns fired, each a single shot, and all three hit, chest, leg and arm. The man dropped, hit the floor, bleeding out. And as if in some horror film for teens, his body slid away through the door, pulled by one of his colleagues.

They looked at each other faces not smiling, not nodding, a recognition of what they needed to do.

"See you when it is done," Cooper said.

He stood into a crouch and moved away toward the room where he had seen Locke.

Charlotte reached out and touched Raucous on the shoulder. They heard other doors open as the one in front of them closed. Raucous reached out and held her shoulder too. Charlotte smiled.

"We have to work on the emotional expression," she said, trying for light and bringing nothing but doubt.

They stood into crouches and started to move in different directions, each toward the doors that had opened.

Bullets pinged, barrels exploded with flashes that were lost in the sound and light of the room. Cooper was a moving target and they knew where he was heading. Raucous looked as well as he could and saw men moving, he couldn't see McClintock, he couldn't see Franklin. He looked up at the balcony and saw nothing but flashes of light from electric strobes and LEDs. Three men from the right and three men for the left, two groups, guns out, converging on the room in which Locke had been held and the room to which Cooper was moving. Charlotte stood and fired, the men on the right saw and changed direction, stopping their slow glide forward and hitting the ground, firing as they went. Raucous moved round, crouched down hoping to be small and unseen and smiling at himself because the idea was impossible. He moved fast, trying to get around their edge, to trap them, to be between them and the door. He glanced but never looked and heard shots but didn't know whose were whose. He looked again to see Charlotte firing, ducking, moving, and firing again. Bobbing up and down and aiming on a whim.

The group had lost him or taken him to be with Charlotte. He edged around, his steps hidden by music and bangs, he came up behind them, the three men looking away and toward the room. He had a clear shot at their backs, an easy out, three men, three bullets and three deaths. He raised his gun aimed, heard a shot and relaxed. He dropped his gun to his side, walked forward, raised his gun again above his head and smashed down on the back of the neck of the man to the right. The man dropped, unconscious and out of action. Raucous turned to his left, spinning at the waist, smashing his gun into the face of the next man, who dropped, eyes rolled back and in danger of choking on his tongue. The third looked down at his fallen friend, not understanding, looking to see a hole, blood or anything to tell the story. He saw Raucous late, raised his gun. Raucous shot, the man's thigh exploded, he dropped, the gun falling, clattering to the floor, the sounds not heard, only imagined. Raucous reached down and picked up the guns. He had no idea about which held most, or which was best for killing. The three men were out of action, two out and not coming back soon, the third in need of a system to stop the blood.

Raucous looked across to where he thought Charlotte was hiding but he saw nothing but space. He looked around the room, looking for movement seeing the other three police, not seeing McClintock.

Raucous crouched down, leaned into the man whose leg was open.

"You need something to stem that flow," Raucous said close up to the man's ear. "I remember you from when you had me in a cell. I'll give you something to help, promise to call in medical help. But you need to tell me where McClintock is."

The man had red spit coming from his mouth, he had bitten through his cheek or tongue because the bullet wound was not close enough to cause that.

The man spat.

"McClintock ran," he said. "You get him, make sure you kill him, the cowardly bastard."

"He's gone?" Raucous asked.

The man nodded, wincing.

"Franklin?"

"I don't know, and I don't care. We need to kill you, and that means we kill Franklin too. He knows that."

Raucous nodded, the noise and sounds only music, no bullets, no guns. Raucous placed his gun down, and lifted his hoodie, pulling it over his head. He pressed the wound hard, trying to push material into the hole he had put there. He grabbed the man's right hand and placed it over the balled up hoodie.

"That's all I can do," Raucous said.

83

Raucous picked up three guns and threw the others toward the door. He looked at the room where Locke had been, the door open, Charlotte near, gun raised, scanning, looking for movement. He saw the three police crouched and moving, converging, believing their colleagues were covering their flank.

The crash and explosion and the wall of heat surprised him. A bottle of petrol and a burning rag exploding on the open door of the room where Locke had been. Cooper ran out, his arm ablaze, the flames licking at his head. He hit the deck and rolled, the flames shrinking and popping back to previous size as he tried to starve them of air. The three police moved quickly, taking chances assuming idiocy in the people they chased. They moved and Charlotte fired, the one in the middle slumping down, letting his gun go and holding his side. Not a kill shot but one that would lead to death if he let it bleed. The other two broke left and right, firing at Cooper but missing as he rolled. Charlotte moved quickly, grabbing Cooper's shirt and lifting and pulling. The flames on the door burning bright, causing heat and melting paint. Bullets whizzed, thumping into walls, and skipping off the floor like stones across a lake. Charlotte pulled and dragged Cooper back through the flames into the room, trapped inside, but shielded from guns. Raucous ducked down as the police looked left and right, scanning, looking for people, trying to see who was where and who was standing.

They would see nothing.

Raucous held his hiding spot, waiting to hear anything to tell him what move to make. Two of them and three of us, he thought. Only two are trapped. No way out unless he created space. He looked at the gun in his right hand, felt another two in his waistband. The music pumping out, the lights flashing, the reverberations hitting his lungs and gut. He waited, tried to picture where the police would move. If they were smart they would go slow, come in at an angle on the door. Face on and they would be shot from inside. Cooper and Charlotte would have smoke and fumes but not stupidity, anything coming through that door was going to be dead.

Raucous took a deep breath, looked at his gun, pulled the second from his waist, two hands, two guns and no way of shooting straight. It was a shock tactic, one that wasn't smart. Two hands gave him aim, two guns gave him nothing but macho bravado and an action shot for an impossible film. He dropped the second gun, gripped the first with both hands. He stood, ready to move his aim based on what he saw.

The first police was lighting a rag on a second bottle of petrol, the flame igniting quick and the air above distorted immediately by heat. Raucous was to their right. He raised his gun, aimed and fired three shots in a quick burst, the first hitting home, the second and third going over their heads as recoil took his aim.

The first bullet was aimed at the bottle, Raucous hoping for a miracle and an explosion of fire. He missed and hit the man in the shoulder. He dropped the bottle, the concrete floor didn't give and the glass smashed, a flame shot up from liquid and fumes and the man was on fire. His trousers burned, his shirt caught next and the second man stepped away as his friend fried and rolled and melted.

Raucous walked slowly, gun raised, pointing at the man who was watching the human match. He saw Raucous, turned, raised his gun, and Raucous shot, the bullet hitting his chest, spinning him around, and dropping to the floor.

Raucous looked down, the burning man was dead, lungs melted inside, no oxygen and no life. Raucous shouted loud for Charlotte and Cooper, his voice not travelling, but enough for them to hear. Charlotte moved slowly out of the room, Cooper followed, his arm blackened by the petrol that had burned its skin. They had their guns raised and Charlotte looked at the burning policeman.

"They are all gone," Raucous said.

"McClintock?" Cooper asked.

"He ran."

"Locke?"

"I don't know."

They looked up at the overhanging balcony. There was no movement, no light and no shots.

84

Cooper said nothing, he moved away without thank or assumption they would follow. He knew the layout and knew where he was going. He burst through the double doors and Raucous and Charlotte ran after. Cooper turned right, looked at the glass shaft and the glass lift and saw it reaching its top. Franklin was inside, holding Locke up by the arm as Locke had no strength to stand on his feet. The lift stopped, Cooper raised his gun, aimed and Franklin smiled watching them all. Cooper fired, the bullets hitting near where he aimed, the glass doing nothing but scratching white and bouncing everything back. Franklin smiled wider as the doors opened into his home and he dragged Locke from view.

Cooper ran to the curved stairs, looking up but placing his feet where they needed to go. The music loud and then gone. A silence and they stopped, looking around to see the reason. They looked at each other, not understanding, not knowing what it meant. They looked for too long, waiting, giving Franklin time. Cooper turned and ran the steps, his feet sounding metal slaps on each contact. Every pace closer was sounding out in the huge empty space. There were sounds of screams that were reduced to groans but they cared nothing for those that had stood to kill them.

Cooper was sprinting, two or three steps at a time, his feet not soft but slapping down. Raucous went slower, his size and age taking any sense of speed he may have once held and Charlotte stayed close. Raucous knew she could sprint away.

The door at the top burst open, two Darts walked out, shirts off, baggy joggers on. Their bodies all lean, no fat but no muscle. They were defined, every sinew to see but they were skinny kids whose muscles showed because they were young and hadn't accumulated the layer of warmth that would come. They held two guns, one in each hand, and Raucous smiled at the fool he nearly was. They shot down alternating hands, left and right and left and right, pot shots in Cooper's direction. They needed to learn to aim rather than taking their cue from a TV show. The shots pinged and ricocheted off walls and into space far from where they wanted. Charlotte raised her gun and sent calm shots their way, bullets hitting the wall behind them, spraying plaster and brick onto their bodies. Raucous raised his gun too and fired methodically, aim, pull trigger, account for recoil, aim and shoot. Each time getting closer. The Darts moved their eyes from Cooper, looking to stop the comeback. They fired again at Raucous and Charlotte, bullets close but not hitting, the angle impossible, the ability to hit down to luck rather than skill.

Cooper was close, he fired at the Darts, plaster exploded from a wall, scattering into their faces. They ducked, turned and stepped back inside.

Cooper slowed, not stupid enough nor crazed to run blindly into a room with men who wanted him dead. The door started to close, Raucous and Charlotte were near. Cooper saw them, judged their distance and speed. He looked at his gun, and Raucous had no idea how many bullets were left.

Cooper stepped and kicked the door, stopping its movement. He didn't step in, didn't take the chance. He waited for support and they reached him quick.

They didn't speak, they looked at each other in a buzz of moving heads. Each to the next looking for ideas or confirmation. The door remained half-open. It looked too easy an invite to accept and too enticing to turn down. They had no idea what was behind, the layout, the furniture, the space or the people, the guns they had, the weapons they would use. They had no information at all beyond the Darts, Franklin and Locke.

The three of them stood with their backs to the wall to the right of the door. There was no choice, no walking away. Raucous wanted to hear voices, an attempt at starting an exchange, a barter or verbal contract. There were none. Silence inside was as quiet as the silence in which they stood.

The lift started to move, doors closing and the glass box sliding to the ground floor. Charlotte watched, looked down over the edge and saw no one. They looked for movement, a person standing pressing buttons but there was nothing beyond the bodies they had left behind. They watched in fascination as the glass lift moved slowly down, stopped and its doors opened.

Charlotte smiled and moved.

She stepped quickly, running and Cooper watched and Raucous knew as she sprinted down flights. They waited, knowing now when the time to start would be.

85

They watched Charlotte be cautious, keeping a look-out from above as she looked and stepped slowly around the open space. She stayed large from the bodies, not wanting to be caught in a trap or shot by a desperate teen. Nothing moved. Charlotte pressed a button, the lift doors opened and she stepped inside. There was no need to go slow, the whole thing transparent and nothing hiding, only the far side was metal with its buttons and alarms. She would need this for protection.

She pressed one of the three buttons, the one at the top and doors moved together slowly as if bored with repetition. The lift started smoothly, and one cable lengthened and one grew slack as the lift ran quietly up.

"Ready?" Raucous asked Cooper.

He nodded, they would go when the doors opened, the only moment those inside would be distracted. Maybe they would plan and set up the ambush, maybe there were hundreds inside. Maybe a lot of things, and not knowing was the cause for anxiety. Raucous needed belief not ignorance, and he braced himself.

The lift reached the top, Raucous watching Charlotte all the way, stopped and there was a pause. Charlotte looked across, through the glass and Raucous stared back. They smiled, not knowing what it meant, not knowing what the other felt. The doors started to open, Charlotte stepped to the side, using the metal panels as a shield to what lay in front. Cooper moved, barging with his shoulder taking his calculated gamble and Raucous followed him in.

The room was a mixture of teen fantasy and a beige Bond Villain. Arcade machines and pinball tables, large screens and large cream comfy chairs. A fake flame fire and bars of expensive gin laid out as if designed by a posh art student with unlimited budget and questionable skill. A build-it-by-numbers den designed to show a lack of original thought and taste alongside the unlimited riches. The edge out to the balcony was a large glass wall looping all the way around, doors opened out onto the walkway where the Darts had fired.

Franklin had chosen the lift as his target, the Darts had wanted Cooper. Cooper was firing in their direction, hoping for luck rather than depending on skill. Franklin was caught, not knowing what to do. The lift was empty from Franklin's view, but he knew someone was inside. He fired two shots as a warning to who was there. But if he turned away they could shoot him back, but if he didn't look to the door he needed to trust the Darts to keep him safe. He edged and panicked and dropped to the floor.

Cooper was firing, trying to force the darts to move. Raucous shot too, but he pulled the trigger three times and the gun ran empty. He pulled the gun from his waistband, fired twice and it had nothing left.

Raucous swore, Cooper understood, and fired some more.

Charlotte walked from the lift, firing at where Franklin hid. A gun popped up and fired, Franklin imagining where to aim and doing nothing but firing into air. The Darts didn't hide, they stood and fired, and Cooper fired back, ducking and bobbing and hitting nothing but wood and glass and walls.

Guns firing, loud bangs and then clicks, and anger and words of insult to weapons that had their limits. Raucous saw Charlotte walking toward Franklin, who was cowering behind a sofa. He wanted to shout warnings of traps and possibilities that Franklin had more weapons, but she was smarter than him and would have thought and seen it all quicker than his own mind.

Franklin stood and ran, but with nowhere to go he stuck close to the Darts, the three of them, two semi-nude like lead singers in a punk band, a diet of whisky leading to the body of a child and Franklin looking like an old man trying to hold on to his youth by wearing what he considered all the cool kids wanted. A hoodie with his brand, joggers and box-new trainers that cost as much as an average family car.

Raucous looked to Charlotte and she nodded, telling him she was Okay. Cooper walked too, toward the Darts, slowly, aware as they all were that while guns had gone, knives were there. The Darts smiled, looking at Cooper under hooded eyes. Cooper stopped. The two groups of three staring each other down and the weak link, the one that had no idea what the game entailed was Franklin. He was trying for control but his eyes darted, looking for escape, and his fingers twitched on a gun that had no bullets and no use. A metallic comfort blanket that had outgrown its owner.

No one moved from their spot, they had chosen where to stand and had chosen how long to wait.

"Which of you was the one that put me in hospital?" Charlotte asked.

The Darts smiled.

"You have names?" she asked.

They shook their heads, smiling all the time.

"Cowards too," Charlotte said. "Not unexpected."

The Darts looked at each other, shirts off, all their ribs clear and counted. Whatever silent language they used to communicate sent a message between the two. They reached behind them and pulled out knives, the hunting kind with no practical application outside the skinning of bears. One side shiny and sharp, the other serrated and angry. Franklin moved too, pulling a knife of a similar kind and Raucous smiled at the way Franklin held himself, copying those who could, hoping he wasn't seen as someone who couldn't. A man who was confident only when on top.

Raucous knew what Charlotte wanted, a straight fight, a challenge, something to repair the scars in her head. They beat her and the only way she could live with calm was to shut the person down. He would have preferred them to be shot, preferred them to already be dead. But he knew what was happening, knew she would not accept him to interfere. She needed one of them to speak, one of them to step up and admit guilt and responsibility and ask for the chance to redeem herself.

Cooper saw Locke lying on the floor, saw his chest rising and falling as he breathed. Raucous nodded, he had it covered, and Cooper moved and knelt down next to his friend. His hands weren't tied, but his body was broken so much he couldn't hold his own weight.

"That was McClintock," Franklin said. "Not us."

Cooper looked up and stared and Raucous saw the old evil he had once possessed. It didn't matter, Franklin was involved and for that he would die. Raucous knew the look of a man who was going to kill.

"He doing Okay?" Charlotte asked without looking away from the Darts.

"Still breathing."

Cooper rolled Locke onto his side, a position so he could inhale with ease, a position he could rest, sleep and wake. Cooper looked at his friend, his face swollen and bruised, his body looking to recuperate through shutting down. Cooper rubbed his face and stood.

"I think all of you are guilty," he said. "And this is the end. Maybe you think you'll walk, I don't know. But I killed your man MarQuick, your big protector, burned him. Because that is what he deserved. I was always coming for you. And this is it."

86

"Your boy begged, cried and squealed," one of the Darts said.

They had heard Cooper, not cared at all about the death of MarQuick and wanted their own confession.

His twin smiled as if they shared a brain and the reasons and thoughts of one were instant in the other.

"We chased Mack down and simply did him. Easy stuff. Would have gone quick but where would be the fun in that?"

Raucous looked at them, these two skinny little fools who wouldn't survive anywhere without a blade and deceit.

"And now here we are," Raucous said. "There's an inevitability about it. Something we all want."

The second Dart spoke.

"None of them respect you, no one with heart," he said. "All those boys you think you are saving or helping. Nothing is true. They think you are nothing, and see you as you are: a nobody with a wasted life. You might as well be trying to convert them to Islam. He was going to grass."

Raucous smiled, wondering where the anger had gone.

"None of this would have been if you hadn't killed our brothers," The Dart said.

Raucous looked at him, not knowing, not truly, but having an idea where he was going.

"The country house?"

The Darts nodded.

"They caused that," Raucous told them.

"You went to kill."

"I went to talk, and then I killed. Easy to do. They had nothing. Poor deaths. Cowardly. A genetic weakness. And that is the reason we are here."

"It is the reason Mack is dead."

The Darts smiled. The first one turned to Charlotte.

"I stabbed you," he said. "But it doesn't matter. I wasn't trying to kill you, just hurt. And it looks like you want more of the same. I guess your big boy friends will try and help. Seems a little unfair."

Charlotte smiled, she was too good for them and she knew.

"Not something that they'd do," she said as a warning to Raucous. "But stabbing from behind and chasing down teens in cars and smashing them into walls. Not exactly the skills of a self-appointed hard man. You don't have it."

"You don't have a knife."

"And you rely on a brother."

He smiled, and they knew they were watching, everyone tensed, ready to go. Franklin's eyes looked to the door and the lift. He didn't have it, Raucous knew it. The man at the top only there because no one else wants it. He was the only one to fear death.

The Dart started to circle Charlotte and she watched him, up on her toes, on balance and ready to move.

Cooper looked to Raucous, asking what to do with a lift of an eye. Raucous smiled, there was nothing but let them go. He nodded at Cooper, telling him it was the way it had to be.

The Dart moved, playing with the knife as if he had a lifetime's experience in combat when all he showed were flash moves learned in front of a mirror. The blade was too big and cumbersome for play, a slashing tool no better than a machete. He danced, moving feet like he believed a fighter should but the movements were off, no training and no skill, skipping and moving a stance too wide and then too narrow like a young boy who has just watched Rocky.

Charlotte was taking him in, looking at triggers and tells, the body motion the Dart gave up when telegraphing what came next. The blade swishing and slashing air, making lines too far from Charlotte for anyone to care. Charlotte feigned to move forward, smiling having seen the weakness. The Dart danced straight back and Charlotte watched, memorising patterns. Everyone had a set of reactions, and The Dart was giving up the secret to his.

The Dart moved forward again, fake or real no longer mattered. Raucous had seen the cue, the shrug of his right shoulder and knew he was coming. Charlotte smiled, slid left as the Dart moved forward, stepped inside his right arm, grabbed his elbow with her right hand and his wrist with her left. She dug her hip into his, twisting his arm, leaning in, lifting and pulling, he flipped over, head going round. In the gym she would help him to the floor, soften the impact, but here she added force, slapping him down, arm bending. The knife fell from his grasp, she rolled to the ground, lifted her right leg up to his shoulder, flipped her left up and around his head. She grasped his wrist, straightening her body, an arm-bar in which he had no means to defend. She pulled and twisted, the point of a tap arrived but The Dart didn't offer and Charlotte would never accept. She pulled and twisted, the pressure and torque all on the ligament and muscles keeping his arm in place. She added force as The Dart screamed, the high-pitched tone of someone defeated and in view of the future. The arm gave way, the socket separated, an arm that no longer resisted. Charlotte released, spun and stood. The Dart on the floor screaming, standing, an arm hanging, the palm facing the wrong way, his skin covered in scratches, the skin reddening where he had scraped the floor.

Raucous smiled, he saw Franklin move. The healthy Dart moved to his brother, but was pushed away. Two kids playing as hard men, and their boss a man-boy with no means to be scary without company.

"Pathetic," Raucous said. "Two kids that couldn't survive outside the bubble of threat their boss provides, and a man who thinks that people fear him. You couldn't last a day in the real world without the help of the law."

Raucous, Charlotte and Cooper looked at the people in front of them, the stupid and dumb, the pathetic and beaten. Raucous had nowhere to go, killing now was an embarrassment to him. They looked around saw nothing that would come as an attack. Franklin sat, one Dart with one arm and the other with a broken heart.

The end of boredom, the challenge too weak. The last of them having nothing to provide resistance.

87

The Darts looked up as one. The anger of the truly delusional in their eyes. They didn't look at each other, they knew, this was their way, this is what they did. They went for her, breaking into a sprint, one fast and the other slow because one arm would not work. They came with knives, slashing and looking to chop through skin, muscle and bone.

Cooper moved fast, he was close and ready and saw and made a decision. He stepped in, blocking a path, the healthy Dart, swinging his hunting knife like a man throwing an axe. Cooper reached with his left arm, pushing up like an old school street fighter blocking a winging right. Cooper moved forward, smashing his forehead against The Dart's nose. It exploded, blood gushing, the Dart staggering and falling to his side, staying upright but not knowing where he was. He slashed with his knife, the serrated edge first, a desperate last shot at winning a fight that needed a miracle. Cooper ducked and threw a sharp right into The Dart's ribs, hitting perfectly, showing his boxing skills. The Dart bent double, and his one-armed brother slashed at Charlotte with his weak hand, Charlotte ducked, drove forward, lifting him up, running to the balcony like a fireman rescuing a hostage and throwing the body over and out into the space, watching it fall, the knife still held in his hand, falling and scrambling backwards, dancing in air and then stopping on impact as the floor tried to push its mass through the young boys back and smashed bones, broke legs and shattered a skull. Blood pooled out as he lay there like a kid trying to make angels in red snow.

His brother screamed, stood, his face a smear of red. He ran to the balcony, stood looking over, oblivious to Charlotte, oblivious to it all. Cooper walked up behind, bent down and picked up his legs, pulling and flipping and the Dart's centre of mass shifted up, forcing him over, forcing him to fall. They watched as he scrambled too, face down, seeing his dead brother come closer, seeing where he would land and where he would die. The impact came, the body bounced, a rib-cage shattered, and a face and neck snapped. They lay, less than a metre apart, legs bent at the knees and through their shins. Blood spreading, joining and being one.

"You okay?" Cooper asked.

Charlotte nodded, looking at the Darts, thinking about how she should not regret.

88

Raucous had watched them dump the Darts, had watched them smile and seen them calm. The deep inhales they took, the smile they exchanged. The Darts dead and Franklin left. He watched them look at each other, a shared experience of which they would never talk, one he had shared with her too. He smiled and waited for her to see him. She looked up, her smile there, a peace.

Raucous looked to Franklin, who was sat, scared, his pair of protective lunatics gone forever. A weak coward, Raucous knew. He wouldn't attack, wouldn't give him the chance to kill in a way that could be explained as justified.

Raucous looked back at Charlotte, smiling, hoping the humour would hold. Charlotte caught his eye, her face without expression. She swore, looking beyond Raucous. And he knew.

"Timing is everything," the voice said.

Raucous heard the smarm and turned slow, no rush needed, to need to try and be a hero.

McClintock was stood at the open door to the stairs, holding a gun, pointing it at the room, smiling and leaning a damaged shoulder against the frame. A kid so desperately wanting to be achingly cool. Raucous saw another gun held in his belt.

"Someone left a lot of guns downstairs," McClintock said.

Franklin stood.

"I'm happy to take one."

"You just stick with the knives," McClintock told him. "Leave this to the big boys."

Raucous looked around the room. They were all too far to make a move, all too isolated to be a group. McClintock had the drop on everyone, no one was getting to him or to safety without being shot.

Cooper stepped, testing the scene.

"It goes without saying that any of you move without my Okay, you get shot. So if you'll kindly put an end to that Cooper that would be grand."

McClintock walked into the room, keeping his distance from everyone. Franklin moved toward Raucous.

"Be careful," McClintock told Franklin. "Tricky people we have here. And if you get in the way, maybe you get shot too. That would make some headlines. Hero policeman takes down fools at gunfight in local hotspot. Medals, promotions and money in that."

McClintock smiled.

"Your friends told me you ran away," Raucous said. "Like a coward."

"Tactical retreat, it is all in the telling. And here I am, unscathed, unmarked and about to kill you. The police killer."

McClintock smiled and so did Raucous.

"It is funny," McClintock said. "So smile away."

McClintock raised his gun, pointed directly at Raucous, aiming for his chest.

"Big target," McClintock said. "I'm not going to miss."

"Me neither," the voice said.

McClintock turned, faster than Raucous thought possible, his gun whipping round but not getting more than half way before his knee exploded, taking away its strength and use and a whole lot of flesh. He fell and Raucous moved quickly, but not fast enough. Franklin was there before him, grabbing the gun from McClintock's hand and firing at the woman in the door.

Simpson had struggled to speak but she had aimed and hit where she wanted. McClintock down but not dead, and this was what Raucous needed. Franklin fired but Simpson had moved out onto the steps, leaving a wall as protection. Franklin turned, pointed the gun at Raucous as he moved in, looking to break a face. Raucous grabbed and pushed the gun up as Franklin fired, the gunshot causing his eardrums to vibrate too hard and leave nothing but a ringing and squealing in his head.

Franklin scrambled, using two hands against one of Raucous. Raucous used his free hand to reach behind and grab Franklin's hair, pulled his head back, pushed the barrel up and under his jaw, pressing hard, trying to drill blunt metal through his skin. Raucous wrapped his finger around the trigger, and started to squeeze. Franklin choked out sounds and kicked with his feet, unable to match power, unable to think. It was a panic that all men face when they know they have nothing left to survive beyond the empathy of the enemy they face.

"It ends one way," Raucous said, his voice quiet, whispering.

Franklin said nothing, using his muscles to struggle against his head pulled back. He tried to talk, tried to use words to explain or express or defend or attack. It made little difference to Raucous, little difference at all. He wouldn't listen, wouldn't care.

"All those kids you ruined for this," Raucous said. "All of them. Led to this."

"Don't do it, Raucous," Simpson said.

She was near him, pointing her gun at his head. Raucous stared at her, not releasing his hold. Franklin tried for sound again, words that would be lies, or pleas for help, or anything to avoid consequence.

"He will talk, he'll help bring them down."

Raucous smiled, understood what she was saying, understood her reasons and knew she believed them. Raucous looked back at Franklin and saw the humour in his eyes, the knowledge that he was saved, that he got to live, that he got a chance to work his way out, to pay, to lie, to bribe his way to a future that had him alive.

"Was it worth it?" Raucous asked.

He released the pressure on the barrel hoping Franklin would speak.

Franklin stared at him, eyes alive with humour, the fear gone, the knowledge he would live outshining the difficulties he would face. Franklin didn't talk, he laughed the fake laugh of someone who needs to know they were better. And Raucous smiled too, and watched Franklin as the reality sunk in, watching his smile fade to fear. Franklin started to shout but the word was lost as Raucous pulled the trigger. Franklin's head exploded, blood splattering, bone and flesh flying, red splashes covering Simpson, covering Raucous.

Franklin's body fell to the floor.

Simpson flinched, but held her gun on him. She straightened her arm, tensed her finger and Raucous watched and waited.

"I needed him alive," she said. "He would talk. Get us others."

"I needed him dead," he told her.

She stared at him, her hand shaking, the gun moving, the anger in every muscle. Raucous stared into her eyes.

"You fire and you become me. You don't want that," he said. "That's no life at all."

She stared, anger debating in her head, pushing the gun forward and pulling it back. She was a witness to murder. She swore and lowered her gun, looked to the ground and swore again. She looked up.

"You going to kill him?" she shouted, turning to McClintock.

McClintock was on the floor, staring at the blood, the dead man and Raucous in red. He tried to crawl away, leaving a streak of red.

Raucous stared at him, saw McClintock's tears well. Raucous shook his head.

"He stays alive. You hear that McClintock? You get to live. It won't be pretty, won't be free."

"Then put the gun down," Simpson said.

Raucous let his shoulders sag, a relaxed stance. He let his grip go and the gun dropped to the ground. He turned and walked to Charlotte, took her hand, hugged her and she him. There should be words he thought, but none came, just a clench and a hold. Cooper sat next to Locke, speaking, talking about survival while Simpson watched, and waited.

They stayed as they were, McClintock screaming for medical attention and no one answering, no one listening to a word, and no noise until the doors burst as police swarmed in. Paramedics hunted the wounded, and then came into the space upstairs. Simpson sat down, men and women in green treated her, they came to McClintock, they came to them all.

Epilogue

Raucous woke on the morning, two months living in a house too big for two and too rich for him, but one he shared with Charlotte. A cohabitation he had always avoided because it was something he didn't want to destroy. The silence he craved available and sure, and one that Charlotte loved too. They had their space and a life.

Charlotte was next to him in the bed they shared, in the house he would say was his home. They dressed, ate and watched the clock to go and spectate at something they didn't need to see.

They went by car and Charlotte drove, parking close and paying a premium to do so. They entered the large historic building, went through detectors without problem, eyes on them because that's how it worked. They walked the stairs saying hello to no one and took their seat in the chamber.

McClintock entered, limping still, not using a cane. Two months gone and he was never getting back to how he was, his left leg seemingly shorter than the other and his face scarred. He was dressed in a three-piece suit, looking as dapper as he could. Expensive material could not hide the fact he looked older and tired, a jaded man before his time. But it was expected, he was a marked man on both sides, a corrupt policeman who sold his soul and a criminal who turned on his people. He had nowhere to go but into hiding.

They had remained in contact, Raucous and Simpson, the story created and their part erased. They were no one to all and onlookers at best. The papers ran the story, the news channels too. The music executive who was a kingpin in County lines and an employer of police who could be turned. The rage and anger flowed for days until other events became more popular. A celebrity, a royal, a killer at large. The limelight died and Simpson and Locke given jobs to hunt down corruption.

McClintock was here to put a final piece on his turn to informer, the murders with planted DNA admitted and people released from prison. Some would go back because they were crooked, but they would go back for what they had done not for what they had been framed. Raucous was free of suspicion.

The powers at the top made moves to show they cared and were making decisions to stop anything happening again, despite the promise being made before. The vacuum was filled as soon as it formed and defeat was never going to happen.

Charlotte and Raucous sat in a row at the back of the courthouse, neither of them required to give evidence, neither named in the case. McClintock had turned, he was there to confirm everything he had told the law was true and to accept his sentence.

Cooper was at the back with the journalists, hiding away, needing to watch but not wanting to be seen. He paid attention, listening and taking glee from the names being taken down. Raucous saw him exchange a smile with Locke.

Simpson and Locke, not looking the same as they had three months before, were sat up front, the heroes of the piece, the names everyone associated with the case. The honest taking down gangs with intelligence and flair and luck. They wore the scars and their minds carried the pain, but they had done what they should, achieved more than anyone.

The network taken down, investigations external and internal started. Simpson and Locke leading teams to root out corruption and hunt down gangs with links to children.

They wouldn't win, they knew that, but they were there to stop it exploding, stop it blowing up unchecked. A brake on growth rather than a means to destruction. Each working away with the fact that they stemmed rather than cured.

Raucous had come to watch, but mostly to be seen. He wanted McClintock to know, but he refused to look their way, refused to acknowledge through a glance that they were present. The judge spoke, the legal teams asked, and McClintock reeled off information he had given before, and would give again as another of his colleagues was sent down, or another criminal was sentenced to years for offences McClintock had seen.

Raucous smiled because he had watched this fake confident man, who was sat in a wooden stand at the front of the room beg and cry and cower.

He had begged for a way out, a way for him to be an undercover agent, an infiltrator and hero. The ideas in his head had swirled and no one had agreed. The recording, the evidence, the word of two police officers and those of his colleagues who had survived, sending his reputation to the place it should be. He was a nobody, and no side would defend him as their own.

Locke had laughed and told him the facts. McClintock was done, a lifetime of being hated, of being no one. The choice he had: stay quiet and live a life of prison where everyone wanted him dead, or talk and live the same fear but in a limited freedom with a different name.

Simpson had told him, "Inform on everyone or be released into the wild with everyone after you."

Raucous didn't check the new name they had given, didn't want to know where a new place and a new career would be found, just like he would never need to talk or think of Franklin, or the Darts. McClintock would have a few years inside to start, in isolation, away from ex-police and gangs. But it was not the lifetime he should serve, not in the way Raucous believed.

They sat and watched for an hour, neither Charlotte nor Raucous talking or looking at each other. When they did it was to acknowledge what they had feared, that the whole process was long and dull and already decided. They walked outside and stood awkwardly in silence.

They knew what the others were doing, there was no need to speak or thank or spout empty words about staying in touch or remaining bonded over events, none of those words would be useful, none of those words would mean anything.

They left, Charlotte driving, heading home, heading to where they lived.

Acknowledgements

Thank you to:

Jo O'Neil for reading all my stuff and giving important feedback suggestions and edit. Hope Smith for letting me talk about my ideas and stories as they come about. Robert Ledger for reading and telling me the good and bad bits, likewise Spencer Conday. Carmella Barbetta, Jane Bradshaw and husband, and Emma Worrel for taking the time to read and give me feedback. And Mark Snell for never reading anything I have ever written and simply telling me it is rubbish – an inspiration to get something out there he may actually read. There really are a lot of great people in the world and these are just a few of them.

Thank you.

Printed in Great Britain
by Amazon

22297945R00142